LORD OF MISRULE

BELOW THE SALT
BOOK EIGHT

ELIZABETH ROSE

OLIVERHEBERBOOKS

Lord of Misrule Copyright 2024 © Elizabeth Rose

Cover art by Dar Albert at Wicked Smart Designs

Published by Oliver-Heber Books

0 9 8 7 6 5 4 3 2 1

FAMILY TREE

<u>**Blake Family Tree:**</u>

Evan & Eleanor Blake
<u>**Their children, spouses, their kids, and books where you can read about them:**</u>

Corbett married (Devon) – *Lord of the Blade*
    Rook 'twin'(Primrose Ashdown) – *A Rose Among Thorns*
    Beowulf
    Raven 'twin' (Jonathon Armstrong) – *Picking up the Gauntlet*
    Sparrow
    Tolin (Kit Baker)
    Daegel

Wren (Storm MacKeefe) – *Lady Renegade*
    Renard – *Lady Renegade*

Lark (Dustin Styles) – *Love Letters for Lady Lark*
Florie (different father)
Elspeth
Finlay (Seen in *Highland Chronicles*)
Hawke (Phoebe MacNab) – *Highland Storm*
Heather (husband)
Liam
(Storm's grandfather is Callum. Storm's parents are Ian & Clarista)

Madoc (Abigail Blackmore) – *Lord of Illusion*
Robin (Sage Hillock) – *Winter Sage*
Martin
Martine (David Stone) – *Sweet Mead for Lady Martine*
Regina
Dorothy

Echo (Garrett Blackmore) – *Lady of the Mist*
Edgar or Gar (different father) (Josefina Waterman) – *Riding out the Storm*
Eleanor (Connor Wyland) – *Dancing on Air*
Evan
Not related – Sorcerer Orrick (Hope Threston) – *Keeper of the Flame*

CHAPTER I
ENGLAND, 1376

Kit Baker's head snapped up as the bells over the bakery entrance jangled and the door slammed open so hard that the pans hanging on the wall crashed to the floor.

"Does this thief belong to you?" came the gruff voice of the man who had entered.

Her heart jumped into her throat when she saw the guard from Blake Castle gripping her eight-year-old son, Parker, by the back of his tunic. Parker's shoulder-length blond hair hung over his eyes, his feet nearly off the ground as the burly guard held him so tightly.

"Parker! What did you do now?" she scolded, running from behind the counter, wiping her hands on a towel and throwing the cloth to the side.

"Mother," said the boy, flashing her a smile that wasn't going to help him get out of the mess he was in this time.

"What did he do?" she demanded to know, her attention shooting up to the angry guard.

"This runt tried to steal my sword," the man answered. "Now I'm going to have to take him to the castle for sentencing."

"I'm not a runt!" shouted Parker, struggling to get free, but the guard wasn't about to let him go.

"Parker?" Kit's focus was back on the boy now. "Did you really try stealing a sword from one of the castle guards? What is the matter with you?" Of all the stupid things her troublesome son had ever done over the years, this was definitely the worst. Kit felt fed up with his tomfoolery of constantly getting into mischief over and over again. She, being a widow and trying to run a business on her own, didn't have the time to give the boy the proper upbringing he needed. Actually, what Parker really needed was a father.

"I didn't do no such thing," said Parker, still struggling against the guard's hold.

"Any," she corrected him under her breath.

"He laid the sword down and I just wanted to hold it. To feel how heavy it was, that's all." Parker looked up at her sheepishly.

Kit released a long sigh. "All right. I believe you," she told her son, knowing that Parker usually admitted to his actions even when he knew he was in trouble.

"Well, I don't believe him," snapped the guard. "And now he can tell his lie to Lord Blake. You, boy, are going to the castle for judgment. Your punishment for stealing will be decided on by Lord Blake himself."

"Did I hear that Parker was stealing?" Kit's brother by marriage, Oliver, hurried out of the back room with Kit's very pregnant sister, Brenna, waddling along right behind him. "Parker, please tell me this isn't so. You don't want to have to pay for a crime like that. You need to learn that lesson while you are young." He raised his hand, minus the two fingers that had been cut off when he'd stolen food, trying to support himself and Brenna after Kit and Brenna's parents kicked them out.

"Ah, I see that stealing is a common trait in this family," sneered the guard.

"Nay. That was an entirely different situation altogether and happened in Ireland, not anywhere near here," Brenna spoke up. "Kit, what are you going to do? You need to help Parker."

"I know that." Kit's attention went back to the guard. "Please," she begged the man. "I'd appreciate you letting my son go with only a warning this time. I promise to watch him more closely." Tears formed in her eyes. "He's just a boy. I beg you not to hurt him."

"You'd appreciate me letting him go, would you?" the guard asked in a mocking voice. Kit already regretted not wording her request more carefully. After all, he was a royal guard and she was naught but a commoner, the town baker.

"I mean, will you? Can you? Just warn him this time?" She tried once more to convince the guard.

"Hmph," sniffed the man. "Bad boys turn into evil men who end up being ruffians and bandits and cutthroats. It won't be tolerated." The guard frowned and shook his head. "Nay, I cannot let this go. I am taking him to the castle to let my lord decide his punishment. Since the boy is so young and you are his mother, I suggest you ride along with us and plead your case to Lord Tolin yourself. Although, I can tell you it will make no difference in his decision."

"Lord Tolin?" Kit repeated, surprised. "Don't you mean

Lord Corbett?" She felt confused, knowing well that Corbett was lord of the castle.

"Nay, not Lord Corbett. I mean his son, Lord Tolin," snapped the guard, giving her a look that could kill. She supposed she shouldn't have questioned him in such a manner. She had a habit of blurting out what she thought before considering the consequences.

"Pardon me," she said, clearing her throat, trying her hardest not to anger the guard more. "But is Lord Tolin standing in for Lord Corbett then?"

"Yes. Yes, he is. Lord Corbett and Lady Devon have traveled to Scotland for the holiday, and they've left Lord Tolin in charge of Blake Castle until their return."

"Oh, I see," Kit answered, secretly having hoped to be able to plead with Lady Devon, since she was kind and fair. Being a woman and a mother, Lady Devon surely would have taken pity on Parker. Now, she could see that plan wouldn't work. Kit knew of the sons of Lord Corbett, but had only met the eldest son in person. Lord Rook along with his twin sister, Lady Raven, sometimes came into her bakery, but not Lord Corbett's other sons. She'd only seen Lords Daegel and Tolin in passing from afar. "Yes, I'll go to the castle with you. Just let me get my bag." Kit hurried back behind the counter.

"You ask me, not tell me," snapped the guard. Once again, Kit had managed to upset the man. She decided not to say anything more to him than need be.

"Kit, your ovens are loaded with bread," her sister pointed out. "Plus, there are an abundance of orders to fill since it is so close to Christmas. You can't leave here now." Brenna shook her head and rubbed her large belly. While Kit was tall and slender, her younger sister was short and round. The baby was due in about a week and it was no secret that Brenna would be of no help to her now or any time in the near future. This was a bad time for Kit to leave her shop, but she had no other choice. She needed to help her son and would do whatever it took. Parker's safety depended on her now, and she would do the best she could to fill the role of both mother and father to the boy.

"I'm sorry, Brenna, but I have to go. I can't leave Parker," Kit told her sister. "I promise I'll be back as soon as I can."

"Please, don't leave, sister." Brenna's brow furrowed in fear, and with good reason. Birthing a baby was difficult. Oftentimes the baby or the mother, or both, didn't even live. And to put the responsibility of the bakery on her shoulders now, too, was only going to cause the girl unneeded stress.

"It's all right, we'll be fine. Just go," said Oliver with a wave of his half-fingerless hand. "We'd do the same for our own son and understand. It's important that you're there with him. We'll take care of things here at the shop for you. When do we take the bread out of the oven?"

Kit hesitated, feeling doomed. It wasn't a smart idea to leave these two to handle her business. They'd only been here for a fortnight now, coming to live with Kit, having nowhere else to go in their time of great need. Neither of them really knew enough about the business or baking to be of much help in this situation. Plus, if Brenna went into labor now, all hell would break loose. Kit would probably lose her business, that is, if the shop didn't burn down first. She needed these sales to help support all of them. Burnt bread wasn't going to do them any good.

"Oliver, fetch Vivian, my sister-by-marriage. She knows

about baking and has helped me many times since Gerold's passing. She will help until I return."

"Vivian?" asked Oliver, squinting his eyes, seeming to try to remember the woman.

"You met her when you first arrived," Kit told him. "She is my late husband's sister and is married to the cordwainer at the edge of town. Now go. Brenna cannot be alone for long."

"Yes. Right. I'll be right back, my love," Oliver told his wife, kissing her and then hurrying out the door.

"We're going to the wagon," snarled the guard, pulling Parker out the door. "And if you're not there when I'm ready to leave, I'm not waiting." The bells over the door jangled again. The guard left with her son, the door swinging closed behind them.

"Brenna, promise me you won't go into labor before I return." Kit picked up a few things and threw them into her bag. Then she eyed up the fresh tarts cooling on a shelf behind her. She grabbed a cherry-almond tart and quickly wrapped it in brown paper and placed it gently into her bag, careful not to break the crust.

"You're taking food with you?" asked Brenna in shock. "Why? Are you planning on being gone that long?"

"Nay, of course not. I'll be back soon, I promise. This is not for me. Lady Othren will be here for tarts soon, so be sure to wrap them gently. She doesn't like when they break." Kit hurried across the room and pulled open the door. "I am hoping to be able to win over Lord Tolin so Parker doesn't end up whipped, without a hand, or in the dungeon."

"You're going to bribe a nobleman?" Brenna sounded horrified.

Kit turned and faced her sister. "If I have to, then yes," she answered calmly. "I will do whatever it takes to protect my son. Now I can only pray that this man is easily persuaded."

CHAPTER 2

L ord Tolin Blake glanced over the top of his cards, eyeing up each of the players sitting at the trestle table in the great hall. He was usually good at deciphering what kind of hands they held. Six of them played a card game he'd invented. Tolin liked games. A lot. He was competitive and didn't tolerate losing. This game was his lucky charm, and so far today he'd won every hand.

"It's your turn, Rook," said Tolin, recognizing the frustrated curve of his older brother's brows. Rook wasn't good at hiding his emotions. He was always so serious and needed to learn to relax more and actually have fun. Tolin lived for fun, not getting caught up in all the troubles that his father or brother always seemed to focus upon. "We don't have all day," he taunted him.

"Brother, I don't think we are setting a good example by gambling during Advent," complained Rook. His eyes scanned the room of onlookers. "It is bad enough that you've promoted drinking during a time that is meant for fasting. Next, you'll be eating meat before the required fasting time is over."

"Oh, ease up, Rook," scoffed Tolin, never being one to follow rules. Even if they were from the church. Tomorrow is Christmas Eve and the required fasting is over then anyway. In my opinion, we're close enough. Now lay down your card and stop worrying so much. Focus on the game."

"Fine." Rook's hand wavered between two cards. Then he threw down a card and released a deep puff of air from his mouth. "Three of acorns."

"Three of acorns?" Tolin eyed the card and chuckled. "Seriously? Brother, that is truly a pathetic move."

"Stop it," grumbled Rook, his eyes glancing back and forth to the onlookers once more. Tolin's older brother always seemed to worry what everyone around them might be thinking. Rook cared too much about the opinions of others. Tolin on the other hand, couldn't care less.

"Even a girl can beat that!" Tolin continued, looking over at his sister, the only female playing cards. "Go ahead, Raven. Show up your twin brother. I know you can do it."

"Convincing a woman who is now a mother to play your silly game during Advent has got to be the worst idea ever," Rook continued to complain.

"Stop fussing. I agreed to it, Brother," said Raven, studying her cards.

"So did I, but Tolin more or less threatened me if I didn't play," spoke up the youngest of the brothers, Daegel. "You know, if Father were here, he'd make you abide by the Advent rules."

"And if Mother were here, she'd be on Tolin's side." Raven's mouth curved up into a sly smile. She was just as competitive as Tolin—a trait that was not normally found in girls. Then again, Raven wasn't your usual female. "I'll play the queen of horses," said Raven proudly, gingerly placing her card atop the others. It was a card depicting a queen riding atop a horse, holding a sword in the air. "I think it is fitting since I'm good with a horse as well as a blade."

Raven wasn't one of those helpless women. She was independent and skilled with weapons. Tolin's sister could best most men on the practice field and was proud of it. However, since birthing a baby seven months ago she didn't have a sword in her hand as much anymore. Instead, she could usually be found in the ladies' solar with a needle and thread in her grip. Or playing with her daughter with some of the other mothers and their children. Raven was truly embracing motherhood lately. Even though she married the blacksmith, Jonathon, they were in love. Raven surprised Tolin by really seeming to be enjoying having a child. There wasn't a day that went by that she wasn't telling Tolin or the rest of her brothers what her perfect daughter, little Sparrow, had learned to do. Rook's son, Beowulf, was the same age as Sparrow. However, Rook's wife Rose never bragged about their child.

"Well, I'm out," spat Daegel, not bothering to throw down his cards face up. Daegel folded his arms over his chest and looked like he was pouting. He'd come in last place every round.

"Daegel, stop fretting," said Tolin, busying himself by rearranging the cards he held close to his chest. "You're going to be dubbed a knight soon and need to start showing a little more pride and honor in everything you do. Like me."

"Like who?" spat Rook, nearly choking on his own spit at

hearing that. "Pride, yes, but honor? You? Seriously? Don't make me laugh, Tolin." Rook made a face and ran his hand through his long, black hair, smoothing it back.

"If Brother Ruford sees me playing cards and drinking during Advent, I might not be dubbed a knight after all," worried Daegel.

"Our father's uncle is at the monastery where he belongs and not here, so don't even think twice about it," Tolin tried to reassure him. "Besides, he is in charge of St. Basil's, but I am in charge of Blake Castle until Father returns. So I make the rules until then."

Rook wanted to tell him it doesn't work that way, but whatever his warning, it was sure to fall on deaf ears. Tolin did things his own way and always had. No silly rules were ever going to change that.

Tolin, Rook, and Daegel all looked so similar that there was no doubt they were brothers. Black hair and blue eyes were a common trait of a Blake. Even so, Tolin thought he was the handsomest of the three. After all, the females were always following him around, wanting him to pay them special attention. And he usually did.

Rook held Tolin's eye and spoke. "Being honorable, little brother, doesn't mean breaking holy rules or inventing silly card games that you are sure to win. Games with stupid names like Awful."

Now it was Tolin's turn to make a face. "Rook, you don't even know the name of the game you play. It's called Tolinoffel, named after the oldest card game known to man, Karnöffle. Not Awful. Get it right."

"All right," said Rook. "Tolin Awful." He smiled sarcastically.

"Tolin's awful, I agree," muttered Daegel, covering his face with his hands. Daegel had always idolized Rook and wanted to be just like him. Tolin, on the other hand, wanted to be as different from Rook as he possibly could.

"Excuse me, my lords and lady." Emeric, the castle steward, stopped at their table in the great hall and bowed.

"What is it, Emeric?" asked Raven, standing in as lady of the castle in their mother's absence.

"Henry the guard wishes an audience with you. He says it is important."

"Hold on." Tolin raised his hand in the air. "It can wait. I still need to play my last card."

"Tolin, I have the queen of horses. Face it, it's over. I won," said Raven, sounding overly confident. "Accept the fact that someone finally beat you at your own game."

"And about time, too," mumbled Rook. "I am so glad this stupid game is over. I don't know why I even let you talk me into playing it in the first place. I should be spending time with Rose and Beowulf."

"I agree about this being a waste of time," chimed in Daegel. "It's over, Tolin. You lose." He started to get up but Tolin stopped him.

"Nay, nay, nay, sit back down," said Tolin in a scolding voice. "All of you." A smile widened across his face. He plucked a card from his hand and plopped it down over his sister's queen of horses. "As you see, I have just played the Tolinoffel of Bells."

"The what?" asked the steward, getting pulled into the conversation. The man squinted and leaned over to look closer at the card in play.

"It's a card that can't lose," explained Tolin. "Each of the

Tolinoffel cards of the deck automatically trumps the others, hence Raven's queen. Therefore, I won! Once again, the pot is mine." Tolin chuckled and scooped the pile of coins together, dragging them across the table to him.

"I feel the need to go pray in the chapel. I hope I haven't risked my chance of becoming a knight because of Tolin's awful game," complained Daegel, getting up and walking away.

"Don't worry, Brother Ruford will never find out," Tolin called after him.

Someone approached behind him, clearing their throat. "Tolin, what are you doing?"

Tolin didn't need to turn around to recognize the voice of the abbot of St. Basil's Monastery, Brother Ruford. The stout, round man was also the uncle of Tolin's father.

"Brother Ruford. How good of you to join us." Tolin slowly turned to face him, his hands still covering the heap of coins he'd won from his siblings.

The screaming of a young child was heard from across the great hall, causing everyone to cover their ears from the piercing shrieks.

"That sounds like my daughter." Raven stood up and brushed off her gown. "Excuse me."

"She sounds more like a Banshee, not a tiny little baby with the fragile name of Sparrow," scoffed Rook. "My son never screams like that!"

Raven frowned at her twin. "Please don't say such things about your niece. She is too young to know now, but someday might hear your insults."

"She's right," said Tolin. "Even if the girl does scream like a Banshee."

"It is a stage my daughter is going through, since she is teething. Rook's son doesn't have teeth yet," Raven replied. "The nursemaid is having problems calming her lately, but it won't last forever."

"We hope," said Rook in not much more than a whisper.

"I'd better go to her." Raven turned to look over at the steward. "Oh, what was it you wanted, Emeric?"

"I'll handle it. Go calm Sparrow before my ears blow out from her noisy crying," said Rook with a wave of his hand in the air.

"Are you really playing cards during Advent?" asked Brother Ruford with a frown.

The monk didn't alarm Tolin in the least. But Tolin almost laughed aloud when he saw the disturbed look on Rook's face. His older brother quickly tried to change the conversation rather than to admit to the monk that he willingly let Tolin lead him astray.

"Emeric, what is it you want?" asked Rook, putting all his attention on the steward.

"My lords," said Emeric clearing his throat. "This is of great importance."

Tolin ignored him, scooping up his winnings and shoving the coins into his pouch.

"Lord Corbett won't be happy when he finds out you are all playing cards during Advent," Brother Ruford told them.

"My father left me in charge, and I didn't think it was a problem," Tolin defended himself. "I mean, I am planning all the entertainment during the Yuletide celebrations and I needed to test out my new game ahead of time to make sure it will go well. That's all."

"I see," said Ruford. His beefy hand shot out, open palm

upwards. "So, then. I am sure you meant for the winnings of this evil gambling during a holy day to be given to the church. As repentance for your sin and to help pay for decorating the church for Christmas. Right?"

Tolin looked at the man's open hand and then over to his brother. Rook nodded slightly and his clenched jaw ticked. While Tolin didn't think he'd done anything wrong, he was sure Brother Ruford would make his life a living hell if he refused. Rook also wouldn't let him hear the end of this if he didn't agree. He let out a sigh. Dangling the pouch of coins from two fingers, he dropped it into the holy man's open hand. "Of course, that's what I had in mind, Brother Ruford. It is all for the church. Until I win it back, at least," he said, the latter under his breath as he collected his cards.

Rook heard and glared at him now. "Tolin, all you ever think about is having fun. Eating, drinking, and making merry is all that's important to you." Rook's hands waved in the air dramatically as he spoke.

"What's wrong with that?" Tolin shrugged. "It sure beats always being frustrated, tired, and grumpy like you."

Emeric cleared his throat once more. "My lords? There is a situation that needs to be handled and I'm afraid, it can wait no longer."

"God's eyes, what is so important?" asked Tolin.

The monk cleared his throat loudly, a silent reminder that Tolin was cursing. Total blasphemy, no doubt. Just one more thing for Brother Ruford to add to his list when he reported back to Tolin's father upon his return.

"The castle guard has caught a thief in town trying to steal from him. He wants to know how the offender should be punished," Emeric relayed the information.

"Well, I'm off to the tavern for a spell. I mean...off to town," Tolin corrected himself in front of the monk. He stood up and stretched and yawned. Tolin had hoped to be able to find some betting men at the tavern who would appreciate a good game of Tolinoffel so he could continue to test out his new game. Still, he figured he'd better not admit it aloud.

"Aren't you forgetting something?" Rook raised a brow.

Tolin looked down at the table. "What? Did I miss a coin?" He stretched his neck and patted the table to double check.

"Nay. I'm sure you'd never forget a coin. I'm talking about the fact that you seem to have forgotten that our father put you in charge of Blake Castle until his return," Rook reminded him.

"Oh, that. Yes. I didn't forget. What about it?"

"You can't leave. You need to decide how to punish the thief." Rook nodded toward the steward. The guard stood a little ways behind him, blocking their view of the offender.

"He's right," said Ruford. "It is your responsibility."

"Me?" Tolin didn't want to punish anyone. He was only watching over the castle during the Christmas celebrations to keep things in good order. To control the crowds during the festival and make sure they didn't run out of sweetmeats or wine. He was there to make sure everyone had a jolly good time. "I'm sure there must be some holy rule that no prisoners can be punished or killed during the holy season. It should wait until my father's return."

"No executions can happen during the holy days, but the thief's future needs to be determined," Ruford informed him.

"That's right," agreed Rook. "We can't let a thief continue to roam the lands. He could very well end up stealing from us, right here at the castle. Something needs to be done right away."

"Now wait a minute," said Tolin with a raised hand. "I decide what we eat and drink during Christmastide and how many musicians will play at the celebrations. It's my job to make sure couples embrace under the kissing bough and dance until morning. I am in charge of food and entertainment only. Father told me that I am in charge until Twelfth Night. However, I must point out, he said nothing, and I repeat *nothing*, about holding court or trials. Or handing out sentences of any kind. I don't really think I'm qualified to do that."

"Nay, not so," Rook objected. "You need to handle every aspect of every matter in Father's absence. Including thieves. Now, tell the guard what to do about it." Rook stretched out his arm with his palm up, forcing Tolin's attention toward the steward. "Make a decision, Tolin. This is all up to you."

"Nay. You do it." Tolin shook his head, wanting nothing more than to leave and head for the tavern. He never agreed to something like this. It wasn't what he was good at. He liked to stick with things where he knew he could exceed.

"No, I will not. This is all on you now, Tolin," Rook stubbornly announced, even though he had much more experience with these kinds of things. "After all, if you are ever lucky enough to have your own manor house or castle someday, you'll need to learn how to run it. So, start practicing now."

"I don't know." Tolin looked down at his cards,

shoving them into the pouch at his side. Only pride kept him from turning and running right now. He loved his freedom and having no ties to anything other than his knightly vows and loyalty in fighting for his king. But this was different. He didn't know nor did he care what the guard did with the petty thief. To him, this was of no importance.

"My lord?" Both the steward and the guard stared at him now. So did Brother Ruford and Rook. He felt heat building up inside him. Normally Tolin liked being the center of attention. But that was when he sparred on the practice field with the other knights, played cards with his friends, or even danced with a pretty woman. This was not the type of attention he liked at all. He didn't need it and certainly didn't want it. Still, he had accepted the responsibility, talking his father into letting him run the castle in his absence and he really didn't want to let him down.

"Tolin? He needs an answer." Rook's prodding was like a knife twisting in the wound.

"I don't really care what happens to the thief. Just put him in the dungeon until Lord Corbett returns," Tolin told the steward, thinking it would now be over. He abruptly turned to go now that he'd made his decision.

"Nay! Please, my lord, don't do that." A woman in a cloak with her head covered, stepped out from behind the guard, holding the hand of a young boy who couldn't be more than seven or eight years of age. She rushed over to the trestle table where he'd played cards and kneeled down in front of him. The girl lowered her head, staring at the floor when she spoke. "Please, my lord, don't put him in the dungeon. He never meant to steal."

Tolin and Rook exchanged confused glances. Who were this woman and child and why were they here?

"He? Do you mean him?" Tolin nodded at the child.

"This is the thief? This young boy?" Rook chuckled lowly, enjoying the fact that Tolin's life just got worse.

"Yes, my lords." The guard hurried over to join them. "When I took the wagon to town for supplies for the holiday celebration, I caught the miscreant lad trying to lift my sword."

"Really?" asked Tolin, in just as much shock as Rook. "Is this true?" The thought of the thief being a child almost made him laugh aloud. But seeing the serious looks on everyone else's faces, he decided he'd better bite his tongue instead.

"It is true that my son lifted the sword," said the woman. "But it isn't what you think."

"*Your* son?" Tolin eyed up the woman kneeling at his feet. He couldn't see her well beneath her hooded cloak, but he surmised that she barely seemed old enough to have a son that was eight or nine. "Tell me, I'm curious," he continued. "What exactly is it that I think?"

The distraught woman continued. "Parker was curious, nothing more. He wanted to feel the sword's weight, not to steal it. Honest, it's the truth. Have pity on him, my lord. He is just a boy." The woman slowly lifted her face. When she did, the hood of her cloak fell back. Sunlight from the window bathed her tanned skin. The rays fell upon her long oaken hair that was twisted into a loose knot at the back of her head. Some of the strands had spilled free and now fell across her face. A powdery white streak was smeared over her cheek. The woman's eyes glowed with the color of acorns, much like the ones painted on Tolin's deck of playing cards. The only difference was that her eyes looked glassy and filled with tears. For some reason, his heart went out to her.

"What should be the thief's punishment, my lord?" The guard asked once again. "Did you still want me to imprison him? Or mayhap a good lashing would teach the boy a lesson not to steal again. Or did you mayhap want something more severe?"

"More severe?" repeated Tolin, thinking of how the child would cry to feel the sting of a whip against his fragile skin.

"Nay! Please, don't hurt him. He's just a child. I beg you, let the boy go." The woman pulled her son to her bosom, clutching him protectively, acting like a lioness defending her cub.

Tolin's eyes traveled back to his brother hoping Rook would give him some insight on how to handle this odd situation. Of course, Rook didn't.

"Well, good luck," whispered Rook with a nod of his head, quickly turning and walking away. Tolin squeezed his eyes shut and slowly opened them again, feeling doomed and trapped. He couldn't believe his own brother would do this to him, leaving him in such a position. Rook was a poor example of a helpful brother. After all, Rook was the eldest and also had his own manor. He was used to these types of things, Tolin wasn't. Surely, this decision would be easy for Rook to handle. He was probably still just being a sore loser from the card game and this was his way of retaliating. He looked back at Brother Ruford. The monk stuck his hands in his cassock, seeming to close his eyes in prayer. No help here either.

"My lord?" asked Henry yet again. "What is to be the boy's punishment for trying to steal from a castle guard?"

Tolin hated this more than anything. He didn't like making decisions unless they directly affected him. And he didn't like women begging at his feet unless it involved pleasures in the bedchamber. He honestly didn't know what to do.

If he didn't punish the boy, he would seem weak in front of everyone, including his brothers. Tolin never cared what people thought of him, but for some reason, with the boy's mother present, this time he kind of did. Letting the little thief get away with this would also send the message to the rest of the commoners that it was all right to steal from guards and even nobles. Tolin's father wouldn't like that in the least. Nay, he couldn't just dismiss the situation even though he wished it was that easy. He'd have to hand out some kind of sentence, he had no other choice. However, he couldn't give the command to hurt the child or throw him in the dungeon either. Parker was just a young boy and would never survive that! Tolin wasn't a cold-hearted bastard. He didn't want to hurt the child, he wanted to protect him, just like his mother was doing. But this boy was a thief.

The boy's mother was still on her knees with tears running down her cheeks. Tolin looked around for Raven to help him, but she'd already left the great hall with her crying baby. Raven would have his head if he did anything to harm a child. Now that she was a mother, she'd been acting as fierce protecting not only her own daughter but the children of any of their family members. Just this morning she was even helping protect the children of the servants as the young ones played in the courtyard. They had chased a ball and got in the way of the mounted guards as they headed out on their rounds. Raven flung herself in front of the horses and ordered the men to stop. Then she collected up the children and huddled with them as she openly shouted at the men for their carelessness. This was something that he'd never seen her do before.

"Please, I beg you once again, my good lord. I will do anything you wish if you spare my son from being punished." The woman kneeling before him sounded desperate. Tolin didn't like to see anyone beg.

He drew in a deep breath and slowly released it. His eyes quickly scanned the room. Every occupant in the great hall watched and listened even though they pretended not to be paying attention.

"Get up," he told the woman in a deep growl. "Stand up and face me instead of groveling at my feet like a dog. That act is pathetic, even for a commoner such as yourself."

When she did nothing to move, Tolin reached out and took her arm, yanking her to her feet. She wore the clothes of a peasant and he figured she lived in town. The rough wool of her gown felt scratchy to his touch. Her simple dress was covered by a white apron that had a bib that traveled up and over her curvy breasts. Even clothed in this manner, she appeared to be a comely wench. At any rate, she was a relatively clean one who shouldn't be on her knees on the floor. Her skin looked smooth and silky. It took everything in his power not to reach out and rub his fingers across her cheek to find out if he was correct. The woman's hair was mussed but clean. It smelled like fresh bread, if he wasn't mistaken. Bread. Mmmm. His stomach growled at the thought. Since he'd slept late this morning he'd missed the meal to break the fast. Now all he could think of was food.

"Don't cry," he told her, not liking to see a woman so upset. He was a gentleman through and through, no matter if his siblings thought of him as naught but a scoundrel or a philanderer. Tolin strived to make women smile. If there was a female frowning in the room, then he wasn't putting his charm to good use and doing his job. Feeling bold as usual, he reached out and brushed away her tears with his thumb. An isolated gasp resonated from the quiet room behind him. The silence served as nothing more than a reminder that he was a noble and she a mere peasant from town. Perhaps he shouldn't have touched her in such a familiar manner. Or at least not in front of half the castle. "You have white powder on your face. What is it?" He made a big show of rubbing his fingers together, hopefully convincing everyone watching that he was reprimanding her for coming to the castle looking unkempt or dusty.

Her hand flew to cover her cheek. "Oh, no. I'm so sorry, my lord. It must be flour. I own a bakery shop in town and we've been very busy lately."

"*You* own a shop?" He cocked his head, not believing how brash she was being by saying this aloud. "Woman, you will refer to yourself as the wife of the baker from now on, as is proper. I do not think your husband would care to hear you claiming his business as your own. No woman has the right to do so."

"You are wrong, my lord," she said, raising her chin slightly, meeting his challenge. Her bottom lip quivered but she stared straight at him and kept her gaze steady. "I do have the right to claim the shop as my own. You see, I am a widow. My husband was in the Baker's Guild, and the law clearly states that the store reverts to me now that he is deceased."

Tolin pressed his lips together in thought and nodded slightly. This was something he hadn't expected in the least. Impressive. Most men would be appalled by this woman's audacity, even if what she said was the truth. He, on the other hand, found her defensive nature rather refreshing. Intriguing. Her actions excited him. Oddly, Tolin found himself impressed by this woman's strength, especially as she was naught but a commoner. He supposed having a sister who was bold and strong, and also very opinionated and acted like a man at times, made him used to seeing a woman behave outside the expected way. But Raven was an exception. And she only got away with it because she was the only daughter of a well-known and well-liked lord.

"I'm sorry, my lord," said the woman in a mere whisper. Her gaze lowered to his feet. Tolin was sure she regretted her words as they might have angered him, and also put her son at risk for a stricter sentence. "Please, forgive me."

Tolin chuckled. "Well, that all depends."

Her eyes snapped upward. "On what, my lord?"

"On if you are any good." Tolin raised a brow, toying with her, letting his eyes rake down her body. He swore he saw her tremble. Still, she proudly held her composure.

"My lord, what exactly do you mean?" Her face blushed and she looked away, not able to let their eyes interlock. The boy stayed still and silent at her side. The guard and the steward shifted their weight back and forth uncomfortably. Brother Ruford swayed his weight from one foot to another as well, quietly mumbling a prayer. Tolin liked this game between he and the woman, and wasn't about to let it end so soon.

"What do *you* think I mean?" he asked her.

She swallowed forcefully, looking as if she were biting the inside of her cheek, keeping herself from saying something she might regret later. "I am sure I don't know, my lord," she answered.

"Then let me tell you."

"My lord, perhaps it would be better if—" The steward was cut short when Tolin raised his hand to silence the man.

"I am curious if you are any good...at baking," Tolin blurted out, and smiled widely when he saw the woman release a relieved breath. "I want to know if you are experienced in the kitchen. Did you perhaps think I was referring to your skills in a different room instead?"

Her face slowly lifted. She looked at him from the corner of her eyes, shocking him with her answer. "Would you like to find out for yourself how good I am, my lord?" Mischief danced in her eyes, making her even more attractive. And alluring.

Tolin groaned inwardly when he felt his loins tightening. She was good at this game and he enjoyed the challenge. Aye, he'd like to find out if she was any good in bed, that thought had crossed his mind. Plus, the woman said she'd do anything if he let the boy go. He'd bet anything that she had stamina that could give him pleasure for hours in lovemaking. But as much as he entertained the thought, he knew she wasn't really talking about coupling. After all, a woman like her would never do so in front of her young son. Instead of answering her question, he asked her another, just like she had done to him. "Would *you* like me to find out? Perhaps you could...show me?" He played with her, throwing words back at her that had double meanings. Games were Tolin's specialty. Games with pretty women were his favorite. This particular one was proving to be more pleasurable than he'd expected. He didn't want it to end.

"I'd like that, my lord," she answered, causing his jaw to drop. The mouths of the steward and guard hung open as well. Brother Ruford's prayers got a little louder. Damn it, he couldn't stop thinking of what this game could really mean, although both of them knew it was nothing of the kind.

"Y-you would?" he asked, coughing, and really needing a drink right now. His mouth felt dry and it was getting hard to swallow.

"Yes." Her eyes lit up and a devilish smile spread across her face. She had to know how her words affected him. Tolin only hoped no one else noticed. He quickly dropped his arms, hoping to hide his loins. "I *desire* to let you *taste* my talents," she continued, only making things worse with the way she stressed certain sensual words. "With your permission, of course, my lord." Her hand slowly traveled up her hip and his gaze followed. Her fingers settled on the bag she carried over her shoulder.

"My lord," the steward whispered in warning, his thoughts probably being on bedding the girl too. "Please, don't answer that. It's not proper."

Tolin's hand shot up in the air to hush the steward once again. All the while, his eyes stayed focused on the vixen standing before him, offering to give him everything his heart desired and so much more. "Yes," he blurted out, triggering off hushed whispers from the crowd. The guard and steward both took a step backward. Brother Ruford held on to the trestle table, slowly lowering himself to the bench. "Yes, I'd like to taste your talents." He purposely moved closer to the girl, bringing his face near hers, teasing her but at the same time only torturing himself. He truly did want to taste those plump lips as well as her tongue. She raised her chin and looked him right in the eye, which was a brash move for a commoner. Still, it made him feel desire stir within him. Mayhap she was going to kiss him. Nothing would surprise him when it came to this woman.

Leaning in even closer, she spoke and all his attention was on her mouth although he didn't hear a word she was saying. He dipped his head down, moving in to taste her sweet lips, his focus on nothing but kissing the wench. If he hadn't been so smitten with her, he would have realized she was making a fool of him in front of everyone. Aye, this woman was better at this game than he. And Tolin didn't like losing.

"Here," she said, raising a hand-sized fruit tart between them. His lips ended up on the pie instead of on her mouth. He pulled back in surprise, ready to chastise her. But when he opened his mouth to speak, he tasted something delicious. Tolin's tongue darted out to lick the sweet flavor from his lips, the action bringing him back to his senses.

"Mmmm," he said, lifting his hand to his mouth. "Is that cherry I'm tasting?"

"Cherry-almond with fresh butter and a sprinkle of saffron. It's my specialty."

"Saffron?" gasped the steward. "That spice is expensive and reserved for nobles. What are you doing with it?"

"Baking with butter during Advent is prohibited," added the monk.

"The baker's guild has the pope's permission to use butter, now that it is so close to Christmas," the woman told them. "I get a lot of orders from nobles who are ordering baked goods for their upcoming celebrations." Her eyes traveled back to Tolin and she held out the pie like a peace offering between them. "I like to please my clients as much as I possibly can."

"Do you, now?" asked Tolin, reaching out for the hand tart. He wondered if she'd still say that if he ever managed to get her in his bed. He took a big bite of the tart and moaned aloud in exaltation. Everyone was supposed to fast during Advent, as instructed by the church. Butter, dairy, and even meat had been forbidden for the last four weeks and it was making everyone cranky. In some places even wine and ale was prohibited, but thankfully Tolin's father had received special permission so they hadn't had to give it up. The church was delusional, thinking that everyone was really going to adhere to these stupid rules. Especially the one of no coupling during Advent. Tolin wasn't the kind of person who could live by rules such as this. Even if the orders supposedly came straight from God himself.

"I take it my talents please you, my lord?" The baker woman looked up at him with big, beautiful brown eyes.

He devoured the tart in several bites and licked the powdery sugar from his lips. It was heaven, and the best thing he'd tasted in a month now. Tolin proceeded to lick the cherry filling from his fingers next. "You have no idea how much I enjoy your talents." His mind went astray again, but when the boy spoke, all lusty thoughts fled his head.

"My mother makes the best tarts as well as the most delicious bread you'll ever taste," said the boy. "Her Christmas stollen has ten different types of fruit in it."

"Does it, now?" Tolin had an idea.

"Parker, don't exaggerate," said the boy's mother. "It is only seven types of fruit in the stollen."

"My lord, what is the boy's punishment?" asked the guard once again.

"Patience," said Tolin, not wanting to be pushed into handing out a sentence in such an awkward situation. Not yet. Mayhap, if he was smart, he could turn this incident around and make it beneficial to him after all. The girl might be good at this game, but he was better and had the final say. There was no way he'd lose, because he was used to winning. "What is your name?" he asked the woman.

"My name is Kit Baker, my lord."

"Kit?" he repeated in question. "Named because you were small like a kitten when you were born?"

A slight grin turned up the corners of her mouth and a blush stained her cheeks. "Nay, my lord. My parents were Katherine and Christopher. My name is a combination of the two."

"I see." Tolin fingered his chin in thought. "Well, I have come up with the lad's punishment," he finally announced.

The girl watched with wide eyes in anticipation.

"Please, don't send him to be locked away," she said in a mere whisper, seeming to be holding her breath, waiting for his answer. Her arms closed tighter around her son. If he was going to take the boy, he was sure he'd have to pry the lad from her fingers.

"On the contrary, I am not sending him anywhere. I am going to keep him right here at the castle," he told her.

"What?" Kit, as well as the steward and the guard, all said at once.

"Your son, as well as you, Kit Baker, will stay at Blake Castle through the holidays and that is my final decision."

"I don't understand, my lord." The girl's thin brows dipped in confusion. "Why would we stay here? Our home is at the bakery. In town."

"I understand that, but I could use a good baker for the upcoming Christmas festivities."

"Excuse me, my lord, but we already have many good bakers in the castle's kitchen," said Emeric.

"I don't care. I want another," Tolin told him, looking over to Kit. "I want your skills, so I think you will do just fine, Kit Baker. The boy will work in the kitchen along with you. He will also help serve tables during the meals."

He could tell by the look on Kit's face that this decision didn't please her in the least. "My son is not a servant and neither am I," she ground out. "I have a business to run, Lord Tolin. This is my busiest season. Not to mention, my very pregnant sister and her husband live with me and I need to be there to support them."

"My lord, I am not sure that is the kind of sentence usually given to a thief," the steward tried to persuade him to change his decision.

"No, it isn't and is quite unusual," Brother Ruford agreed.

"Whether it is usual or not, it doesn't matter. It is the sentence I have decided upon," Tolin told them in finality.

"My lord, is there any other way?" Kit's eyes held anguish and determination.

"Didn't you say you'd be willing to do anything if I didn't harm your son or put him in the dungeon?" Tolin folded his arms over his chest and waited.

"Well, yes. Yes, I did." Kit's eyes moved back and forth from him to his steward and next his guard and back again. "But to walk away from my business? That could ruin me. Please, there must be another way."

"Yes. Of course, you are right," said Tolin with a shrug. He looked over to the guard. "Let the girl go back to her bakery."

"Thank you," said Kit, smiling until she heard the rest of what he had to say.

"The girl is free to leave but be sure to put the boy in the dungeon," Tolin told the guard. "He is a thief and must pay for his mistake."

"Nay! That's not what I meant, my lord." Kit's eyes filled with tears again. It was almost enough to make Tolin let them both walk away. Almost. The taste of her tart still lingered on his tongue, causing him to stick to his original decision, wanting more of her delicious desserts.

"It is either you both work in the castle kitchen until the end of Twelfth Night, or you go back to your shop and your son spends the holidays locked up in a cell. So, what will it be?"

He watched the woman turn white and sway slightly when her eyes closed. Then she opened her eyes again and pulled her son to her even closer, wrapping her arms around him so tightly that Tolin was sure the boy couldn't breathe.

"I will never abandon my son," she told him. "Although I

don't agree with your decision, my lord, I would risk my business to keep Parker from being hurt or imprisoned."

"Good," said Tolin with a slight nod. "Then it's done. You will both report to my kitchen first thing in the morning. And I'll expect more of those tantalizing tarts amongst other baked goods that will intrigue and amaze all those at the Christmastide celebrations."

As he walked away, he felt the satisfaction of having won the challenge and getting what he really wanted. He had no desire to harm a child or put the boy behind bars. Neither did he want to ruin the woman's business. Thankfully, the woman agreed to his terms because if she hadn't, he wasn't sure what he would have done. He bluffed his way through this game, but had a feeling the woman named Kit was going to prove to be a challenge and true competitor before this was over. She was amazingly good at not only baking but also getting what she wanted. He liked her competitive nature! And he was already devising more games in his mind that he and the pretty baker from town could play together.

CHAPTER 3

"**K**it, you can't really leave your bakery unattended. Please. I don't want to birth my baby without you," said Brenna the next morning, not wanting Kit to go.

"She doesn't have a choice, sweetheart." Oliver took Brenna's hands in his as Kit dragged a loaded-down bag to the door of her shop.

"That's right," agreed Kit. "It was Lord Tolin's decision, not mine. Still, it is better that Parker and I live at the castle for the holiday season rather than my child ending up in the dungeon. Parker, are you ready to go?" Kit called out to her son.

The bells jangled over the door and Kit's sister-by-marriage walked in.

"Oh, good, you're here, Vivian. I'm counting on you to fill the orders until I return." Kit's saving grace was this woman. Without her, there would be no one qualified to run her shop. By law, Kit needed to leave the business in the hands of someone who was a guild member. If she didn't and the guild checked up on her, she'd be fined or mayhap would have her bakery taken away from her. There were rules to be followed. And although Vivian was in the cordwainer's guild now and no longer in the baker's guild, it would still be a great risk, but she had to try it. Vivian was her best chance at securing her future. Kit was counting on the fact the woman was in some kind of guild. Hopefully, it would keep Kit out of trouble until her return.

"I can't do this. I'm sorry." Vivian was a small woman with red hair. She never said much but tended to her job and kept to herself, not wanting to create waves. This objection now coming from her was surprising and unexpected.

Kit stood upright and blinked several times in succession, not able to believe what she was hearing. "What did you say, Vivian?"

"I can't cover for you," the girl repeated, letting her gaze drop to the floor. She obviously felt as uncomfortable about this situation as Kit did at the moment.

"I know it's not much that I can pay you, but I promise to give you more later as I can."

"It's not the pay. I just can't."

"You can't? Why not?" Kit put down her things and moved closer to the girl. It wasn't hard to see Vivian's whole body was shaking. "You've helped me out before," Kit continued. "My husband was your brother. I need your help now. Please, don't abandon me."

"I'm sorry, Kit. Willis won't let me do it," Vivian blurted out, wringing her hands together.

"Willis," said Kit with a nod, releasing a deep breath. Why had she even thought that the man wouldn't try to cause her trouble?

"Why won't he let you help us?" Oliver demanded to know. "You helped us out yesterday. What changed?"

"And we are so grateful you helped us, aren't we darling?" Brenna grabbed Oliver's arm and scowled at him. It was her silent warning to be kind to the poor girl.

"Willis never got along with Gerold," said Kit, speaking aloud about her late husband who was also Vivian's brother. "And he also always thought I was a harlot, since I got pregnant with Parker out of wedlock," Kit spoke brashly, stating the truth. "Most people still think I am a strumpet, thanks to him and his untrue gossip."

"Oh, Kit, please don't say that." Vivian wrung her hands together. "It's not true. No one thinks of you in that manner."

When Kit became pregnant by Gerold's brother Crispin, they had planned to be married. But Crispin died quickly and unexpectedly. Gerold, being a widower and having no children of his own, took Kit in and made her his wife. Eyebrows raised in town when the story started to circulate. Especially when Parker was born a mere five months later. It had taken years for the townsfolk to accept Kit as Gerold's wife, but Willis never could seem to befriend Gerold, even though he was married to the man's sister.

"Let me make something clear. I don't care what anyone thinks of me," said Kit, walking back to where she was packing, pulling the strings of the full bag closed tightly. "Vivian, you know how to bake and how to run this business just as well as I do," said Kit. "You have skills and a true talent. You also used to help Gerold before I married him. You once belonged to the baker's guild, and it is not easy to be accepted by them. If I don't have you here in my absence,

I'm afraid I will truly lose the business. Forever. Why does Willis despise me so much that he'd order you to stay away and doom me to this fate?"

"It's not that he despises you, Kit," said the nervous woman. "Well, not really. Willis heard that Parker was caught stealing. I'm sorry, but he doesn't want me to associate with thieves."

"Are you talking about me?" Parker walked into the room with a bag of his things thrown over his shoulder. "I'm not a thief, no matter what you've heard. I wasn't stealin' nothin,' I swear."

"Anything," Kit corrected him. "Vivian, my son won't even be here at the shop, so why does it even matter?" Please. I need you. Can't you try to change your husband's mind?"

"I'm sorry, Kit, I wish I could help you, but he was adamant with his decision. And I swear I hold nothing against you or Parker. But it is our busy season, too, at the cordwainer's shop. Willis needs my help with the shoes. I wish you the best. Honest, I do." Without waiting for a reply, she turned abruptly and left the shop.

Kit felt her heart sink as the door closed behind her friend, separating them, putting distance between them. She was doomed now and there was nothing she could do about it. She would lose all her customers, not be able to pay the rent, and she and her son as well as her sister and brother by marriage would all be living on the streets by the time she returned from Blake Castle.

"We'll handle the shop for you," promised Oliver, meaning well but doing nothing to ease her worries. The man didn't even know how to build a proper fire in the ovens let alone make a batch of tarts or knead bread.

"I can't lay my burdens on the shoulders of the two of you," Kit said softly. "I won't be here if something should happen."

"Nothing is going to happen," said Oliver.

"That's right. And mayhap I'll be late birthing my baby." Brenna rubbed her very pregnant belly and groaned. With Oliver's help she slowly got seated atop a stool. Ever since their mother had told Brenna and Oliver to leave, Kit's sister was feeling insecure and abandoned. The last thing Kit wanted was to make Brenna feel alone once again. Kit lived through the rejection of her parents when she became pregnant with Parker and had no ring on her finger. It was the hardest time of her life. She didn't wish these kinds of hardships on even her worst enemy.

"Nay, it won't work. I won't leave the two of you here alone." Kit continued to pack her things as she spoke. Then she stopped and pushed the bag away from her. "I just won't do it, that's all. I will refuse to go."

"Mother, nay," gasped Parker. "I don't want to go to the dungeon, and that will be exactly what happens if you resist." The poor boy looked as if he were about to cry. Kit realized he thought she was abandoning him, choosing to stay at the bakery instead of living at the castle with him.

"Nay, you don't understand. I won't leave you, baby, don't worry." She pulled Parker to her in a half-hug. "Oliver, pack up your things as well as a bag for Brenna."

"What?" Brenna's eyes opened wide. "You're asking us to leave here?" Fear washed over the girl's face. "Where will we go? We have no jobs or any other place to live. Oh, please don't do this to us."

"Nay, of course I would never do that." Kit let go of Parker's hand and ran over to comfort her sister now. "I only meant that you two are coming with us."

"We are?" asked Oliver in confusion. "With you...where exactly?"

"Yes," said Kit with a sharp nod. "And I am talking about you two coming with me to the castle."

"Nay!" Brenna shook her head so hard she nearly fell from the stool.

"Aye," said Kit, trying to give a confident nod even though she really wasn't feeling confident with this decision at all. "Why not? If Lord Tolin demands that Parker and I stay at Blake Castle, then you two, being my family, will just join us."

"But we're not nobles. We are naught but common folk," cried Brenna.

"The royals won't want us at the castle," agreed Oliver. "Besides, it won't be allowed."

"Why not?" She faked a smile. "The nobles invite all the peasants and commoners to the Christmas feasts. You won't be asked to leave."

"But what if we are?" Oliver wanted to know. "Where will we go then?"

"I'm sure Lord Tolin can use the extra help during their Christmas celebrations. That is exactly what we will give them."

"We will?" asked Oliver.

"Sister, be serious," said Brenna, shaking her head and

still rubbing her large belly. "What kind of job could I possibly do in my condition?"

"Mother, Lord Tolin is mean," added Parker. "He won't allow them to stay."

"We don't know that." Kit spied her favorite baking pan and went to collect it from the wall. "And Lord Tolin is not mean. After all, he didn't harm you or put you in the dungeon. It will be fine." Kit already started coming up with some sort of plan to make this happen. Lord Tolin seemed to like games and challenges. So that is exactly how she planned on presenting it to him.

"He hates me," said Parker with a pout.

Kit opened up a canvas bag and started shoving baking pans inside. Then she hurriedly collected any leftover bread and baked goods and started wrapping them with brown paper. "Parker, you're being silly. He doesn't hate you. You're just a child."

"And a thief," said Oliver from the side of his mouth, as he headed to the back room.

"I'm not a thief!" Parker huffed, crossing his arms over his chest. Then he ran after Oliver into the other room.

"We must hurry," Kit called out, wrapping the pastries. "Lord Tolin is sending a wagon to collect us and I know how impatient that guard can be. Brenna, can you please help me put the loaves of bread into the bag?" She helped her sister off the stool and shoved a bag into her hand.

"I'm scared, Kit." Brenna slowly placed loaves of freshly baked bread into the bag, taking a second to sniff each one first.

"There is nothing to be frightened about. Women have babies every day. It's a common thing."

"Not that. Well, not *just* that," Brenna corrected herself. "What if Lord Tolin turns us away? Where will we go? I don't want to birth my baby in a trough inside a barn with cows breathing down upon it."

Kit giggled, dragging the heavy bag to the door. "Neither will you have to. We'll be back here in our own home before that baby arrives, I promise you that." Kit said it aloud to calm her sister, but honestly had the same fears as Brenna floating through her mind.

"Back here?" Brenna looked around the room. "Do you really think the business will still be here if we close up shop from now through Twelfth Night?"

"Yes," Kit answered, not able to meet her sister's gaze.

"I know what you're doing, Kit. What you always do. You are trying to cover up the fact that things are about to change and we can do nothing about it."

"Sometimes change is good."

"Mayhap. But don't you think by believing this, you are being a little too optimistic?"

Before anything more could be said, Kit noticed a horse and wagon from the king's castle stop in front of her shop. People gathered around it in the street, wondering if one of the nobles was at her door for a reason.

"The wagon is here!" Kit called out to the others. "Oliver, make certain the fires are out in the ovens. Parker, help me take our things outside. Brenna, bring that bag of bread and don't forget your cloak as it is cold outside. We don't want that baby to freeze. Everyone hurry!" Kit turned the sign around on the door, telling everyone that the bakery was closed.

She half-expected the grumpy guard or mayhap even

Lord Tolin himself to be there to collect them. However, a different man came through her door instead. She had never seen him before. He stopped and looked directly at her.

"I'm here for Kit Barker and the thief," said the red-haired man who looked to be in his early twenties. He was tall and lanky, but carried himself proudly, standing straight and pushing back his shoulders. He wore the clothes of a noble. Her eyes scanned down his form and she realized he wore a weapon belt with a sword at his side under his cloak. He was a fighting man, and mayhap a noble.

"It's Baker, not Barker," she corrected him. "I am Kit Baker and my son is Parker. Who are you?"

"I'm Jarvis, Lord Tolin's squire," said the man. "Which one of these bags is yours?" He looked to the ground where she had piled the things she wanted to bring along with them to the castle.

"They're all mine. And my son's of course," she added, not yet wanting to say anything about Oliver and Brenna.

"I've never seen anyone with so much baggage." He started to pick them up.

"I have a job to do, to bake at the castle. I will need my good pans for that. And recipes, of course."

"Of course," he mumbled, grumbling under his breath about having to haul the things of commoners. The bags were filled to the brim and not light. Yet, the thin man picked them all up at once. "Get the boy and let's go. It looks like rain and I don't plan on getting wet."

"We're leaving," she called over her shoulder to her family. "Now. Hurry!"

Brenna waddled up with her cloak over her shoulders, struggling with the large bag of bread.

"I'll take that." Kit collected the bread bag and followed Jarvis out the door. The rest of her family fell in line. Jarvis was busy loading the things into the back of the wagon and complaining to himself or he would have noticed the entourage behind him. Kit took advantage of the situation. She had Oliver help Brenna up to the bench seat where the driver rode. Then, she helped Oliver up as well. "Oliver, you'll have to ride in back," she said, hoisting herself up next to Brenna and her son.

"Wait a minute. What's all this? What's going on?" Jarvis looked confused as he climbed up to the bench seat to drive the wagon.

"Where is the guard? Or Lord Tolin?" asked Kit, changing the subject by asking a question without answering his. "We need to be protected on our trip to the castle."

By the dark look on the man's face, she knew her distraction had worked. She had purposely wanted the man to feel insulted, hoping he'd forget about them and think about himself instead. "I'm Lord Tolin's squire and I assure you I am quite capable of protecting commoners," spat Jarvis. "I have even saved my lord's life on the battlefield on more than one occasion. I am able to protect the lot of you if trouble should break out, don't worry."

"Good," said Kit. "That makes me feel better." She repositioned herself on the seat, fanning out her cloak that reached to her feet.

"Oh no, I think I felt a raindrop." Brenna held out the palm of her hand. "It's going to rain."

"It is getting colder." Jarvis glanced up at the sky. "By the looks of those clouds, I wouldn't be surprised if it turned into a bad squall or perhaps even a snowstorm before we make it back."

"Then we'd better leave before we get wet," suggested Kit.

Jarvis looked at her from the corner of his eyes with suspicion. "Ms. Barker, I am familiar with games, since Lord Tolin craves them. So, I know this is a game you're playing with me. I must tell you that your distraction will not work with me. Now, answer me. Who are all these people?"

Kit let out a deep sigh, seeing the man was sharper than she'd thought. Just not with remembering names. "Baker, not Barker," she corrected him once again. "This is my son, Parker, and my sister, Brenna, who is going to have a baby any day," she told him, motioning to the two seated next to her.

"A baby. Yes, I see that." Jarvis' gaze dropped to Brenna's large belly. "What about the man in the back who thought I didn't see him get in in the cart? Who is he?"

"That's Oliver. My husband," Brenna relayed the information.

"Mother, it is starting to rain," whined her son. "Can I go in the back with Oliver and get under a blanket?"

"Sure," she said, helping Parker climb over the seat to the open wagon. Oliver helped him get settled. She looked over at Jarvis who wasn't moving. "It would be a shame to see your cloak ruined from the rain," she said, trying to coax him to leave.

"Cloaks are made for all kinds of weather. I'm not worried about it." Jarvis sat there, not in any hurry to leave. "We will stay here as long as we have to, but I'm not leaving until you answer me."

"I told you who these people are," she protested.

"Yes, but you refrained from mentioning why they are traveling with us."

"I knew this was a bad idea," said Brenna, her eyes starting to close from being tired. Kit wanted to muffle her because she was going to spoil her plan.

"I never go anywhere without my other bakers," Kit blurted out hoping Brenna wouldn't say anything else.

"Your other bakers?" asked Brenna. Kit put her finger to her lips, turning her head so only Brenna could see her.

"My orders from Lord Tolin were to pick up the baker and her son. No one else. I'm afraid they're not coming with us on this journey." Jarvis wasn't budging with his decision. This was not turning out well at all. Kit needed to come up with another plan quickly.

The sky was about ready to open up, and the last thing she wanted was to leave Oliver and Brenna here in the midst of a storm. They wouldn't know what to do. Nay, they would never survive on their own. They needed her, and she didn't want to disappoint them.

"Lord Tolin told me he wanted me to bake tarts," said Kit. "And bread. Also, enough food for the celebrations he has planned from now until Twelfth Night. For that kind of volume, more bakers then normal are needed. That is why they are here and coming to the castle with us."

"Oh," said Jarvis, seeming to ponder the thought. "I suppose that makes sense. Lord Tolin does tend to get quite carried away with celebrations and the amount of people he invites to join him. His father left him in charge of the feast days from Christmas until Twelfth Night. I suppose a few extra bakers would come in handy."

"So, we can leave now?" Kit raised her head and looked up at the sky. "I would hate for all the bread and baked goods I am bringing along for Lord Tolin to get ruined by the storm."

"You have food in those bags?" Jarvis sounded hungry. He turned to look over his shoulder at the bags in the back of the wagon.

"Plenty of it," Kit assured him. "Freshly baked this morning, I might add."

The squire looked over at her and nodded. "You're right. We wouldn't want the food to get wet and ruined. Lord Tolin would never forgive me if that happened. We'd better go." Jarvis took the reins and they finally started moving toward the castle.

Kit looked over at her sister and nodded slightly. They'd made it past the first obstacle, but would they be as lucky once they entered the castle courtyard? It was going to be hard enough getting Oliver and Brenna past that obnoxious guard. But Lord Tolin was a different story altogether. Would he see this as an opportunity to make the situation into another one of his silly games by sending Oliver and Brenna away? That, she could not allow. Even from the short time she'd spent with the obnoxious man, she knew better than anyone that competition was everything to him. Another thing that was clear was that he was a man who wasn't used to losing.

∾

Tolin lounged atop the battlements, drinking and playing dice with the guards. He'd rather be at the tavern, but

Brother Ruford had been following him around and he was trying to shake him. At least he knew the overweight monk wouldn't attempt to climb the steep stairs to the top of the castle walls.

He was about to throw the dice again when he heard the squeak of the wheels of the wagon driven by his squire as it arrived. By the loud rumbling sound he knew they were crossing the drawbridge. A second rumble filled the air, and that one was the threatening weather overhead.

"Stop. Who goezzz there?" Henry the guard called down, looking over the battlements. They'd been playing a drinking game and Henry had become a little too familiar with the bottle of whisky they were using. Tolin could already hear the man slurring his words.

"It's me, Jarvis," came Tolin's squire's voice from below. "Raise the gate, quickly. It is raining and we have a very pregnant woman here."

"What?" Tolin looked up and over to the guard. "Did Jarvis say something about a pregnant woman?" He didn't remember the fair wench named Kit looking pregnant at all.

"Aye. Certainly looks that way." Henry took another swig of whisky, peering down over the battlements, almost losing his balance and teetering on the edge. "Raise the gate," he ordered the other men, throwing his hand in the air.

Tolin jumped up, sticking the dice back in his pouch. He hurriedly made his way to the battlements. Glancing over the edge, he saw only the back end of the wagon as it rolled through the gate. "Damn it, what is going on here?" He pulled the bottle out of Henry's hand. "The only ones allowed to enter were the wench and her son. Are you telling me there was a pregnant woman with them?"

"Yes. And a man and a boy too. And a boy. Did I already say that?" Henry squinted as if thinking, trying his best to hold back a burp.

"Henry, go sleep it off in the armory. And no more whisky for you." Tolin took a swig as the sky opened up and the rain pelted down. "Take this," he said, shoving the bottle into the hands of another guard and running down the stairs to the courtyard to meet his prisoners. Something was amiss and he had a feeling the wench was trying to pull something over on him. She was a sly one. He knew that from the moment he'd met her. Aye, he needed to keep a closer eye on her than even with the light-fingered lad.

When he got to the courtyard, everyone was running from the rain, trying to take shelter inside. He dodged a couple of washwomen, a group of children, two barking dogs, and the jester, who was already soaking wet.

"Out of my way," he grumbled, getting to the wagon just in time to see the backs of a woman and a man entering the great hall. The boy was dragging a bag behind him and following them.

"Lord Tolin," said Jarvis, taking the rest of the baggage out of the back of the wagon. He was so loaded down he could barely walk while carrying all these things.

"Jarvis, who were those people who just entered the castle?" He pointed to the great hall, extending his arm outward.

"Oh, thank you. I could use a little help." Kit surprised him when she appeared, coming around the wagon, looping the handle of a very full and heavy bag over his extended arm. She held on to another full bag. Then she turned and headed toward the great hall.

"Stop!" he called out, purposely dropping the bag she'd looped over his arm. The contents inside clanged together as it hit the ground.

"Nay! Careful with that," Kit cried, running back to inspect the contents of the bag. "I have some of my best baking pans in there, not to mention glass jars of herbs and spices. I hope you didn't break them." She bent over, digging through the bag as the rain continued to fall all around them.

"Pardon me, my lord, but these are getting heavier with the rain." Jarvis stepped around him, hauling the things to the great hall.

"What is all this?" bellowed Tolin.

"These are our things," Kit answered him, since Jarvis was in no position to turn around without dropping something.

"This is ridiculous. No one travels with so many belongings," grumbled Tolin.

"I do."

"You couldn't possibly use all the things you've brought with you."

She looked up at him when she answered. "If we're going to be living here until Twelfth Night, then these things will all be needed, I assure you." She tried to pick up the bag but it was bulky and she slipped on the wet cobblestones. Tolin's arms shot out to catch her. He pulled her to his chest to steady her and keep her from falling.

A mistake.

Feeling the warmth of her body pressed up against him,

smelling the floral scent of her hair, and noticing each one of her delectable curves, it had his mind racing. Once again.

"Thank you," she said, looking directly at him. Their faces were close. So close that he could have easily bent over and kissed her lush lips. But he didn't. "If you don't mind, I am getting wet. I have fresh bread and baked goods in these bags that will be ruined if we stand here a minute longer."

"Huh? Baked goods? Oh, yes." Tolin blindly released her. He picked up the bag of pans and carried it as they headed to the great hall together.

"I'll require a private room for my accommodations during my visit. For me and my family, that is," she added catching him off guard.

"Private room," he repeated, confused by the family part and thinking about that instead. "Wait a minute. You said during your visit."

"That's right." She continued to walk.

"But you're not here visiting and are not a guest. You are here as part of a punishment for what your son did, if I must remind you. Therefore, there will be no private room or any room at all."

"What he *supposedly* did," she corrected him, once again taking control of the conversation as he kept pace at her side. "Of course, you believe that a little boy is capable of stealing a sword from a royal guard, even though it is the furthest thing from the truth."

"That is what my guard told me. I have no reason not to believe it."

"I see," she answered with a sniff. "Well, if that is what you believe, then perhaps you need to think about getting a new guard. One who can fend off an eight-year-old boy."

He wanted to object, but after just seeing Henry well in his cups, he was having his doubts that the guard was worth much at all. Perhaps the girl was right, but he couldn't admit it. Nor would he ever let the wench tell him what to do.

"I am still waiting for an answer. Who are those other people who arrived here with you?"

She stopped in her tracks and turned to face him in the rain. "That is my pregnant sister and her husband."

"Why are they here?"

"To help me bake, of course. For your celebrations from Christmas until Twelfth Night."

"I didn't say they could come here."

"I thought you wanted successful festivities during Christmastide since you are in charge during your father's absence. Did you not?"

"I assure you, I know how to plan a celebration."

"I'm sure you do, my lord. But when you said you liked my tarts, I thought you wanted more."

She was still standing close and it was driving him mad. The raindrops on her long eyelashes only made her eyes even more alluring.

"Yes, I do," he answered, his hand resting on her shoulder. "You have no idea how much I crave your tarts."

"My sister helps me make them, so it might be wise to let her stay."

"Of course," he said, getting lost in her eyes. "Wait a minute," he mumbled, realizing she was catching him off guard yet again. "What about the man? He doesn't look like a baker to me."

"He's not. But I figured you could use more help for

the holidays. In the stable perhaps? He is good with horses and also very strong. He also likes dogs, so mayhap he'd be better suited for the kennels. I suppose you will be inviting some of the finest nobles to the castle for Christmastide?"

"Well...I...I, yes, I suppose so. Yes. Yes, I will."

"Then you'll need extra help. Oliver is your man."

"I suppose I could use more help. All right. They can stay."

"In a private room with me and my son."

"You will be working in the kitchen. I can't give you a room to yourself."

"We are not serfs nor servants, my lord, if I must remind you. I own a business. A flourishing bakery that might fail now that you've taken me away during my busiest season. I'd think a small private room off the kitchen for my family would be a fair trade."

"Fine, fine," he said, not liking anyone to say he wasn't fair. "There is an empty room off the kitchen. You need to move the extra food supplies in the room to the undercroft but you can use the space for yourself and the boy during your stay."

"And my sister, too? I mean, she is very pregnant and won't be able to sleep on the floor of the great hall in her condition."

"Nay, I suppose not," he found himself saying, not even sure why. "All right, but the man will sleep in the stable. I won't have him in the same room as the women."

"Oliver is married to my sister," she told him. "It's not like he is a lusty stranger."

"I don't care. I won't have rumors stirring in my father's

castle in his absence. No man, just the boy in the room with the women, and that is final."

"Fine." She snatched up the heavy bag and continued to walk. "However, I think you should be the one to tell Oliver that he won't be able to see to his wife's needs during this crucial time."

"Well, it's not like she's having the baby now. Is she?" He hurried to catch up with her.

"She is due in a week's time. And I am sure you know that births cannot be planned. A child will come when it is time, no matter what you or anyone else says."

"That is just great," he mumbled, taking the heavy bag back from her and escorting her into the castle. He could just hear his brother Rook right now, reprimanding him, telling him that he was doing everything wrong. It would be hard enough to confront Rook when he found out he didn't really punish the thief after all. But if Tolin gave a private room to not only the baker wench and the boy thief, but a pregnant woman and a strange man, too, all hell was probably going to break loose. He couldn't lose control so easily. Nay, the wench was not getting everything she wanted. This was supposed to be a punishment, not a reward. Still Tolin didn't have it in him to turn away a child and pregnant woman.

"I'll tell Oliver he needs to sleep in the barn," he said, not wanting to lose. He needed to keep the upper hand. Once again, the wench bested him with her little games and he didn't like it. Well, he had games he'd play with her and next time he would be the one to win. That was something he would be sure to make happen. Now, he just needed to keep a close eye on the wench because he had a feeling wherever Kit Baker was, trouble was about to follow.

CHAPTER 4

The next day was Christmas Eve, and there was still so much to be done. The main meal was set to take place today right after Mass. The holiday celebrations were now in motion. Tolin walked swiftly toward the kitchen, his squire following close on his heels.

"Why didn't you wake me?" asked Tolin, using his hand to block a yawn. "I told you that I wanted to get up early today."

"I know, my lord, and I did wake you just like instructed."

Tolin stopped in his tracks and turned to his squire, his hands on his hips. "This is early?"

"Mayhap not for most people who wake before the rise of the sun, my lord," answered his squire. "But for you, Lord Tolin, yes, this is very early indeed."

"I see I will need to be more direct with my instructions from now on."

"My lord," said Emeric, hurrying across the great hall to

join them. "I'm afraid the head baker, Arvid became ill last night. It was very unexpected, indeed."

"I'm sorry to hear that." Tolin kept walking. "Tell him I need to meet with him to give him instructions for everything I want regarding the Christmas feast. I've already spoken with the head cook, but need my bakery requests heard as well. We are short on time. I have a few changes I need to go over with him before I head to Mass."

"But my lord, I'm afraid that is not possible." Emeric was in charge of the household but acting odd today, looking twice as worried as usual. Tolin needed people he could count on in order to bring his festive plans to fruition. Somehow, Emeric didn't seem like a good choice at the moment to make this happen.

Tolin needed to set things straight. "I am Lord of Blake Castle until the return of my father. Tell the head baker that I don't care how ill he is, it is Christmas Eve and there is so much to be done. He can rest after Twelfth Night. I want to see him in the kitchen in ten minutes, and that is an order." He turned to leave.

"I'm afraid Arvid is dead, my lord."

Tolin stopped in his tracks, hoping he'd misheard the steward. He slowly turned to face the man.

"What did you say?" he asked, already feeling a sense of doom washing over him. All Tolin's plans for the best sweet treats in England were riding on the expertise of the head baker. Today was Christmas Eve. This was of vital importance. His hall would be filled with people soon, all expecting a stupendous Christmas dinner along with exquisite desserts. He needed that head baker to finish off the meals with exciting sweets or this wasn't going to go as planned.

"Arvid died in his bed as he slept, my lord," continued Emeric. "The healer said it looks as if the man had a bad heart, but he can't be sure."

"This cannot be happening." Just as he said it, two men walked by carrying a stretcher with a body atop it. The dead one's face was covered. "Wait!" Tolin called out, hurrying over and pulling back the sheet to reveal the dead man's identity. Sure enough, it was the head baker. He had truly died, and with the death Tolin's aspirations of presenting the best and most elaborate baked goods for Christmastide died with him. Kit popped into his mind. She was a baker and good at it. But she came from town. She'd never worked with servants from the castle. Nay, he decided, she was here as part of a punishment. He couldn't reward her after what her son was accused of doing.

"Did you want us to put down the stretcher?" asked one of the men carrying Arvid.

"Nay." Tolin covered the dead man's face back up. "Get him out of here anon. And go quickly. It is best that his death stays quiet for now. Or at least until I figure out what to do now that he is gone."

"Shall we bury him, my lord?" asked the second man whom Tolin recognized as the gravedigger.

"Yes. The ground will be frozen, but use pickaxes and warm the earth first with fires. Just get this man buried and out of my sight."

"Aye, my lord." The men carrying the body left.

"Don't you think that was a little cold-hearted?" came a

woman's voice from behind him. Tolin turned to see Kit and her son standing there watching him.

"Cold-hearted?" Tolin raised a brow. "The man is dead, my dear. I hardly think he'd take offense to anything I've said."

"I'm sure the man has family. They'll want to mourn his loss," she continued. "They deserve a little compassion at a time like this."

"Nay, he didn't, so no, they don't. Arvid had no one, so don't worry your pretty little head about it." Tolin felt frustration sweep through him. This woman was not making his worries any less.

"Well, shouldn't there at least be a ceremony for his burial?" Kit continued to press the issue. "I'm sure he had friends who will miss him."

"It is Christmas Eve," he told her. "His body will be buried, but any kind of actual funeral will have to wait until after Twelfth Night."

"So, it seems the festivities are more important to you than a man's life?"

Tolin was about to reprimand her for speaking this way to a noble when Emeric interrupted.

"Excuse me, my lord," said Emeric. "But the servants in the kitchen will be needing instructions. Who will lead them regarding the baking for the Christmas feast?"

Tolin's eyes swept over to Kit and he released a deep sigh. There was no other choice. He had an idea and hoped to hell this would work. "There is a new head baker as of today."

"There is?" asked Emeric.

"Yes. All of you, follow me. I am going to address the

kitchen help." He made his way to the kitchen with his squire, his steward, Kit and her son following. He stepped into the room where all the servants seemed to be in a dither, needing a leader, upset about Arvid's passing.

"Attention, everyone," said Tolin, raising his voice as well as a hand in the air. The kitchen servants became quiet, venturing closer to hear him. "It has been brought to my attention that Arvid passed away peacefully in his sleep."

Murmurs went up from the bystanders.

"Although this is a sad occasion, the mourning for the man will have to wait until after Twelfth Night. It is Christmastide and plans need to be carried out."

"Tolin, I heard about the head baker." Rook walked into the kitchen with Brother Ruford at his side. They were the last people he wanted to see right now. Raven entered right after them, not saying a word.

"That's right," Tolin answered. "It is a misfortunate situation, but being Christmastide things must continue as planned."

"Then you need to appoint a new head baker anon," Rook told him. "The great hall will be filled with people soon expecting the normal Christmastide treats."

"I was just about to do that," Tolin remarked.

"Who is it?" The monk looked around the room. "It needs to be someone who will carry out your orders as well as be able to act swiftly in an emergency such as this. Someone who is as proficient as Arvid was at turning out the delicious baked goods."

"I couldn't agree with you more," said Tolin. "That is why I have chosen a new head baker who will not only fill

Arvid's shoes but make the Christmastide celebrations the best that Blake Castle has ever had."

"Well, who is it?" asked Raven. "No one can bake like Arvid could."

"The castle's new head baker is none other than the owner of the village bakery. Kit Baker." He held out his arm as he announced it. The room became silent while Kit's jaw dropped.

Kit couldn't believe that Tolin had just put her in such a horrendous situation. He announced her as the castle's new head baker and she didn't like it in the least. She was only here until Twelfth Night to work off her son's debt. He made this sound like a permanent position.

"Her? The girl from town is the castle's new head baker?" asked Rook. "Really, Tolin."

"You can't be serious," said the monk, shaking his head. "She knows nothing about the castle's kitchen. She won't be able to carry out the task."

"The mother of the thief?" asked Jarvis. "She is the new head baker?"

"We don't even know her," came a comment from the servants.

"She doesn't belong here," came another lone voice from the crowd.

"Quiet!" shouted Tolin. "I will not hear another word about it. You will all get to know her quickly. She will take her orders from me, and you will carry out the orders she gives you regarding all the bread and castle's baked goods.

Now get back to work. Everyone. There is a Christmas feast to prepare and I expect it to be up to my high standards."

Kit found herself so shocked that it took a moment for her to even respond.

"My lord," she said, her mouth feeling so dry that she could barely swallow. "I need to talk with you."

"Emeric will show you around the kitchen," said Tolin.

"But I need to speak to you about this new position."

"We will talk later. We are already late for Mass." He looked at his siblings and the monk and nodded. "Let's go."

They started to leave the kitchen, and Kit took her son's hand and followed. Tolin noticed and stopped, turning around slowly.

"Where do you think you are going?"

"To Mass of course," she told him. "It is Christmas Eve. I will just stop at my room to get my sister first. We'll collect her husband when we go to the stables."

"Nay, you won't. None of you are going to the church. You are staying right here."

"What? Why?" she asked.

Rook cleared his throat. "I'll find Daegel and wait in the courtyard for you. Rose should already be there by now wondering where I am," he said, speaking of his wife.

"I'll join you," said Raven. "But first I must fetch Jonathon from the smithy." Raven spoke of her husband. Kit had met the nobles' spouses yesterday and thought they were kind people. It surprised her that they were commoners who married the nobles of the Blake family. She liked the idea that rules had been broken where true love was involved.

"We'll be right there," Kit called after them, but Tolin's

dark gaze made her realize she really wasn't going. "Do you mean to stop me from attending Mass with my son?" she asked. Parker stayed silent at her side.

"The servants don't attend Mass during Christmastide," he told her. "They stay and prepare the meal so it will be ready upon our return."

"But I'm not a servant," she reminded him.

"Not normally, but for the duration of your son's sentence, you are. Now go to the kitchen and find Emeric. He will tell you all that you need to know. I've left him with my instructions."

Kit watched in frustration as Tolin left the great hall without her. This would be the first Christmas that she and her son didn't attend Mass. An emptiness gnawed at her gut. This wasn't at all how it was supposed to be.

"So, we don't have to go to Mass, Mother?" asked Parker with a big smile on his face.

"Don't look so happy about it," she scolded. "As soon as we get home you will attend extra Masses to make up for it."

A big white dog ran across the great hall and up to Kit, jumping on her and licking her face.

"Down!" she commanded, pushing the hound back to the floor.

"Hello, doggy," said Parker, throwing his arms around the dog's neck in a hug. Parker giggled as the hound licked his face next.

"Parker, put that dog outside and meet me in the kitchen. I am going to collect Brenna. We have a job to do."

"I don't want to work, Mother. I want to play with the dog." Parker ran around in circles and the dog barked, jumping and playing with him.

"This is your sentence, Parker, and the reason why we are even here. You need to work in the kitchen to make up for stealing."

"I didn't steal nothing, Mother. I told you that."

"Anything," she said under her breath. "I know, sweetheart. But until we convince Lord Tolin of that fact, I'm afraid we will be nothing more than his servants from now until Twelfth Night."

"Servants?" asked the boy. "I don't want to be a servant. I want to go home."

"Me too," she said, pulling her son against her, running her hand through his hair. "Me too." The hound laid down and whimpered, putting his nose between his paws, seeming to feel her sadness.

"This is going to be the worst Christmas ever," cried the boy.

"Nay, don't say that." She held her son to her, feeling like crying. She was now a servant, her son was falsely accused of stealing, her sister was about to birth a child, and they were most likely going to all be homeless soon when she lost her business. How could things get any worse? "Everything will be fine," she told her son, trying to stay strong even if she didn't believe it. Something was going to have to change because Kit would not allow her life to crumble like this. She'd worked too hard to have everything taken away from her and would do whatever she had to in order to get it back. Yes, she decided, she would go along with Lord Tolin's sentence, but he would be sorry he ever brought her here to begin with. Because Kit was going to beat the cur at his own game or die trying.

CHAPTER 5

"Here is a list of the bread and baked goods that Lord Tolin requires." Emeric handed Kit the piece of parchment. "It also explains the different days until Twelfth Night that he wants certain items."

"I see," said Kit, glancing at the list, not seeing anything that excited her. Her sister sat on a bench rubbing her belly while Parker played with the dog under the table. "I have some items I would like to add to the list," she told the steward. "Things I bake at my shop that the customers love."

"You'll have to take that up with Lord Tolin, I'm afraid." Emeric looked at the small group of servants standing nearby. "These bakers will assist you."

She looked up to see nearly a dozen servants watching her with wide eyes. "I have never had or needed this much assistance," she told the steward.

"You also haven't had to bake for so many people before, Kit." Brenna stretched her neck to see the list as well. "Does that say two hundred mincemeat pies?"

"What?" Kit's eyes snapped down to the parchment in her hand. Sure enough, her sister was right. "Nay. I don't bake with meat. I do sweets only."

"Lord Tolin prefers his mincemeat pie with lots of extra apples, dates and raisins. And a variety of spices. He likes it as a dessert. I've given you the recipe." The steward nodded to the papers in her hand.

"This is absurd."

"Lord Tolin invited the serfs as well as the villagers to join the nobles and castle occupants to the Christmas festivities. Use the servants to help you. There is a lot of work to be completed."

"Of course, he invited the villagers too," moaned Kit, knowing this was common but not wanting her friends to see her as naught but a servant of the castle. She was in a humiliating situation. If her sister-by-marriage showed up with her husband, she was sure that Willis would go back and tell all the villagers rumors about Kit and her family. She was a proud business owner, but after Christmas, she'd be naught but a homeless, jobless woman. She would have no choice but to keep being Lord Tolin's servant.

"Oh, what is going on out there?" asked Brenna, stretching her neck to see out the door of the kitchen, down the corridor to the great hall.

"The servants are stringing up mistletoe and holly to decorate the hall," said Emeric. "I'm afraid they are not very creative and that it will not meet Lord Tolin's expectations."

"I like to decorate," said Brenna, still looking out the door. "Perhaps I could help them?"

"I don't know," said Emeric. "I thought you were brought here to bake. Lord Tolin might not like that."

Kit saw the shadow darken her sister's face. Brenna was a very creative person and had always wanted to make things look pretty. She wasn't a baker and would only get in Kit's way in the kitchen, not able to move fast because of her big belly. "I'll take responsibility should Lord Tolin object. Brenna, why don't you go see if you can help them. I'm sure it will be fine."

"I would like that." Brenna got up off the bench, nearly falling when the dog shot out from under the table and knocked into her. Kit caught her and helped her balance.

"Parker, I told you to get that dog out of here," scolded Kit.

"I like him and don't want him to leave. At least I have someone to play with now," Parker answered.

"Oh, you can't make King leave," said Emeric. "Lord Tolin won't allow it. King likes to stay in the keep and Lord Tolin lets him go wherever he pleases."

"King? Oh, is that the dog's name?" asked Kit.

"Yes, King is Lord Tolin's dog."

"It figures," Kit mumbled under her breath. Just one more thing about the man that aggravated her. "Parker, I'll need your help gathering some ingredients," Kit told her son, running her finger down the list.

"But I want to play with the dog," protested the boy. "I don't know what to do in a kitchen."

"It'll be just like helping me at the bakery," she tried to assure him. "And once Lord Tolin sees you working so hard, he'll hopefully lift your punishment sooner. Now, go find me the raisins."

"All right," said the boy, moping away to do a job that no eight-year-old should be expected to do.

∽

Tolin left the church on horseback anxious to return to the castle where a feast would be waiting, now that the fasting from the last four weeks had ended. He'd purposely ordered lots of meat and dairy, since these were foods banned by the church during Advent. He'd left in such a hurry that he hadn't had a chance to tell Kit the changes he'd made concerning the desserts for the Christmas Eve meal. He hoped Emeric had explained the way Tolin liked things to be.

Since it would be hours yet before the food was ready, he had planned a joust to take place in the practice yard. A good joust would work up a powerful hunger. Actually, he decided to stop by the kitchen on his way to the joust to make sure Kit was following orders. He was secretly already starving and had hoped to sneak a taste early.

Tolin's squire walked with him, pointing out the obvious. "Oh, look, my lord. The decorations are up in the great hall. I see strings of holly and even ornate kissing boughs."

"Yes, I see that." He stopped under one of the kissing boughs, inspecting it hanging from the rafters. Dozens graced the room. Each was a wire structure in the shape of a ball. To his surprise they had apples and oranges hanging down, with lots of holly and pine branches with mistletoe attached in the center. Some of the oranges even had cloves stuck into them. It was quite nice. More elaborate than he'd ever seen. Just the scent alone made the normally stale air smell spicy and sweet. "This is quite good," he said aloud, noticing the details of colorful ribbons woven into curious bows and loops from which the kissing boughs were attached. A beeswax scented candle was placed in the center of each. Once the candles were lit later tonight, the kissing boughs would fill the room with a soft light, giving off a mysterious glow. He nodded his approval. "I have never seen such elaborate kissing boughs before. I like it."

"I'm glad you approve because my sister had a hand in making the kissing boughs."

Tolin turned to see Kit standing there holding a tray of small loaves of bread. The aroma wafted up into the air, making Tolin salivate. There was nothing like the scent of freshly baked bread.

"Your sister did this?" He glanced upward.

"Yes. And her name is Brenna. She might not be that much help in the kitchen being so pregnant, but I sent her out to assist the servants with the decorations. I hope it is to your approval."

"*You* sent her out to help? Not Emeric?"

"Yes, it was me. I take full responsibility."

He was about to reprimand Kit for giving orders that weren't approved by him when his dog ran into the great hall being chased by the boy.

"King," Tolin called to the dog, always being greeted by the hound jumping on him and licking his face. King heard him and ran in his direction. Unfortunately, the dog knocked into Kit and she lost her balance. The tray of bread fell to the floor and Kit somehow ended up in Tolin's arms.

"Ooomph," she said with a breath of air escaping her lips. She clung to Tolin, looking up at him through tangled strands of hair.

"You're under the kissing bough, my lord," his squire pointed out.

"Tolin's already making use of the kissing boughs? Why am I not surprised?" His brother, Daegel entered the great hall with Rook and Raven following.

"I'm sorry, my lord," Kit said in a whisper. Tolin held her securely, not wanting the beautiful woman to fall.

"It wasn't your fault," he told her. Her eyes held innocence but at the same time he saw passion and determination. Once again she had flour spewed across her cheek and he had to stop himself from reaching out to brush it away. Long dark lashes curled upward as she blinked several times in succession. He swore he saw her gaze settle on his mouth. When it did, it made his attention go to the girl's full lips that looked like they needed...or wanted kissing. It would be so easy to kiss her right now and no one could question it as they were under the kissing bough. He wanted to taste those lips desperately, but he wasn't sure the wench wouldn't slap him if he did. Thinking it best not to act on this right now, he gently righted her position and released her. "I'm sorry my hound is so forceful."

She bent down to collect the small palm-sized loaves of bread. Without thinking it through, he hunkered down and helped her to put them back on the tray.

"I'm sorry about the bread. I will clean it off. I should have left it in the kitchen to cool."

"No harm done." He put his arm under her elbow and helped her to her feet.

"I wanted to ask you why the list specifically called for such small loaves? Was that a mistake?" She looked down at the dirty bread and then back up at him.

He smiled, wanting to break the tension. He didn't want her to feel uncomfortable here at the castle.

"The loaves are perfect, Kit." He picked one up and tossed it to his dog.

Kit watched in confusion as Tolin gave the loaf of bread to his dog to eat. "My lord, I thought those were for the meal. And did you not say they were perfect?"

"They are," he said, taking the tray from her and handing it to his squire. "These are Christmas treats for the hounds. Jarvis, take these loaves to the kennels and tell the kennel groom that every hound gets one. If he needs more, let me know."

"But those are white bread," protested Kit, not able to believe something that was reserved for nobles was being given to the animals instead of the servants. He was revering the hounds and wouldn't even let the servants worship in church. What kind of a place was this?

"That's right, these are white bread," said Tolin, laughing and petting King's head with two hands as the dog devoured the loaf of bread in three bites. "Only the best for the castle hounds."

"Make sure Copper and Brindy get some too," Raven called after the squire.

"Yes, my lady," said Jarvis.

"Who?" asked Kit.

"My mastiffs," said Raven with a kind smile. "Of course, they'll want several loaves since they are large and tend to eat a lot." She called after the squire once more. "Make sure their pups get some too. They're getting big now and can't seem to stop eating."

"Yes, my lady," Jarvis' voice got softer as he headed out to the courtyard.

"Just kiss her already," growled Daegel. "And then let's get to the practice yard for the joust."

"Kiss?" Alarm ran through Kit when she realized both she and Tolin were still standing under the kissing bough. "Oh, no. I couldn't."

"It's Christmas, and everyone does it." Tolin reached out and pulled her to him, pressing his lips up against hers before she could stop him. His lips were surprisingly soft and sensuous. Her eyes closed and she returned the kiss, putting her hands on his shoulders. It felt so damned good to be kissed by a handsome man. Lord Tolin might be crass and rude, but his looks made up for all his shortcomings. Kit felt something come to life deep inside her. Something that had died the day Crispin was killed. Even after having married Crispin's brother, Gerold, she had never felt the same way. Until now.

"Well, get back to the kitchen and make me up some of those enticing tarts," he said, quickly releasing her and pulling away.

"Tarts? But I thought you wanted mincemeat pies today."

"I've had a change of heart. Tarts today and mincemeat pies tomorrow." He pushed a strand of his long black hair behind his ear and glanced at his brother. "Daegel, Rook and I will show you how real knights joust. Come."

"I know how to joust," complained Daegel.

"Prove it," said Rook with a chuckle. "Beat Tolin and me and mayhap we'll buy you a whisky when we're done."

"I prefer beer," said Daegel as the men all walked away

ignoring Kit. It was as if nothing had happened. Or, at least to them. She watched them exit the great hall, her hand going to her lips, wanting to savor the kiss.

"My brothers are all pig-headed curs. Sorry about that," said Raven, who Kit had almost forgotten was still standing there.

"Whatever do you mean?" Kit hoped Raven couldn't see her blush. She still felt hot and heady from Tolin's kiss. It embarrassed her that she felt this way. After all, he was a noble and she was just a commoner. One kiss under the kissing bough might mean the world to her but she was sure it was just another motion to him. Tolin Blake wouldn't give it another thought.

"I saw the way your eyes closed and your cheeks reddened when my brother kissed you just now."

"Oh." She flashed a smile. "It is only because I am a widow and haven't been kissed in quite a while."

"Is it really?" Now it was Raven's turn to flash a smile.

"Excuse me, my lady, but Lord Tolin wants tarts for the meal and it takes a while to make them. I really should go. I already have my hands full with the mincemeat pies. Parker, come help me," she called to her son who was still playing with Tolin's hound.

Raven's hand shot out and her fingers clasped Kit's wrist. Kit's eyes snapped upward.

"I'm actually glad you are here. Tolin needs someone like you to put him in his place once in a while."

"Me? Put him in his place? I could never."

"Yes, you could and you know it as well as I," said Raven, slowly releasing Kit's arm.

"Pardon me for saying this, my lady, and I mean no

disrespect, but I could never be interested in a man like Tolin."

"Whatever do you mean?" Raven repeated her words back. "Because he is immature, likes to show off, constantly plays games, drinks and gambles too much, is not responsible for anything but having fun, and cannot stand losing to anyone? Especially a woman?" She raised her brows and smiled again.

Kit and Raven both burst out laughing.

"I suppose that about covers it," said Kit.

"And now you see why my little brother needs a good woman."

Kit's smile slowly disappeared. "I am a widow with a son out of wedlock from a second man. I have worked hard to change my reputation and was even running the bakery on my own successfully before my son was accused of something he didn't do. Now, I am naught more than a servant. I am at risk of losing my business as well as my home. I am responsible for not only my son, but also my very pregnant sister and her husband who has no job. So tell me, why on earth would I ever want someone in my life with all the vices you just listed regarding Tolin?"

"Oh, I'm sorry. I had no idea your life was so hard. I suppose you wouldn't." She smiled and shrugged. "I must go joust now, to show all of my brothers that I can still beat them."

"You're a mother, aren't you?" asked Kit.

"I am."

"And you still joust? Isn't that dangerous?"

"Whether something is dangerous or not is only an opinion. I like to feel alive. Being a mother and jousting and using weapons are all things that make me feel that way. Why should I give any of them up?"

"I see what you mean," said Kit in deep thought.

"Kit Baker, I will leave you with a thought. I don't want you to answer but just think about it."

"What is that?" asked Kit.

"What makes you feel alive? And are you ready to do something dangerous so you can start living and stop just surviving? There is a difference, you know." Raven nodded and walked away, leaving Kit standing there pondering the woman's words of wisdom.

She supposed mayhap she wasn't living but only surviving, just like Raven said. All of her problems would still be there tomorrow and no amount of being cautious was going to change that. Yes, mayhap she should start living after all. And to her, the most dangerous thing in her life right now was having been kissed by Lord Tolin Blake.

CHAPTER 6

God's eyes, he'd never meant to kiss her! Even though he'd wanted to. Tolin held out his arms as his squire buckled his armor in place. The joust had already started and Tolin was up next.

"Is something the matter, my lord?" asked Jarvis.

"Nay. Of course not."

"You seem upset about something. Or distracted. What is it?" Jarvis pulled the last strap tight and secured it in place with the buckle. "Is it something about the joust?"

"Huh? Nay, I'm not worried about the joust. I could win a joust with my eyes closed."

"Eyes closed?" His squire stood upright to get his helm. "Like the way that baker woman closed her eyes when you kissed her under the kissing bough?"

"I don't feel guilty about that, no matter what you think."

"I never said anything about feeling guilty, my lord.

Why? Do you feel guilty for having kissed her?" Jarvis picked up the helm.

"Why should I? She's just a servant."

"A servant?" Jarvis shined the top of the metal helm with his sleeve. "I thought she was a widow who owned a bakery in town. Has she been demoted to a servant now?"

"Nay! I didn't mean that. I just meant—why am I explaining anything to you? Now give me my helm and get out there and hand me my lance. I have a joust to win."

"Aye, my lord." Jarvis handed the helm over and ran out to the practice field.

Tolin looked down, able to see his reflection on the surface. Why had kissing Kit Baker shaken him up so much? Mayhap because she was different than most women he knew. She was spry and confident and not afraid to stand up to him. She could also bake better than anyone he knew. Damn, the woman was also attractive. He had wanted to kiss her badly, but was going to refrain from doing so. After all, she was there with her thief of a son and working off his sentence. Something warned him not to do it. But he'd wanted to so badly. And when his brothers walked up and more or less challenged him, he did what he always did. He took the challenge. But this was one challenge that didn't make him feel like a winner. Part of him felt as if he'd used her somehow. That didn't sit right with him. He'd never felt this way in his life and didn't understand it.

"Ready to lose?" It was Daegel, suited up, ready for the joust.

"I won't lose." Tolin put his helm under one arm and tightened his weapon belt.

"You did today."

"What do you mean?"

"You didn't get the girl."

"Brother, you are spouting nonsense, now stop it."

"Am I? I saw the way you looked at Kit and the way she reacted to your kiss as well."

Tolin's head snapped up. "What do you mean?"

"She was disappointed that you stopped. I could see it on her face."

"You don't know that. And since when are you an expert on knowing what a woman is feeling?" Tolin figured Daegel was goading him again.

"I might not know for sure, but at least I am not as blind as you are when it comes to women. That one likes you, Tolin. You'd better watch out."

"Watch out for what?" He headed to the door.

"If she gets her hooks in you, you'll be no different than Rook and Raven."

"There you go with spouting nonsense again. You make no sense, Daegel."

"I make all the sense in the world, Tolin. You're going to end up marrying a commoner. Just like Rook and Raven."

"That is where you are wrong, brother. Because I am never going to marry at all. And if I do change my mind, I can promise you it'll be with a noblewoman."

"You'll crumble, just like the others. And Father will return to discover that you disappointed him too."

Tolin stopped in his tracks and turned back to his brother. "I don't disappoint Father. If I did, do you think he would put me in charge of the castle in his absence?"

"That does surprise the rest of us immensely," said

Daegel. "The only thing we can figure is that it is a test of some kind."

"It's not a test. It is because Father knows I am the only one capable of planning a successful string of celebrations from now until Twelfth Night."

"Aye, that must be it. Now, let's go joust so I can show you just how full of yourself you really are."

～

"Kit, do you really think it was wise for us to come to watch the joust when there is so much yet to be done?" Brenna struggled to keep up with Kit as they made their way to the practice field. Her legs were a lot shorter than Kit's. Her pregnancy being so advanced made it hard for her to walk at all.

"Parker wanted to watch the knights joust and I don't see why he can't." Kit reached back for her son. "Parker, keep up. It is so crowded that I don't want to lose you." She took his hand in hers.

"I don't want to watch the joust, I want to play with the dog," the boy answered with a pout.

Brenna rubbed her belly and gave Kit a knowing glance. "Mmm hmm. It was Parker who wanted to be here. Right."

Kit was caught in her lie and felt embarrassed that she hadn't been honest from the start. "All right, I admit it, I was curious to see Tolin joust. Do you think he is any good?"

"Lord Tolin seems to be good at anything he does, if you haven't noticed," answered her sister. "Did you know that I overheard the servants talking. There isn't a game he's lost in years now. They say he is so competitive that if it looks like he might not win, he makes everyone keep playing until he does. He is a man who doesn't tolerate losing."

"He does seem to put a lot of importance on games, celebrating, and having fun. Especially when he wins. I believe the man has too much self-importance."

"You say that like you are disgusted, but I can tell you're not. Admit it. You like him, don't you?" Brenna was direct and to the point.

"Brenna, please." Kit glanced over at her sister and then down to her son. "This is a conversation for a later date." She didn't want Parker to hear this, but she also didn't want to answer because she wasn't sure yet what she thought or felt about Lord Tolin. All she knew was that he was handsome and sparked her interest with his passionate kiss. Then again, he did sentence her son for something he didn't even do. She needed to be careful.

"All right. We will talk later," said Brenna. "Oh, Kit, look!" She grabbed Kit's arm. I see an open spot on the bench right up front. Let's get it, fast. I cannot remain on my feet much longer."

"No, not up there," protested Kit, not wanting Tolin to know she was there watching him. Brenna hurried for the bench, anyway. Not wanting to lose her in the crowd, Kit followed her sister, taking Parker with her. They had just gotten seated when the herald announced that Lord Tolin was going to joust with his brother, Lord Daegel. Cheers and shouts went up from the crowd. It seemed as if Lord Tolin was a favorite on the jousting field. And with the ladies.

"Tolin will win, he always does," said a woman nearby. "He is so strong and handsome."

"I heard he kissed a servant under the kissing bough today," said another woman behind her hand.

Kit gasped and tried to hide her face from them.

"I wish he'd kiss me under the kissing bough," said the first woman. "Every girl in the castle hopes they will find the bean in their cake so they can order him to spend the day with them and kiss them under the mistletoe."

"Find the bean? What does that mean?" Brenna had started up a conversation with the women and Kit wished she hadn't. She didn't want anyone to know she was the one who'd received the kiss. For some reason, it embarrassed her even though she didn't understand why.

"The Bean King or Bean Queen is the one who finds a bean in their cake during the Christmas dinner," the first servant girl explained. "It can be anyone. Even a servant, it doesn't matter."

"I still don't understand," said Brenna. "Why would they want to?"

"Don't you know? The one who finds the bean has power," explained the other girl.

"What kind of power?" asked Brenna.

"They can tell nobles what to do."

"Really?"

"Yes," said the first girl. "Until their rule is over, they can ask a noble for anything, and the nobles have to give it to them."

"Their rule?" asked Kit, trying to get into the conversation without showing too much of her face. "What kind of things can they ask for?"

"Anything at all, until the end of their rule," said the girl. "Until Twelfth Night, they can live like kings or queens for the first time ever. This is a very coveted position. I always wanted to find the bean but never have. But if I did, the first thing I'd do is to order Lord Tolin to kiss me." She and her friend giggled at that, but the giggles were drowned out by the shouting of the crowd. Tolin had easily won the joust against his brother.

The servants next to her stood and waved their hands in the air, trying to get Tolin's attention. Tolin rode over to collect all the support he could. He really knew how to excite a crowd.

"Take my favor," called out one of the servant girls, ripping her sleeve from her gown and holding it out, waving it in the air. If Tolin accepted it, he would lower the tip of his lance and the girl would slip it onto the pole.

All of the women held out a sleeve or veil or some kind of personal belonging, hoping Tolin would choose theirs. Kit sat quietly watching.

"Lord Tolin! Lord Tolin, we came to see you win the joust!" Parker jumped up and down waving his arms, shouting to be heard.

"Shhhh. Sit down, Parker. That is not appropriate behavior." Kit tried to still her son, hoping Tolin didn't notice them.

"This is a joust and a very appropriate time to shout," came Tolin's voice as he rode up and stopped directly across from her. "However, to leave the kitchen when you are supposed to be preparing my meal is far from proper or tolerated." Tolin sat atop his horse on the opposite side of the wooden fence scowling at her.

"Lord Tolin." Kit meekly looked up. Their eyes interlocked for a mere second before she dropped her gaze. "I'm sorry for leaving the kitchen. Parker wanted to see the joust. I'll leave at once." She started to stand, but one of the servants next to her called out.

"He wants your favor! He chose you. You are so lucky. Give it to him, quickly."

"What?" Kit was confused. "I don't have a favor and neither did I offer him one."

"Use your hair ribbon, Kit." Brenna jumped up and untied it from Kit's hair.

"Brenna, what are you doing?" Kit asked from the side of her mouth.

"Having fun." Brenna giggled. "What are *you* doing, sister? Being too serious again? Relax, Kit. It is just a game."

Kit swallowed hard and looked back up at Tolin, expecting to see his eyes of fire. The crowd chanted his name and called to him. It was all so overwhelming and felt like thunder pounding in her ears, making her head spin. Brenna looped the green hair ribbon and pushed it into Kit's hand.

"I'm sorry," Kit said once again, clutching her hair ribbon like a lifeline. Heat rose in her body making her feel as if she would faint. She didn't like to be the center of attention. Now, everyone was staring at her.

"Put the ribbon on the end of his lance," called out one of the servants who was crazy for Lord Tolin. "You are so lucky. He's chosen your favor! I wish I was you right now."

Kit looked over at the girls. "Nay, you have it wrong," she tried to tell them, but stopped when she felt a tap on her shoulder. She looked back to see Tolin touching her with the tip of his lance.

"I don't have all day, baker. I have a joust to win," he told her. "Now give me your favor."

"Oh, Kit, hurry!" Brenna took Kit's hand and pushed it closer to the end of the lance. "Slip the loop over the end. Everyone is watching."

Kit felt her blood coursing through her. She was sure her face had turned bright red the way it always did giving away her emotions. Everyone watched her, when all she had wanted to do was to keep hidden in the sea of onlookers. Too late now. With shaking hands she reached up and slipped her hair ribbon onto Tolin's proffered lance. Her knees shook. In the past, whenever she was around a handsome man she couldn't control her nerves. It was happening once again. But this time, with Tolin.

Tolin lifted his lance high in the air and the ribbon slipped down to the hilt of the pole. He held his lance high in the air and rode back to the lists. The crowd cheered wildly. The noise in the stands became unbearably loud.

"Brenna, I don't feel well. I need to get back to the kitchen," she told her sister. She looked down to see her hands shaking uncontrollably. Her anxiety was taking over.

"But don't you want to stay and watch Lord Tolin joust?" asked Brenna. "He is up against Lord Rook next. And he is wearing your favor."

"Nay, I really don't. Come, Parker, we need to get back to the castle." She quickly got up, and Brenna followed as they made their way through the rowdy crowd. Kit needed to get back to the safety of the kitchen where she knew what was expected of her. Where she knew she could perform well. She was out of her element here at the joust, giving hair ribbons to a nobleman. What was she thinking? Kit now realized that she never should have come at all.

~

Tolin couldn't help but feel smitten as he rode back to the lists with Kit's favor looped over his lance. So, she did like the kiss under the mistletoe after all, just like Daegel had said. If not, she wouldn't have come to watch him joust.

"Lord Tolin, are you ready?" His squire looked up at him. "Lord Rook and you are tied. Whoever wins this round will be the champion of the joust this Christmas."

"And that will be me," he said, feeling more alive and powerful than ever. He wanted more than anything to look good in front of Kit. And now that he had her favor, he was sure her eyes would be fastened on him the entire time.

The joust began. Tolin didn't bother to lower the faceplate on his helm. He wanted to have a good view of Kit watching him win the competition against his brother. He steadied his lance and kicked his heels into his horse as he bolted forward down the list. One last time his eyes sought out Kit. To his dismay he saw her leaving her seat and pushing her way through the crowd. Why was she leaving now? He wanted her to see him win again.

The crowd screamed and Tolin brought his attention back to the joust, but it was too late. His distraction had been a fatal mistake. Rook's lance knocked into him, catching him off guard and pushing him backwards. He tried to regain his balance, but the weight of his own lance pulled at him. He dropped the pole and flipped backward over his horse, landing facedown in the mud. The crowd went wild. And then the master of ceremonies proclaimed Rook the winner of the Christmas joust.

"Damn it," swore Tolin, pushing up from the mud. With his attention on Kit, it cost him the win.

"Brother, you made that so easy for me." Rook rode over, looking down at him from atop his horse. "I guess your winning streak is broken now."

"Nay, it isn't. I was distracted, or I would have won."

"Distracted?" Rook laughed, turning a full circle on his horse, holding his lance high in the air. "Perhaps it was that ribbon fluttering in your face? I'm sure the lady whose favor you chose won't be so infatuated with you anymore."

Tolin looked over to his lance covered in mud. Kit's green hair ribbon was wrapped around it and covered with mud as well. All he'd wanted was to look good in her eyes, even if she was naught but a commoner. Any other woman would have clung to the lists and watched intently as he jousted with her favor attached to his pole. This wench got up and walked away as if she didn't even care. He didn't like that at all.

"My lord, are you hurt?" Jarvis ran to help him up from the mud.

"He's not hurt," spat Rook. "Not physically. He's taken blows much worse than this. However, I think his pride might be bruised. Well, excuse me, Tolin, I need to take my victory lap. I'll meet you inside where we can celebrate my win with a tankard of ale." Rook rode away, circling the field, working the crowd into a frenzy.

"I can't believe you lost a joust to Lord Rook," said Jarvis, helping him up as his armor was heavy and bulky. "You've beaten him at the joust for years now. What happened?"

"*She* happened," he spat, storming away, ready to wring the girl's neck for ever leaving the kitchen in the first place.

Tolin lost today in more ways than one. Jarvis was right. He hadn't lost a joust to Rook in years now. Plus, he had never *ever* lost the attention of a woman, especially when he'd chosen her favor. No noblewoman would have walked away. Kit shouldn't affect him this way. He shouldn't care. But the more she ignored him, the more he wanted her. And he wouldn't stop trying until he had her. Because Tolin Blake was not a man who would tolerate losing again.

CHAPTER 7

Kit and the servants all attended an early Mass the next morning since it was Christmas Day. Because of Raven, they'd actually been allowed to go to the service, but were instructed to return directly to the kitchen afterward. The meal yesterday had been hectic. She'd been lucky enough to manage to complete all the fruit tarts in time. But since she'd gone to the joust, she was short on time and had to give up eating her meal in order to complete things. She'd been so busy that she never got out to the great hall at all.

However, the word around the kitchen was that Tolin lost the joust and ended up facedown in the mud. Mayhap she should have stayed to watch, after all. From what she'd heard, Tolin never lost. Then again, she was glad he lost. Mayhap his self-importance would go down a notch. After all, the man had too much pride.

"Mother, I see King. Can I go pet him?" Parker tugged on her arm.

"What?" She looked up to see Lord Tolin atop his horse,

watching as the servants exited St. Basil's Cathedral. Her heart sped up. What was *he* doing here? The sun had just risen and she'd heard the man liked to sleep late. Besides, the nobles wouldn't go to Mass until a little later.

"I'll bring him over there," offered her sister's husband, Oliver, taking the boy and heading right to Lord Tolin.

"Aren't you going too?" asked Brenna from behind her.

"Nay," said Kit, her gaze dropping to the ground. She didn't want to talk to Tolin. He would probably only reprimand her for having left the kitchen to come to the joust. "Oliver will bring Parker back to the castle. Let's keep walking."

She headed in the opposite direction with Brenna at her side. Kit felt the need to sprint, but her sister moved slowly and she wouldn't leave her behind.

"Kit, I thought you liked Lord Tolin. So, why are you trying so hard to avoid him?"

Kit slowed down to talk with her sister.

"I don't know. He makes me...nervous when I'm around him. He didn't at first, but now whenever he is near, I feel flooded with anxiety and my whole body shakes."

"Oh, I understand. You mean, ever since he kissed you."

Kit supposed that was right. It made sense in a way. She had felt bold and stood up to the man when she'd first met him. Now when he was near, her hands and knees started shaking.

"Mayhap that's it," she said softly under her breath.

The clip-clop of a horse's hooves from behind her led her to believe that it was Lord Tolin and that he was following her for some reason. This only caused her to become anxious once again.

"Baker," he called out, making her stop in her tracks.

"I think he's talking to you," her sister whispered.

"Yes, I believe so." There was no way she could avoid him now. To do so would be defying a noble. She was trying her hardest to help work off Parker's punishment, and she didn't need him adding more time to the sentence. She had no choice but to heed his call.

"I would have a word with you. Alone." His deep and sexy voice sounded so demanding.

"I'll leave," offered Brenna.

Kit looked over to her sister and shook her head. "Nay," she whispered. "Don't leave me, Brenna. Please."

"He said he wants to speak to you alone. I cannot ignore his wishes. He's a noble." Her sister grabbed her hand and squeezed it. "Everything will be fine, I promise. Just be yourself. I will join Oliver and Parker until you are finished." Brenna left, leaving Kit standing there alone with Lord Tolin.

"My lord," she said, forcing a smile and curtseying to him. He sat high atop his horse, towering over her and making her feel inferior. He did this on purpose she was sure.

"So, did you enjoy the joust yesterday?" he asked. She couldn't be sure if he was being sincere or just facetious.

"Yes, my lord, I did." By the look on his face she realized she'd said the wrong thing. Mayhap he thought she was saying that she'd enjoyed the fact he'd lost. "I mean, no, I didn't. I mean, I'm sorry to hear you lost and ended up face-down in the mud. My lord." She squeezed her eyes shut thinking how silly she must sound. Damn her nerves. Kit already regretted mentioning his failure and the mud in the same sentence. She probably should have left that part out altogether.

"You do realize that I chose your favor over all the others," he continued. "Yet, it was brought to my attention that you didn't bother to stick around for the joust afterwards." He dangled her hair ribbon from his fingers. It was caked with mud. Her eyes settled on it and her heart skipped a beat. So he'd kept it. It made her wonder why. Especially after he'd lost the joust.

"I'm sorry, but I had work to do in the kitchen. I shouldn't have gone to the lists at all." She tried to retrieve the ribbon from him but he snatched it up in his hand just out of her reach. Her eyes raised to his face as she slowly dropped her hand to her side.

"Nay, you never should have been there to begin with, that is right. I should have made you return to the castle at once instead of rewarding you by choosing your favor over all the others. I never should have taken a favor from a commoner to begin with. It only brought me ill luck." He dangled the ribbon from his fingers again. This time she didn't bother to try to get it. He was toying with her like a cat and mouse and she didn't like that. Nay, she decided, she wouldn't play his game anymore.

"Are you here now to punish me, my lord?" she asked, being bold enough to stand up to him again. "Or are you here perhaps to tell me that it was my fault that you lost the joust? After all, you always win is what I've heard. Surely, I must be nothing to you but bad luck." She was too angry right now to feel nervous. Perhaps what she'd felt when he'd kissed her was not affection or attraction to him like she'd initially thought. Mayhap it was nothing more than the longing to have a man in her life once again.

Kit needed to learn to ignore these feelings. Men in her life had only brought her despair in the past. Kit didn't want that and she certainly didn't need this one. Tolin Blake was not someone whom she would ever choose to purposely have in her life. Nay, it was a silly mistake to think so in the first place, and she wouldn't be so careless again.

"If you must know, I am here to give you this." He held out his closed fist. At first she thought he was giving her back her hair ribbon, but then she realized he still held that in his other hand. She slowly reached up and her opened her hand. His fingers brushed against hers as he dropped something into her palm. All she could feel was a surge of excitement wash through her when his skin touched hers.

Why did she feel this way? Nay, she didn't want to think about it. Quickly, she pulled her hand back, looking at a dried bean that he'd placed in her palm.

"What is this?" she asked.

"A bean," he answered.

"Yes, I can see that. But why are you giving it to me?"

"It is to be used tonight."

"In the mincemeat pies?"

"Nay. I've decided we'll have cake instead."

"What?" She didn't like him changing his mind so often. "Cake, my lord?"

"Yes. You will put that bean into the cake for tonight's meal."

Her thoughts went back to the servants at the joust who were talking about the Bean King.

"It's for a game. Right?"

"Yes, it is. Whoever finds the bean in their cake will be the Bean King or Queen. Or as I prefer to call them, the Lord or Lady of Misrule. Their reign will last until Twelfth Night."

"So then, anyone can find this bean and earn the title?" she asked, staring at the bean in her hand. Already a thousand thoughts swarmed her head. This could be the answer to all her prayers.

"Aye, that's right."

"And this Lord or Lady of Misrule can make anyone, even nobles, do whatever they want? Even if the one who finds the bean is naught but a servant or a commoner?" Her eyes slowly lifted to his face.

"Yes, the game is for servants and commoners," he said slowly, studying her intensely. "That's the way it works. Why do you ask?"

He started to sound suspicious and she needed him to trust her. She had a plan that was going to bring wealth and success to her family, but she didn't want him to know it. Luck was finally on her side, and Lord Tolin Blake had just put the answer to all her problems right in the palm of her hand.

"No reason. I just wanted to understand the game, that's all." She smiled and curtseyed again. "Good day, my lord. And good luck to the next Lord...or Lady of Misrule."

～

"Damn it!" cursed Tolin several hours later, after having been on the losing team of the Christmas football game. The nobles had taken on the villagers in a game that involved kicking around a pigskin bladder filled with air. It was a rough game with many injuries, but he didn't care. He'd needed to get out his frustrations somehow.

Kit wasn't falling for him like most women did. This only made him want the wench even more. Breathing hard, he stopped at a horse trough filled with water. Since it was winter the water was cold and nearly frozen. He splashed it on his face, liking the sting of the bite. It made him feel alive.

He looked down and pulled the hair ribbon from where he'd tied it to his belt. Mayhap it really was bad luck after all. About to throw it down, he felt the soft silk under his fingers and that only made him think of Kit's soft skin and her enticing lips. He dipped the ribbon in the water to cleanse it.

"My lord, did we really just lose to the villagers?" Jarvis came up beside him, rinsing his face with the cold water as well. "Aaaaaah, that's cold. Brrrr."

"We would have won if Tolin hadn't been such a bad aim," said Raven, walking up with Rook. She brushed the dirt off her gown.

"Aye," said Rook. "Tolin, what is the matter with you lately? You couldn't even seem to kick the ball straight today. You're usually our best player."

"Don't forget, he lost the joust yesterday, too," Jarvis so diligently pointed out. "Mayhap he's cursed or something to be losing so much lately."

"Aye, that must be what it is," said Tolin, looking at the wet hair ribbon in his hand.

"Or mayhap his mind is on something...or someone else." Raven smiled and nodded to the ribbon. Tolin quickly shoved it into his pouch.

"Oh, do you mean the baker woman he kissed under the mistletoe?" asked Jarvis.

"Ah, my little brother has been bitten by the love bug," said Rook with a chuckle. "And so soon after meeting the woman, too."

"Nay, that is ridiculous!" spat Tolin, not wanting to believe he was under anyone's spell. Especially not the baker wench even if she was lovely and a big distraction. No girl had ever affected him this way. He needed to stop this losing streak before he also lost his reputation. "I just had some ill luck, that's all. But I assure you, it will all end tonight. After the main meal. I will challenge any of you to any game and I assure you I will not lose again."

~

Kit couldn't believe the feast being served at the castle's Christmas dinner. She had never attended this meal before and now wondered why she hadn't.

The food was fantastic, delicious, and a work of art. The castle cooks were truly amazing. The servants kept bringing out course after course, starting with soup, lampreys, and vegetables, followed by eight different kinds of meat. There were dishes she'd never seen before, like the stuffed chickens made to look like knights riding atop pigs. The chickens were cooked and dressed in clothes and had little jousting poles in their hands. No expense was too much for Blake Castle. Or perhaps Tolin was trying to show off, she wasn't sure. Either way, it truly was impressive.

"Mother, did you see all the meat?" asked Parker, helping her to mix the ingredients for the cakes that were to be served as part of the Bean King game that would take place after the main meal. "They even have a swan with feathers on it yet!"

"No, Parker. They reattached the feathers after the bird was cooked," she explained, ladling the contents of the fruit-and-nut cake into the proper pans, getting it ready for the oven.

"Try this!" Oliver walked over and held up a piece of roasted boar to her mouth. Kit tasted it and robust flavor exploded on her tongue.

"That is really delicious," she said, licking her lips.

"Kit, look at the boar's head," Brenna called out from the table as she helped with the baking. She pointed to a large tray being carried by two male servants. On the center of the tray was the cooked head of a huge wild boar. In its mouth was a baked apple. Around the boar's head were stewed figs and baked quinces sprinkled with lots of currants and what looked like spices.

"Look, Mother, what's that?" Parker stood up on the bench to see over the heads of all the people working in the kitchen.

"It looks like a peacock," said Kit. "Oh my!" She held her hand to her mouth in shock. The cooked bird also had its feathers reattached and they were spread out in a colorful and wide display of the bird's elaborate plumage. It was surrounded by cooked root vegetables that were somehow carved to look like flowers.

"Don't forget the salt cellar for the main table," called out one of the servants. "Where is it?"

"Oh, here it is." Kit ran over and picked up the large silver dish that was shaped like a boat. Inside, it was filled to the top with salt to be used by the nobles. Salt was expensive and not everyone had the luxury of seasoning their food with it. The servants and peasants sitting below the royal dais would not have this luxury as they were from 'below the salt.'

"Take that out to the dais right away," commanded the man who was the head cook.

"Who? Me?" asked Kit.

"Yes. The nobles need the salt. Don't forget to bring a spoon. Hurry."

"But I need to—"

"Hurry, before we are reprimanded by Lord Tolin," shouted the cook.

"Oliver, perhaps you could do it?" asked Kit, holding the salt cellar with two hands.

"Nay." He shook his head. "I'm supposed to be in the stables. Besides, and it wouldn't bode well for me if Lord Tolin knew I was in here snitching food."

"I suppose you're right," said Kit with a sigh. Since Oliver was missing fingers, she couldn't take the chance that he might drop or spill it. Kit looked over to Brenna next who was rubbing her belly. Her sister could barely walk let alone carry a cellar filled with salt. Nay, this would never work.

"Here's a spoon, Mother." Parker stood on his tiptoes and placed a spoon into the salt cellar. She considered having Parker bring it out, but figured he was too small and wouldn't be able to lift it to the raised table.

"All right, I'll do it. I'll be right back. We need to get those cakes in the oven." Kit took a deep breath and slowly released it. She didn't want to walk up to the dais where the nobles sat to hand them salt. But if she refused, all the servants might get in trouble. They'd been working so hard and were so tired. They didn't deserve to be punished, especially on Christmas. Nay, she would just go quickly and deliver the salt herself.

Tolin looked up from his meal surprised to see Kit heading right toward the dais with the salt cellar balanced between her hands. Her hair was tied back but mussed. Her cheeks were ruddy and her apron was smattered with flour.

Never had such a bedraggled wench looked so enticing to him as she did right now. She was about to hand the salt cellar up to Raven, but he raised his hand to call her over.

"Bring the salt here, please," he told her. He watched as her eyes darted back and forth. She hesitated, but then carefully carried the salt over to him. He stood up and reached down over the table to take it from her. When he grabbed it, he swore he saw her hands shaking. "Thank you," he said.

"My lord." She nodded quickly and turned to go, but he didn't want her to leave just yet. Actually, he wanted her to sit next to him and share a trencher, but knew that would never happen. She was naught but a commoner, and only nobles were allowed to sit at the dais. Besides, she was a baker and belonged in the kitchen.

"Wait!" he called out, still holding the salt cellar. From the corner of his eyes he saw his brothers and sister watching him intently.

Kit slowly turned around. "Is there something else you require, my lord?"

"Yes," he said, clearing his throat, trying to think of something. He slowly put the salt cellar down on the table.

King sat next to his chair whining and wagging his tail. "It's King," he said.

"Your...hound?" She looked confused. "What about him?"

"I'd like you to take him into the kitchen."

"You would? Why?"

"Tolin? What are you doing?" asked Rook. "Your hound is always at your feet during a meal. You are sending him away?"

"I want you to bring my dog to the boy so he can watch him."

"The boy?" One of Kit's brows lifted into an arch.

"Parker. That's his name, right?"

"Yes, my lord," she answered with a stiff upper lip. "My son's name is Parker. I would have thought you'd know that by now. Especially after sentencing him."

"He's good with the hound. Make certain he feeds King whatever he wants to eat. Go King," he told the dog, giving him a small push until the dog jumped down from the dais.

"Whatever the dog wants to eat he gets?" she asked, sounding as if she thought it was absurd.

"Yes," he answered. "And make certain you and your family get some food too."

"I have cakes to bake for the bean game, my lord. I'm afraid I might not get the luxury of eating until later tonight and only if there is anything left at all." She reached out and took the dog by the collar. "Now, if you'll excuse me, I have much work to do." She turned and left before she was dismissed.

Tolin raised a finger meaning to reprimand her, but then

decided he didn't want to do that. Not with everyone watching. He slowly lowered his hand and sat back down.

"Isn't that the girl who is the mother of the boy thief?" Raven's husband Jonathon leaned forward and looked down the dais past Raven to talk to Tolin.

"She's the baker," he said. "Her name is Kit." Tolin took the spoon and some salt, sprinkling it on his food. He kept thinking of what Kit said. That she might not have time to eat. Why did this bother him so much?

"Tolin? Tolin, can you pass the salt?" asked Rook.

"Sure," he said, handing it to Rook's wife, Rose who sat next to him.

"Is something the matter?" asked Rose, passing the dish to her husband.

"Nay. Why would you think that?" asked Tolin, busying himself pushing his food around his plate with his spoon.

"It just seems like something is taking your concern," Rose answered, taking a sip of wine.

"Nay. Not at all."

"Mayhap he's afraid he'll lose any game he plays tonight," Daegel said from down the table. "After all, he is on a losing streak lately."

"That is all about to change," said Tolin, lifting his goblet to his mouth. Over the rim, he saw Kit bringing his hound into the kitchen. Parker ran out and hugged the dog. Together they left the great hall. This didn't feel right to him. He didn't want to think of Kit and her son working so hard on Christmas. Even the serfs had the week off from working the land.

"How are things going with that little thief?" Rook broke him from his thoughts.

"I'm not so sure the boy really is a thief," said Tolin.

"Then why don't you let him and his mother go back home?" asked Rook.

Tolin could very well decide to do that. But if he did, he would never have the chance to get to know Kit better.

"Nay. I've made my decision and they will work in the kitchen until Twelfth Night," said Tolin.

"Good, good." Rook nodded and took a swig of ale. "It seems you are getting the hang of things after all. I'm glad to see you are taking proper measures and teaching the peasants a valuable lesson."

"Yes. I suppose so." Tolin pushed his food around his plate, no longer hungry.

CHAPTER 8

"It's time to serve the cake," Kit instructed, putting the final touches of sprinkled sugar atop the cooling fruit-and-nut cakes. The sweet and tangy aroma wafted up into the air. "Everyone take a platter of cakes and be sure to serve the nobles first," she told the other bakers who were assisting her.

"Mother, is this cake for the Green Bean game?" asked her son, kneeling on a stool and reaching out to pluck a currant from atop one of the cakes. He popped it into his mouth and smiled. Then he snitched another currant and handed it to King who was begging under the table.

Kit giggled. Her son was so cute. "Parker, it is not a green bean, it is a dried bean that someone will find in their cake tonight. And yes, it is for the game. Now go and watch King so he doesn't trip the servers on their way to the great hall with the cakes." The boy had taken a liking to the dog. Lately the dog followed him just about everywhere he went. They were inseparable.

"Yes, Mother." Parker skipped off with his new friend, King following on his heels.

"Kit, did you remember to put the bean in the batter?" Brenna waddled over, holding on to Oliver's arm. Her face was flushed and she breathed heavily. The baby was getting closer to being born, and it made her sister very tired.

"Of course she did," said Oliver. "Kit knows the rules of the game."

"Actually, I didn't do it. Yet." Kit pulled the bean out of her pouch and held it between two fingers.

"Kit, you were supposed to put it in the batter," said Brenna in shock. Her eyes opened wide. "We will be punished for that."

"Nay, we won't," said Kit. "Don't worry. I have a plan that involves this bean and it will solve all our problems."

"What is it?" asked Oliver. "I don't understand."

"The rules of the game are that whoever finds this bean in their cake is Lord or Lady of Misrule until Twelfth Night."

"Yes, but no one is going to find it if you haven't put it in the cake," said Oliver.

"It will be in the cake, don't worry." Kit grinned and pushed the bean into one of the small cakes that she'd kept on the side.

"Sister? What are you doing?" Brenna looked horrified.

"Oliver, go out into the great hall and sit down. Quickly. I am going to serve you this cake. Then you will announce to everyone that you have found the bean. You will be the Bean King."

"I am? I will?" Oliver made a face, not understanding.

"Yes, you are going to be the winner," said Kit. "Don't you see? Once you find the bean, we will not have to worry about where we'll live or the bakery shop or finding a job or anything ever again."

"Kit, this makes no sense at all," said Brenna. "Why not?"

"Because, Oliver will hold the power to tell the nobles to send us back to the bakery anon. Or he can have them give us money. Or possibly even a new home. We will have no more worries as soon as Oliver finds the bean. This is the answer to our prayers. Don't you understand? Our troubles will be over and all because of this." She held up the plate with the hand-sized cake on it and smiled.

"Oh, Kit, I hope you are right," cried Brenna, still rubbing her belly.

"Do you really think this will work?" asked Oliver.

"I know it will." Kit felt confident. Nothing was going to ruin her plan. Her son's punishment by being here at the castle was to thank, because they were about to get everything they ever wanted.

"I would also like Oliver to hold a job at the castle," said her sister excitedly. "And you to be able to hire enough help at the bakery so your business can flourish again."

"We'll have all that, and more." Kit felt smug and she didn't care. It might be dishonest, but then again, her son was being punished and blamed for something that he never even did. Her boy was not a thief. Life was about to smile on them. This was one of Lord Tolin's games that she was about to win. "I have some ideas of more things we can demand from Lord Tolin and I'll tell you about them later. Mayhap we can even get him to give Parker a dog of his own. I know that would be a wonderful present for my son."

"I'm starting to like this idea," said Oliver with a nod.

"I've got my eye on a fine steed in the stables. I've never had a horse of my own, but would like to have one."

"Then you shall have it," said Kit, giving her promise.

"Oliver can ride it to his job at the castle every day," added Brenna, getting swept up in the excitement now.

"Yes," said Kit. "This is all going to be perfect. You see, before Twelfth Night is here, Lord Tolin will have made us the richest people in town. Now go! I will bring out the cake as soon as you sit down, Oliver."

I'm going, I'm going," said Oliver, taking off for the great hall at a near run.

Kit took off her apron, brushed off her clothes, and ran a hand over her head to smooth down her hair.

"Oh, Kit, this all sounds so wonderful but are you sure we should be doing this?" asked Brenna. "What if someone finds out? We might all be thrown into the dungeon because of it."

"Nay, don't even say that. No one is going to be the wiser." Kit smiled and picked up the plate with the special cake on it. "Besides, isn't it time that a commoner had something good happen to them? Why should the nobles have all the luck, wealth, and riches?" She took the plate and made her way to the great hall. Taking a quick look around, she spied Oliver waving to her from one of the far tables. Kit was so excited she could barely stand it. She took one step into the room but was abruptly halted.

"Hold on, there," said Tolin, seeming to come from nowhere. His big body blocked her path and her view of Oliver. She needed to get around him and give her brother by marriage the cake so her plan could be set into action.

"Lord Tolin," she gasped. He was the last person she

wanted to see right now. Especially since she was deceiving him.

"What have you got there?" he asked, looking down at the cake.

"Huh?" Her head snapped up and her eyes widened in fear. "Oh, this is the cake. You know, the cake that is being used for your game," she told him. "This is the last one to be served."

"That looks delicious." He started to reach for it, but she pulled the plate away.

"I told the servers to bring cake to the nobles first. I'm sure if you return to your seat you'll find some waiting for you."

"Mmmm, that smells good," he said, closing his eyes and sniffing the air. "What kind of cake is it?"

"It is fruit-and-nut cake, my lord. With a sprinkle of cinnamon on top and a splash of dark ale inside. Now, excuse me. I need to deliver this last cake and get back to work." She stepped around him, but with one stride from his long legs, he was blocking her way once again.

"Those are some of my favorite ingredients, you realize."

"That's nice. Pardon me." She tried again, but his hand on her arm stopped her this time.

"Wait."

"Is there something you need, my lord?" She glanced up at him. Heat started to rise within her. She and her family were so close to having a good life, but Lord Tolin was the only thing right now standing in her way.

"Were you able to get some food to eat in the kitchen?" he asked her, sounding sincerely concerned.

"Nay. Not yet. But don't worry, I will as soon as I deliver

this last cake." She flashed him a fake smile. "So, excuse me so I can bring it to the table."

"No need for that. I'll help you get rid of it." He reached out and plucked the cake off the plate.

Kit's eyes focused on the empty dish and her mouth fell open. "Nay. What are you doing?" she gasped.

"I am helping you to finish your work quicker so you can go and enjoy the Christmas feast."

Kit wasn't interested in food right now. The only feast she desired was her dreams that would be granted once Oliver found the bean in the cake.

"Don't eat that, my lord," she blurted out, having to refrain herself from ripping it out of his hand.

"Why not?" His dark eyes narrowed slightly as he studied her.

"Because! Because your cake is at the dais, my lord. That one is for the commoners." She held out the plate but he didn't return the cake.

"If we're short because of this one, I'll give my cake at the dais to a commoner, don't worry."

She tried to actually reach out for it, but she was too late. Tolin opened his mouth and took a big bite.

"Mmmm, this is delicious," he said as he chewed. "You must be the finest baker in the land, Kit. This is the best fruit and nut cake I have ever tasted."

"Thank you," she said, horrified by his act. Her eyes flashed down to the rest of the cake in his fingers. She wondered if the bean was still inside the piece left. He hadn't seemed to bite into it yet. Mayhap if she got the rest of the cake away from him before he found the bean, she'd still be able to slip it to Oliver in time.

"I'm sure you'd like to sit down and eat, my lord. Allow me to carry that cake to your table for you." She held out the plate, wanting him to put the remainder of the small hand cake atop the dish, but Tolin had other intentions. The man couldn't seem to be parted from his sweets.

"No need to do that. This is so good that I'll finish it right here." He shoved the rest of the cake into his mouth and chewed. Kit held her breath and her body stiffened. How was this really happening? Why? This couldn't be true! Then she heard his tooth hit the bean and he moaned and held his hand up to his mouth.

"What the hell." He spit the bean out into his hand. "What is this? A shell from a nut?"

"Lord Tolin," called out his squire walking up to join them. "No one seems to have found the bean. Oh, look, there it is. You've found the bean in your cake! Doesn't that make you the Bean King then?"

"Yes. I suppose it does," said Tolin, studying the bean.

Daegel was right behind Jarvis, stretching his neck to see what was going on. "Hey, you can't be the Bean King, Tolin. That is a game devised for peasants to get that privilege."

"Yes, I believe he is right," said Kit, feeling her heart drumming so loud in her ears that she wondered if they heard it too. "I would be more than happy to put the bean into another batch of cakes." She held out her hand for it. Tolin started to give it to her, but at the last minute he pulled his hand away and closed the bean into his fist.

"Nay, nay. I think I'll keep this after all."

"What? Why?" Kit felt her world come crashing down around her.

"Well, I am in charge of the games during Christmastide, so I can make or even change the rules if I feel like it."

"Oh, I don't think that would be a good idea," said Kit. "Won't everyone be disappointed?"

"Nay, why would they? Actually, I think it would be a lot more fun this way. Yes, I think I will bend the rules after all."

He looked up and called out so everyone could hear him. "Attention, everyone! This year, anyone, including nobles, can win the title of Bean King. And that said, I have just found the bean in my cake." He held it up high so everyone could see.

A soft lull of talking and comments filled the hall. Kit could tell that the commoners were not at all pleased by Tolin's decision.

Rook rushed over, stepping around several servers along the way. "Tolin, nay. What are you doing? This is a game for the peasants, not the nobles."

"Well, I can't help it if I won." He looked at the bean and chuckled. "I guess my winning streak is back."

"Put it back," said Rook through his teeth. "You cannot be the winner of this game. It isn't right."

"He's correct," said Kit, her heart still drumming against her ribs.

"I won fair and square," said Tolin with a shrug. "Besides, I decide the games and the rules for Christmastide. I say this is the way we will do it this year."

Jarvis grabbed two tankards of ale from the tray of a passing serving girl, giving one to Tolin. "Then let's all drink to this year's Bean King, Lord Tolin."

"Lord of Misrule," Tolin bellowed. "That is the proper

title. Now, let's all drink and dance and have some fun. That is what this year's Lord of Misrule orders you all to do."

Kit slowly slunk away, making her way back to the kitchen. Of all the rotten luck, why did Lord Tolin have to be the one to get the bean instead of Oliver? Her plan had been perfect, but that man just ruined everything. Why couldn't he have stayed up at the dais where a noble belonged?

"It looks like your winning streak truly has returned, Lord Tolin," she heard his squire say as she left the great hall.

"Yes. I'm back," shouted Tolin with a chuckle. "Hail to the winner—the Lord of Misrule."

Tolin couldn't believe his good luck. He raised his tankard and drank with his friends, then attended the group by the fire as the servants brought in the Yule log. It was a piece of the leftover log from last Christmas, to be burned for good luck. More logs would be added to it, and the fire would keep being fed and burning bright until the end of Twelfth Night. Then, a piece of the new Yule log would be saved to use next year for good luck as well.

"Tolin, your cake was up at the dais," his sister Raven told him. "What were you even doing down on the floor, and why were you eating cake with the peasants?"

"I was looking for King. My dog keeps disappearing lately. That's when I saw Kit enter the great hall with a plate with one lone cake atop it. She said she had to deliver it before she could get any food to eat. I was only trying to help her out, since I didn't want her to go hungry. So I ate the cake, enabling her to get back to the kitchen quicker."

"She only had one piece of cake to deliver?" Jarvis made a face. "Why only one? The servants always have huge platters filled with desserts to hand out."

"That's true," said Tolin. "I suppose it was a little odd. Mayhap it was the last of what was left."

"Oh, that makes sense," said Jarvis. "I mean, I saw Oliver, your new stableman, come out and sit down just before this happened. He was waving to Kit to bring the cake over to him. Mayhap that is what she was doing."

"You saw what?" Tolin's smile faded. "Are you sure it was Oliver? That is her brother-by-marriage."

"I'm positive." Jarvis nodded. "I know who he is. He was in the kitchen most of the night. I saw him there earlier. I guess Kit wanted him to eat the cake out in the great hall for some reason. I'm surprised Kit took the time to deliver it herself when she has been so busy baking. I would have thought she'd have the boy deliver it instead."

"Yes, now that you mention it. It would seem so." Tolin started to get a bad feeling about this. His eyes shot over to the kitchen. He wondered exactly what the wench was up to.

"I'm sure she was just trying to help," said Raven, sticking up for Kit. "Remember, she did take the time to bring the salt cellar to our table during the meal."

"Aye, she did," said Tolin, remembering how flustered Kit had seemed when she did it. And how she couldn't wait to run back to the kitchen. He couldn't help thinking it was a little odd that she would personally deliver a cake to her family member. Twice as odd that she kept trying to stop him from eating it, too. "Damn, she played me," he spat, knowing now exactly what she had been trying to do.

"Pardon me, Lord of Misrule?" asked his squire.

"Who played you?" asked Daegel.

"If you'll excuse me, I have a stop to make." Tolin made straight for the kitchen, knowing now that Kit had tried to cheat and he just happened to have caught her in the act. Most of the servants were sitting down in the kitchen, finally able to eat, when he stormed in.

They all jumped up at his presence.

"Sit back down and eat," he said, with a wave of his hand. He scanned the kitchen but didn't see the wench anywhere. "Where is the baker named Kit?"

He saw the boy and his dog across the room, as well as the pregnant woman and her husband. He hurried over to them. "There's my dog," he grumbled. "Where is Kit?" he asked. I need to talk to her at once."

"I think she went out for a breath of fresh air," said Brenna, looking up from her meal. "Is there something you need, my lord? Mayhap we can help you?"

"What I need is to speak to the liar and the cheat." He stormed away before giving anyone a chance to answer and headed for the door leading to the courtyard.

"My lord," called out Jarvis, seeing him and running over with Tolin's cloak in hand. "If you are going outside you'll need this." He handed the cloak to him.

"Thank you, squire." Tolin grabbed his cloak from Jarvis, donning it as he made his way out to the courtyard. Once outside, the wind picked up and he realized that it had started to snow. He saw a woman by the well and went to meet her. "Kit?" he called, walking up behind her. She slowly turned around. Her face was red and her body shivered from the cold. "Kit? Why are you out here in the cold without a covering?"

"I—I just needed some fresh air, that's all." She flashed a quick smile that didn't meet her eyes. Then he noticed her swipe her cheek with the back of her hand. Was that a tear she was trying to hide? "Was there something you needed, Lord Tolin? I mean, Lord of Misrule?"

Her words only made the situation worse. He had meant to reprimand her, but instead, he found himself removing his cloak, wanting to comfort her instead. She looked up at him and blinked away a tear. Those eyes drew him in and clenched around his heart. He actually felt sorry for her.

"You need this more than me. To keep warm." He gently wrapped his cloak around her. She reached up with one hand and clutched it to keep it closed. "However, I must say that I also know what you tried to do and I am not happy about it."

Her head jerked upward. "Whatever do you mean?"

"I'm talking about this." He held up the bean in two fingers. "You were trying to give it to Oliver weren't you? Just admit it. You wanted him to be the winner of the game."

Fear showed in her eyes. Then it changed to sadness. She looked down but didn't answer. There was an awkward silence between them.

"The cake was delicious," he said quietly, wanting to pay her a compliment. "You are an exceptional baker, Kit."

"It is who I am. It's my life. It's what I do." Her words came out sounding forceful. "If you'll excuse me, my lord, I need to get back to the kitchen and finish my work for the night. The morning comes quickly." She removed the cloak and handed it to him. "Thank you, but I have my own cloak and won't be foolish enough to venture out into the cold without it again." She walked away but he didn't want to let her go.

"Kit," he called after her, causing her to stop and turn around. "I would like a dance with you tonight."

At first she looked pleased, but then she looked angry. "I'm sorry, but I have work to do."

"It's not a request," he told her, not liking the way she was trying her best to turn him down.

"Not a request?" She cocked her head. "I see. So, it is the first order from the Lord of Misrule, then."

"Nay, I didn't say that."

"You didn't need to. I know the way the game works, my lord."

"Don't be that way, Kit," he said in a deep voice, not wanting the girl to think it was an order. He only said it because he wanted to spend more time with her. Why couldn't she see that?

"What way did you want me to be?" she asked coldly.

"Why do you hate me so much?"

"Hate...you?" Her voice was broken and breathy. "Is that what you think?"

"What else can I think?" He took a few steps closer to her. "Every time I'm near you, you are either fighting with me, or trying to run away."

"I—I'm not. Not doing that, my lord."

"Then you'll meet me on the dance floor when you finish your work."

Her eyes snapped up and drilled into him. He wasn't sure at all what she was thinking.

"As you wish, Lord of Misrule." She turned and ran back to the keep, leaving him standing alone, feeling like a loser even though he'd just won the title of Lord of Misrule.

CHAPTER 9

Tolin didn't think she would come. It was already getting late into the night, and it was hours ago that the dishes from the meal were cleared away and the trestle tables were taken down, making room for the Christmas games as well as dancing.

Tolin had kept one eye on the door leading to the kitchen as he first watched the mummers put on a Christmas play. Then the jester made the rounds, playing pranks on everyone. Jugglers and musicians filled the room. Everyone seemed to be having a good time. Everyone but him. He couldn't stop being bothered by what had happened with Kit.

"Let's play Blind Man's Buff," said Raven, taking a cloak and putting it backward over Tolin with the hood covering his face.

"Nay. I don't want to play," he protested, trying to push it away, but Raven held it in place.

"You love this game," said his sister. "And there hasn't

been a time yet where you weren't able to identify the person you catch. Now, come on, Tolin. You are usually a lot more fun than this! Especially at Christmas."

"All right," he mumbled, handing her his tankard of ale.

"Hold on," said Rook, spinning him around so hard that Tolin got dizzy and nearly fell.

"Rook, you'll pay for that!" Tolin reached out to catch his brother, but Rook darted away.

"Over here, Bean King," shouted Daegel, causing Tolin to spin around the other way and reach out once again.

"Back here," cried Jarvis from behind him.

Tolin wasn't at his best tonight, being so distracted by Kit and the way she'd reacted earlier. Every time someone taunted him and he tried to catch them blindly, they jumped out of the way leaving him empty-handed.

"That's enough!" he shouted, rushing forward, grabbing for whoever might be too slow to get away. He latched on to someone, and by her gasp he could tell it was a woman. "Hold still. I will identify you," he said.

Kit froze, not expecting to have Tolin rush forward and grab her like that. She had just entered the great hall looking for him to join him for the required dance, when she stumbled into the middle of a game called Blind Man's Buff. She didn't know at first who was under the cloak. Not until she had heard his voice. It was Tolin. And although he was not able to see her, he was using his hands to feel her and to guess who she was.

"I can tell by the coarseness of your gown that you are not a noble," he said.

She opened her mouth to say something, but spied Raven with her finger to her lips telling Kit to stay silent.

"Go on," Raven called out. "What else?"

"Well, let me see." His hands slid up her arms ever so slowly and then around to her back as he pulled her closer to him. Instantly, her body became hot. This was such an intimate position she was in. And right in front of everyone! Kit wanted to turn and run, but knew she couldn't. This was just a game she reminded herself. She couldn't leave now even though she wanted to.

"I feel something else," he said, letting his hands slide down to her waist. She wickedly liked the way he touched her, even if he didn't know it was her. "You seem to be wearing an apron. That tells me that you are probably a kitchen worker. A cook or a scullery maid, perhaps."

His hands brushed past the sides of her breasts and she couldn't help but gasp aloud once more. He came so close to touching her too familiarly.

"I need to feel your face," he told her. His big palms cupped her cheeks. "You feel warm to the touch," he surmised, getting a lot of whistles and off-colored comments from the men. "That either means you desire me, or mayhap that you work close to the kitchen ovens."

She really wanted to say something, but once again Raven motioned to her to stay silent.

"You need to make your guess," called out Rook. "Who is she, Brother?"

"Well, let me check one more thing."

• • •

116

Tolin knew damned well the woman in his arms was Kit. He could smell the scent of bread on her, as well as feel a streak of flour on her cheek under his fingers. He purposely stalled, not wanting to make his guess yet. The longer he kept her there the better. At least right now she couldn't leave him.

"I need to feel your hair," he said, his hands going to her head, his fingers rubbing her soft locks together. "Nice. Soft. Pleasant."

More whistles and shouts came from the crowd.

"God's eyes, Tolin," growled Rook. "Stop fondling the girl and make your guess."

"Hold on. I need to be sure," he said, stroking her cheek with the back of his hand, feeling her head tilt and lean in to his touch. Good. That meant she liked being touched by him, even if she wouldn't admit it. "Soft skin. Let me feel her lips." He cupped her chin in his hand and gently stroked his thumb first over her top lip and then her bottom one. He swore he heard her stifle a soft moan. Her mouth opened, her lips parted. Damn, her actions were making him hard. Even if he couldn't see her. "I smell the aroma of bread," he finished, not able to stand here any longer stroking her cheeks and lips without being able to stop himself from wanting to do so much more.

"Who is it?" asked Raven.

"My guess is that she is the beautiful new baker of Blake Castle, named Kit." He lowered the hood from his face, staring directly into her eyes. With their gazes interlocked, time seemed to stand still. He had never wanted a woman as badly as he did right now.

"You win again, Lord of Misrule," said Jarvis, slapping him on the back. When he said his title aloud, Kit's eyes lowered and she pouted slightly. "Do you want to go again, or should someone else try?" asked Jarvis.

"Neither," he answered, his gaze still locked on the beautiful woman standing before him. "Musicians, play a song," he called out. "It is time for everyone to dance."

"I'm sorry. I need to get back to the kitchen." Kit turned to go, but Tolin's hand clamped over her arm to keep her there. Slowly, she turned back to look at him.

"There is nowhere you need to be right now but here," he said in a soft voice.

"I—I don't dance. Not really."

"It's the command of the Lord of Misrule to dance with him." Jarvis walked up with a smile on his face and a tankard of ale in his hand. "You can't say no. That's not the way the game works."

The musicians started playing a lively tune. Before she could object again, Tolin took her hand and bowed. She, in turn, curtseyed to him. He could see now that she knew how to dance but just hadn't wanted to do so with him.

"I didn't think you were coming," he said, trying to make small talk which was something he wasn't very good at.

"I didn't want to, but as we both know, I didn't have a choice."

"What does that mean?" He spun her around, and when she turned he put his hand on her shoulder.

"You are the Lord of Misrule. You can demand anything of me and I would have to do it."

"Now, now," he said, shaking his head. "I am a noble and right now lord of the castle. I could do that anyway."

By the look on her face he could tell this wasn't going well.

"I mean...what I meant was that I never ordered you to dance with me. As Lord of Misrule."

"But as Lord of Blake Castle you did?"

Why did she always have to answer him with another question?

"Kit, I am trying my best for us to get along." He twirled her around again, followed by a promenade.

"I don't believe that."

"Why not?" he asked.

"Because, if you were sincere, you'd never have commanded me to leave my home and work in your kitchen until Twelfth Night. You realize that I'll lose my business now. And my sister will be with a new baby and nowhere to live."

"Oh, is that what you think?" They continued to dance.

"That is what I know."

"Well, you're wrong. I'd never let that happen," he assured her, but she didn't seem to believe him. They stopped dancing and happened to be standing right under the mistletoe. "Oh, look." He motioned upward with his eyes. "We're under the kissing bough again, it seems."

"Are you going to command me to kiss you?"

"Nay," he said, pulling her into his arms. "I'm not going to command, I'm not going to ask. This time, I'm just going to kiss you before you have a chance to run away."

Kit was caught by surprise when Tolin's lips came down and covered her mouth. Without meaning to, her eyes closed and she was wrapped in the magic of Tolin Blake's intimate move. He held her gently but protectively in his arms. His kiss was passionate but not forceful. With her eyes closed she got lost in the moment. Music filled the room and when her eyes opened, the light from the candles atop the kissing boughs lit up the place in a romantic, soft glow.

"There now," he whispered, his finger tapping her on the nose. "That wasn't so horrible, was it?"

Being this close to Tolin made her feel weak. And vulnerable. Her nerves started to shake because anxiety coursed through her. Damn, this always happened to her when she was with a man she really liked. Double damn, because although her mind told her she despised Tolin, her body was telling her otherwise. Kit felt as if she couldn't breathe. She needed to get away from him quickly.

Turning, she darted out of his arms and ran for her room that adjoined to the kitchen. She didn't stop until she'd entered the small living area and slammed the door behind her. Kit dove to the blankets on the floor that served as her bed, wanting to hide away from the world.

The sound of the door opening made her freeze.

"Kit? Are you in here?" It was Tolin. He had followed her to the room and entered without bothering to knock first. "It is dark in here. I can't see a thing."

"This is my private room. Please leave," she told him.

"I can tell you are upset. I won't leave you while you are feeling this way."

A soft light illuminated the small room as he lit a candle that was on a table near the door. Kit slowly sat up to face him.

"Egads, this is a small room." He looked around. "Didn't you say your son and sister are staying in here with you?"

"Yes," she answered.

"Where do you all sleep?"

"On the blankets on the floor," she told him.

"I had no idea that you didn't have pallets."

"It is more than Oliver has in the stable. I gave up my blanket to let him have it to keep him from the cold."

"I'm sorry. I didn't know."

"Was there something you wanted, Lord Tolin?"

He ran a hand through his long black hair in thought. "I'd like you to stop despising me. Tell me what I can do to make you like me and to be my friend."

"Friendship and respect are earned, not demanded, my lord." Slowly, she stood up to face him.

"Well, then. What can I do to earn your friendship and respect?"

"There might be one thing." Hugging her arms around her, she decided to just come out and tell him what she was feeling.

"What's that?"

"You could let a member of my family be the Lord or Lady of Misrule until Twelfth Night."

"Oh. I see." His penetrating eyes perused her. "So you *were* trying to cheat where the bean in the cake is concerned. I must say I am disappointed in you, Kit. You didn't strike me as a liar and a cheat. Even if your son is a thief."

"You know none of that is true! I am only trying to protect and take care of my family in the only way I can."

"There are other things you could have done. Like ask me for what it is you wanted, instead of trying to cheat and get it for yourself."

"Quit calling me a cheater. You are the cheater by taking the title of Lord of Misrule when it was meant for a commoner. This is the only time of year when the poor peasants have a hope and a chance to be something more than a slave and pitifully poor. You, Lord Tolin, took that hope from every peasant when you decided to keep the title of Bean King for yourself."

"Lord of Misrule," he told her, seeming aggravated and irritated by the way she was talking to him. But since Kit was so upset she pushed all her anxiety away and stood up to this arrogant man. She might be punished for it, but how could her life possibly get worse than it was right now? He turned to leave and she called out to stop him.

"Give me the bean. Let me be Lady of Misrule. Then, my lord, I promise I will respect you."

"Nay," he answered talking over his shoulder to her. "Because the day I let a commoner tell me what to do is the day I lose all respect for myself. And I assure you, Kit Baker, that will never happen to me."

He left the room and closed the door behind him. Kit's body shook like a leaf in the wind now, because she was sure her words upset him so much that she just doomed herself and her family. Forever.

CHAPTER 10

"Tell me again. What did Lord Tolin say when you told him you wanted to be the Bean Queen?" Brenna asked the next morning, as she helped Kit knead dough for the bread that she'd make for this day's meal.

"He said he'd never let a commoner tell him what to do," explained Kit, using the back of her hand to push aside a stray hair as her hands were covered in flour.

"Is he going to punish us? Oh, Kit, now he knows we were trying to deceive him. He's a noble. He will never let that go."

"I don't know and neither do I care." Kit let out a puff of air from her mouth and looked around the kitchen. "Where is Parker? I told him to take those dirty pans to the scullery and to come right back. This floor needs sweeping. I swear that boy is doing less and less every day."

"That's because he has a new friend now," Brenna told her, stretching and holding one hand on her lower back. "He and King are nearly inseparable."

"Well, not so today, I guess. Look." Kit nodded at the door to the kitchen. Parker was standing there by himself staring out at the great hall. "Parker, come here, sweetheart."

"Yes, Mother." He shuffled over slowly with his head down.

"What's the matter?" she asked. "You look so sad."

"I am sad," the boy admitted with a sigh, climbing onto the bench, dragging his finger through the flour dusting the table. "Lord Tolin took King away from me."

"What?" Kit's head snapped around. "What do you mean?"

"He said he wanted his dog back and that I needed to work off my punishment."

"Well, this is going too far." Kit took off her apron and wiped her hands.

"Kit? What are you doing?" asked her sister with concern in her voice.

"I am going right out there to find Lord Tolin and to show him my wrath."

"About what?" asked Brenna. "It's his dog! And he's right. Parker is supposed to be here working off a punishment, not just playing with King."

"I don't care. He has no right to take it out on my son since he and I had heated words. I won't allow him to do this." She stormed toward the door.

"Please don't. Kit, come back," cried Brenna, but Kit kept on walking. Sure enough, when she got to the great hall, she saw Tolin standing there talking to his brothers and his squire. His hand was on his dog's head. The dog sat at his side.

"Lord Tolin," she said, storming up to him, not caring that she was interrupting.

"Excuse me?" Lord Tolin scowled at her. "I am in the middle of a conversation with other nobles. You'll wait until I am finished."

Kit bit her tongue and waited, knowing there was nothing else she could do.

"Tolin, this has gone too far," complained Rook. "It has got to stop."

"I'm the Lord of Misrule, and so it is the way it is going to be. It'll stop after Twelfth Night. Now go. I'll be out in the stable as soon as I talk with my baker."

Daegel and Rook headed off one way, while Jarvis went another.

"Now, what is it, baker?" asked Tolin, giving her his undivided attention.

"Parker told me you no longer are letting him play with King. I want to know why."

"You do, do you?" He raised a brow. "Walk with me."

"My lord?" she asked, but followed when he started to walk away. The dog led the way.

"Why is the boy even here?" asked Tolin, not looking at her when they walked.

"That is exactly what I keep asking myself," she answered.

He stopped and looked at her and sighed. "He is supposed to be working off a punishment. A sentence, that is, which I gave him in order to keep him out of the dungeon. Isn't that what you wished? That the child be spared from being put behind bars?"

"Well, yes, of course I didn't want that to happen."

"And isn't that what we agreed upon? That he and you would work off his sentence in the kitchen until Twelfth Night?"

"I—I suppose so."

"Suppose so?" His eyes narrowed.

"I mean, yes. Yes, that was the agreement."

"So tell me. How much work has Parker actually been doing?"

She knew Tolin was right and that she really couldn't fight him on this. Her son had become so infatuated with the hound and she let him play rather than work, picking up the slack for him.

"Parker is just a child, my lord. Please, don't be so hard on him."

"Perhaps you should be more strict with the boy."

"I feel I am doing all that I can as a single mother."

"I know." He nodded and continued to walk. "That is why I decided to take the boy into my care for the rest of the time until his sentence is over."

"What?" she gasped, stopping in her tracks. "Nay. Please, don't take my son away from me, I beg you. He is all I have."

"Calm down, I am not taking him away from you. Since you are his mother, I decided you need to come with us."

"Come with you? Where?"

"I leave in an hour for a hunting trip with some of my men."

"What? You are going hunting? But it's winter, my lord." Kit couldn't believe what she was hearing.

"Aye, it is. But we could use more food and the only way

to get it is to hunt it down. We'll be gone for two days, so pack appropriately."

"Wait. What? I don't understand, my lord. You are taking my son with you to hunt?"

"Did you not hear me the first time?"

"And I am to come with you? Why? How? I am needed here. In the castle kitchen."

"Your sister and the other bakers will cover for you until we return. I need someone to cook over an open fire and serve those in the hunting party. That will be done by you and the boy." He got to the door leading to the courtyard and stopped. "We leave in an hour. Be at the stables with your son and ready to go. And I warn you, don't be late."

He left her there blinking in confusion. Did the man really think she was going to go on a hunting trip in the middle of winter? She wanted to refuse. But even if she did, he would still take Parker with him. Nay, she couldn't allow her son to be away from her. The poor child was scared of the dark as it was. Kit had no choice but to do this. It was crazy, but she couldn't think of a way to get out of it and only had an hour to prepare. By the rood, would life ever get any easier?

She stormed back to the kitchen, seeing two servants carrying what looked like a large pallet over their shoulders. Several women followed carrying pillows and blankets. Then Jarvis walked by with a rolled-up smaller pallet over his shoulder.

"Jarvis, where are you all going?" she asked.

"To your room just off the kitchen," he answered, not sounding particularly happy about it.

"Wait. Why?" She ran after them and Brenna followed with Parker right behind her.

The servants entered her family's room and threw down the pallet. Then the women started putting the soft blankets and pillows on top of them.

"Mother, what is all this?" asked Parker.

"I'm not sure," she answered.

"That is Lord Rook's pallet," said Jarvis nodding toward the larger one. "And this one is mine." He tossed the smaller one down on the floor.

"I don't understand," said Kit. "Why are you and Lord Rook going to sleep in here?"

"We're not," said Jarvis, nodding as the servants left the room. "They are for you and your family to use."

"Really? But why?" she asked.

"To sleep on," said Jarvis. "It is by the Lord of Misrule's orders."

"Oh," she said, looking at the comfortable-looking pallets and all the soft pillows and blankets.

"Oliver has also been allowed to sleep inside the great hall by the fire from now on."

"Oh," she said again. "Thank you. But I don't want to take Lord Rook's bed. Or yours."

"Lord Rook doesn't live at Blake Castle, he's just visiting. This is just the pallet he was using."

"And his wife, Rose? And their baby? Please don't tell me they are going to be sleeping on the floor now."

"Nay. She's sharing a bed with Raven and the children. But Raven's husband Jonathon as well as Rook will be sleeping in the great hall by the fire along with me. I can't say any of us are happy about it. Excuse me, I need to get the food that the cook packed up for the hunting trip."

"Thank you," she said softly, as the squire left.

"Kit, can you believe this?" asked Brenna, her eyes sparkling. "It will be so much more comfortable to sleep on this pallet rather than the floor. Mayhap my back will stop aching now." With her hand on her large belly she slowly lowered herself atop the larger pallet to test it out.

"Is this my bed?" asked Parker, jumping atop the smaller pallet and hugging a pillow.

"Yes, Parker. I'll share the larger one with Brenna, but that one can be yours."

"I want to go to bed right now," said Parker, snuggling into the blankets.

"Nay, you can't," she told him. "We need to pack to go on the hunting trip."

"I'd rather stay here," said Parker.

"Believe me, so would I, but we can't."

As much as Kit didn't want to go along on the hunting trip, she almost felt as if she owed it to Tolin now. She had thought he was angry with her when she left. Especially since he made a big deal about never letting a commoner tell him what to do.

Mayhap the man had a heart after all. Of course, Rook and Jarvis were going to hate him. But like the games the man liked to play, this was no different. Tolin was still playing games, and this time using the title of the Lord of Misrule to get away with his silly decisions.

Then again, he'd made sure she and her family were comfortable. Mayhap his decisions weren't so silly after all.

~

"The horses are ready my lord. Will there be anything else?" Oliver bowed before Tolin, having prepared things for the hunting trip.

"Yes. I want you to join the hunting party."

"Me?" asked Oliver.

"Yes. Not to hunt, but to care for the horses until our return."

"But my wife is here at the castle and about to give birth, my lord."

"She will be fine," Tolin assured him. "Lord Rook's wife, Rose will be here. She has a child now so understands the needs of a pregnant woman. Plus, there is a midwife at the castle who will be checking in on her per my request."

"Thank you, my lord, but I am new to the stables. Are you sure you want me along?"

"We're here," came Kit's voice from behind him. "We're ready to go as you instructed." Kit had a bag over her shoulder and held her son's hand. They were both dressed in traveling clothes and capes.

Oliver looked at them in confusion, his eyes darting back to Tolin.

"I'm sure," Tolin told him with a nod. "Now, make haste. We have no time to waste."

"Mother, there's King!" shouted Parker excitedly, letting go of her hand to run over and hug the dog. "Is he coming on the hunting trip too?" asked Parker, looking up at Tolin.

"Of course. He always comes along on my hunting expeditions," Tolin told him. "I was hoping you'd be able to take care of him for me while we're there."

"I will, I will," cried the boy. "King can even sleep with me. I'll feed him and brush him and play with him a lot."

"That will be fine." Tolin's eyes darted over to Kit. She looked up at him and swallowed deeply. So this seemed to be all part of his plan. He'd never meant to take the dog from the boy or the boy from her. It was a roundabout way of making Parker happy...and also her, she supposed.

She smiled at him and nodded slightly.

"All right, we're ready to go." Raven walked into the stable pulling on a pair of leather gloves. She had a bow and arrows over her shoulder.

"You're going to hunt too?" asked Kit in awe. This woman was a true inspiration to Kit and possibly to every woman at the castle.

"Yes. I'm one of the best hunters we have," said Raven.

"But what about your baby?" asked Kit.

"My daughter is being watched by my husband and my nursemaid and Lady Rose until my return. Sparrow will be well taken care of, so I am not worried."

"I see," said Kit. She liked the idea of this woman's blacksmith husband caring for a child. Matter of fact, she admired any man who would take the care of any child into his own hands. She looked back over at Tolin who was talking to her son.

"You'll ride with me, Parker," he told the boy.

"I will?" Parker's eyes grew wide and he slowly got to his feet. "I've never ridden on a horse with a knight before. I've never even been on a horse at all."

"Then it's time you learn how to ride. After all, you are

eight years old already. I have been riding a horse since I was five." He mounted his horse, the sound of leather creaking as he settled himself in the saddle. "Up you go, son." He reached down and grabbed Parker, pulling him up into the saddle in front of him. Parker smiled more than Kit had seen in a long, long time.

"Will you be riding your own horse?" asked Raven.

Kit turned to realize she was talking to her. "Oh, I don't know."

"Kit you'll ride with Oliver," said Tolin, having over-heard them. "I don't have another spare horse at the moment."

"Yes, my lord," she said, hurrying over to Oliver who had a horse saddled and waiting for them. When they got out of the stable she saw Jarvis with an extra horse. It had some supplies it was carrying but had more than enough room for a person to ride it. Rook and Daegel and two other men whom she didn't know were all mounted and ready to go.

"What about that horse?" asked Kit. "That seems to be extra."

"That's for our supplies. And for all the kill we'll bring back from the hunt," Tolin told her. "Hold on, Parker." He kicked his heels into the sides of his horse and the animal shot off, leading the way. King barked and stayed steady at his side. The rest of them fell in line. Kit and Oliver were in the rear.

By the time they made it to the camp, it had started to snow. The temperature was dropping quickly.

"Jarvis, get the tents set up and find wood for a fire," called out Tolin, getting off the horse and helping Parker to the ground. King was there immediately barking, wanting to play with the boy. "Men, get your weapons. We're hunting wild pheasant and hopefully we will bag a deer." Tolin busied himself with his weapons.

"My lord, I can help Jarvis tend to the fire," said Kit, wanting to be helpful.

"Good," he answered with a nod. "I've got enough food packed, so you'll just need to cook it. We should be back in a few hours. Hopefully we'll catch enough game to have food to eat for tomorrow."

"A few hours?" she asked, looking around. She didn't feel comfortable out here alone in the woods. "Who will be here to protect me and my son?"

"Jarvis is quite capable, and I'll leave Oliver here as well. We won't be far. Just give a shout if you get in trouble."

"Great," she said, letting out a deep sigh. When the men left for the hunt with Raven, the dog followed. Parker ran over to Kit.

"Mother, I'm cold and hungry," said the little boy.

"So am I," she said, pulling her son close to her, still not able to believe Tolin had just left them here like this. What she would give right now to be back in the hot kitchen warming her bones, baking something to fill their bellies.

"Are we going to have to stay out here all night?" asked the boy.

"I'm afraid so." She watched Oliver and Jarvis unloading the supplies from the horses.

"Is this part of my punishment?"

"I'm no longer sure," she told him. "It might just be another game that the Lord of Misrule decided to play with us. Either way, we're going to have to make the best of it, so we will. Come, Parker. Help me find some wood for the fire.

We'll be warm and have something to eat very soon, I promise."

~

"Why did you bring Kit and Parker along on the hunt?" asked Raven, as the hunting party rode to an area where they would be sure to catch prey.

"To cook and to serve us," Tolin answered.

"I know that is what you what everyone to think, but now I want the real answer." His sister was too observant. He might be able to fool his brothers, but Raven was not going to settle for any answer but the right one.

"All right, I admit it. I wanted to spend some time with Kit. It is too hard to do so at the castle. She has too much work to do and there are too many prying eyes."

"Ah ha! I thought so." Raven smiled. "Why did you bring the boy? There is no reason for him to be here."

Tolin hesitated. When Raven kept staring at him as they rode, he figured he'd better tell her everything after all. "I knew Kit would never leave her son, so I figured if I commanded him to be here, she sure as hell wouldn't stay behind. I have to admit I am growing fond of the child and realize he could never be a thief as he was accused of being."

"You're playing your silly games again, Tolin," Raven warned him.

"Games? What do you mean?"

"Why don't you come right out and admit to Kit that you want to spend time with her? That you like her?"

"I couldn't."

"You could, but you won't. You're afraid it might make you seem weak, aren't you?"

"Nay. I don't think that at all." He was afraid Kit wouldn't like him back, and that was the reason he hadn't told her. Tolin didn't do well with rejection.

"I'm sure she'd like you if you gave her a chance."

"I have given her a chance. Several."

Raven scowled at him. "I'm not sure dragging her and her child out here in the cold to wait on you hand and foot is a good attempt at courtship."

"Huh?" His head snapped up with a jerk. "Who said I wanted to court her?"

"You didn't need to say it. I'm a woman. I know these things."

"Raven, she's a commoner and I'm a noble. I'm not looking to court or even marry beneath my status."

"Oh, like I did?" She raised a brow.

"I didn't say that. Jonathon is a great guy and a talented blacksmith."

"Kit is a wonderful, strong woman and an excellent baker. There is no difference. Where love is concerned, status doesn't matter."

"Love? Slow down. I barely know the wench."

Raven's eyes narrowed. "If you at all want her to like you, then I suggest not using the word 'wench' when you refer to her or talk to her."

"I didn't mean anything derogative by it."

"Tolin, if you don't tell her soon that you are attracted to her, then I am going to do it for you."

"Nay!" He held up a hand. "I'll do it. Just give me a chance."

"Twelfth Night is approaching quickly. She'll be gone from the castle before you get around to it if you don't move a little quicker."

"I've been busy. Father put me in charge of the Christmastide events."

"Well, you're not at Blake Castle to oversee things, are you?" She shook her head. "I only came along on the hunt to keep an eye on Kit and her son."

"You didn't think I'd protect them?"

"They're back at camp now, and you're here. That proves my point."

"There is nothing to protect them from. Besides Jarvis and Oliver are with them."

"We'll bring back food from the hunt," Raven told him. "You need to return and talk to Kit now while you have a chance to be alone with her. Don't think Rook or Daegel are going to give you that chance you're looking for. As soon as they return you will have missed your opportunity."

"But I'm leading this hunting expedition. I need to bring back a kill."

"You need to stop being so competitive and delegate authority when needed."

"Do you really think so?" Tolin supposed that mayhap his sister had a point. He didn't want to waste this opportunity.

"I know so. Now go. We'll be back soon with enough meat that we won't have to spend two nights in the cold."

"Mayhap I will return to camp after all. Just to keep an eye on Kit and the boy. Kit seemed nervous that I was leaving them."

"She needs you."

"I'm not sure about that, but I'd like to think so. Kit is a very independent woman. I've never met anyone like her before."

"What's taking you two so long?" Daegel shouted from up ahead. "I could crawl faster than you're riding."

"See you back at camp." Raven sped off to join her brothers and the rest of the hunting party.

Tolin looked one way and the then the other, not knowing what to do. "What the hell. I just hate it when Raven is right." He turned his horse and rode back to camp. When he got there he found Kit down on her knees trying to build a fire. She looked up as he rode into camp.

"Lord Tolin?" She got up and brushed off her hands. "Why are you back so soon?"

"Where is everyone?" He dismounted and looked around.

"Jarvis went out to collect firewood with Parker. Oliver has the pack horses down by the creek, watering them."

Perfect, he thought. He would finally have a minute alone with her. "Let me help you with that." He walked over and hunkered down and restacked the sticks.

Kit watched as Tolin started a fire with little to no effort at all.

"There you go." Still hunkered down, he rested one arm on his knee, watching the fire. The flames glowed, lighting up his face, making him look even more handsome. His rugged body was clothed in a tunic covered by a surcoat and cloak. His breeches were tight, clinging to his sturdy legs. The breeze picked up, blowing his long black hair back behind his shoulders. Snowflakes continued to flutter in the air, settling atop him in a dusting of white.

"Thank you," she said in a mere whisper.

"Bring me some more kindling. We need to keep the fire going until they return with more wood." He held out his hand.

Kit picked up a few dry sticks and hunkered down next to him, breaking them up and tossing them into the fire.

"You never told me why you left the hunting party and returned here." She wanted to think it was because of her, but it was too bold to even imagine.

"I have my reasons." He stood up and brushed his hands together. Then he looked around and rolled a log over for them to sit on. "Have a seat by the fire and warm up. You look cold." He nodded at the log and held out his hand to help her.

"I'm not cold," she told him, feeling warm and alive when she was around him.

"Then why are you shivering?"

That was when she realized her body was shaking again. How could she tell him it wasn't from the cold but from being in his presence?

"Mayhap it would be good to warm myself for a few minutes after all." She gently reached out and laid her hand on his arm. He led her to the log and with his other hand on her back he helped her to get settled. Then he sat next to her and they both looked at the fire and didn't say a word.

Her anxiety became worse. She decided keeping busy would stop her from being so nervous around this handsome man.

"I'd better get started with the food." She tried to get up

but his large hand clamped around her arm to keep her from going.

"Nay," he said surprising her. She would have thought he'd be giving her one order after another of what he wanted her to do.

"Nay?" she asked, her eyes on his hand.

"I want you to stay here, Kit."

"Y—you do?" Her gaze slid up his arm and to his face. His bright blue eyes captivated her as he stared at her so deeply that she couldn't move right now if she tried.

"Yes," he answered, and cleared his throat. "I thought this would be a good time for us to talk."

"Talk?" She didn't understand. "Is this about Parker's punishment? I'm sorry he's been ignoring his duties and spending so much time with King, but that dog has him infatuated. He's always wanted a dog but we couldn't afford one. King is more of a friend to Parker than any of the children back in town."

"Shhhh," he said, releasing her arm and raising his finger to her lips. The soft touch of his skin against her mouth had her thinking about their kiss under the mistletoe again. "I don't want to talk about punishments or dogs or boys right now."

"Then...what?" she asked, as he slowly lowered his hand.

"I want to know more about *you*, Kit."

"Me?" That truly surprised her, because she didn't really think he cared.

"Yes. Tell me about your life. You said you are a widow? Tell me about Parker's late father."

She wished he hadn't asked that. She would rather talk

about anything else. Still, she had to answer. "Crispin was Parker's birth father," she said. "We weren't married."

"Really?" That seemed to take him by surprise.

"We had plans to become married, but he met his untimely death before we could. He was assisting the woodward in the forest during a storm. Lightning struck and he was hit by a falling tree limb. He died instantly when it hit his head."

"Oh, that is unfortunate. I'm sorry." His face remained stone-like, but she saw caring in his eyes. "So when you say he was Parker's birth father, that means you ended up marrying another man?"

"I did. Crispin's brother Gerold was a widower with no children. He was the town baker. He took me in and married me, stepping into the role of Parker's father after he lost his wife."

"You don't sound happy about that."

"I wasn't. But I knew I would never be able to raise Parker on my own, so I took him up on his offer."

"Was he a good husband and father to your boy?"

Kit held back her tears, slowly shaking her head. "Nay, I can't say that he was. He was too busy with work and drinking and bedding other women to pay much attention to me or Parker."

"Oh. I'm sorry."

"Don't be. His ill deeds were probably what took his life."

"I don't understand."

"I was away with Parker at the time, visiting friends in another town. I guess he was drunk and tripped and hit his head. He passed out and bled to death. It was late at night. He died before anyone found him."

"My, your life has been tragic."

"Yes, it has."

"Are your parents still alive?"

"My mother is and she's remarried. They moved overseas and live in Ireland now."

"Why didn't you go to Ireland to live with your parents after this happened?"

"My stepfather didn't want us. He never got over the embarrassment of me getting pregnant out of wedlock. My parents disowned me, and now they've done the same to my sister."

"I'm sorry, Kit. I didn't know." He reached out and put his hand over hers.

"I had a hard time rebuilding the business after Gerold's death, but I did it. At first the customers didn't want to come back to the bakery. I was the widow of a guild member, so I was able to keep the shop. It took a while for people to accept that."

"How did you run the place by yourself? Isn't that a lot of work?"

"Yes. But Gerold's sister Vivian lived with me for a while and helped me out. She used to help Gerold before I came along, so she knew the business. But then Vivian married Willis, the town's cordwainer. So I've been on my own with only Parker's help and occasional help from Vivian since then."

Kit couldn't help becoming emotional. Life had been so hard and just kept getting more difficult. She felt as if she were about to burst. A stray tear dripped down her cheek.

Before she could brush it away Tolin reached up and gently did so for her.

"Enough about me. Tell me about you," she said, finally feeling better as the flames from the fire as well as Tolin's body heat warmed her.

"There's not much to tell," said Tolin. "I'm the second eldest son of Lord Corbett Blake. I'm a knight and...that's it."

"What do you mean that's it?" She smiled. "That is much to be proud of."

"I fight for the king, and I must admit I like games and I don't like losing."

"I could tell that from the first day I met you."

"I like you, Kit." He reached up to stroke a stray lock of hair from her face. "You are a survivor and I admire that. With all the despair in your life, you seem to keep a positive attitude and don't let things get you down. You are perhaps one of the strongest women I have ever met."

"I am only doing what I need to do. For my son's sake. If it wasn't for him, I am sure I would have given up long ago."

"Don't ever stop being who you are." He reached over and kissed her on the mouth. Kit's eyes closed and she reached up and put her hands on his shoulders. She returned the kiss, feeling herself becoming alive again after so many years of thinking she could never have feelings for another man after Crispin died. Their lips parted gently and he still cupped her cheek.

"Have you ever been married?" she asked him.

"Me?" He chuckled in a low voice. "Nay, and I don't plan on ever doing so, if I am lucky enough. I like not being tied down to anyone or anything. I enjoy being free as the wind, no ties to bind me."

She wanted to ask him what he meant, but the sound of approaching voices startled her and she jumped to her feet. "I believe Jarvis and Parker have returned. I will tend to the fire and then start preparing the food."

Kit darted away, almost grateful for the interruption. If her son hadn't returned just then she might have been tempted to kiss Tolin again. Her heart swelled when she was with him. Even though she'd despised him at first, her attraction to him was growing steadily, even though her feelings seemed to waver back and forth. He'd been kind enough to keep Parker out of the dungeon and to devise a punishment that kept her with her son. Life in the castle seemed to have kept Parker out of trouble. Being with Tolin's dog kept the boy from getting into mischief.

Kit had started to have feelings for Tolin. More than once now he'd kissed her, making her feel as if she could possibly open her heart to love again someday. But after Tolin's comment about never wanting to marry or get tied down, she realized he was not the man for her.

While Kit was strong and independent, it was only because she had to be. But she was at a point in her life where having a husband and father for her son was the only thing that would keep her from losing her business. She needed to remarry soon in order to keep her entire family from ending up homeless out on the street. Nay, Tolin wasn't the man she needed. He liked his freedom way too much. In time it would become an addiction to him and that would only lead to her heartbreak, as she'd already seen in her past.

"Parker, help me with the fire and then to prepare the

food," she told her son, glancing quickly over her shoulder to take one last look at Tolin. Sadly, he was gone.

CHAPTER II

Tolin had returned to the hunting party, not sure things had really gone well between him and Kit. He'd felt her passion in the kiss, but after hearing her sad stories, he felt like an ogre for having handed out a punishment to her and Parker to begin with. He'd hunted mainly by himself today, but had been too distracted to focus on catching anything but small game.

"It's getting dark. We won't catch much more today," said Rook, as the hunting party joined together. Between them they had managed to kill a few rabbits, a dozen pheasants, and three wild geese. King barked, having been a good help in retrieving the birds when they fell from the sky.

"Yes, let's get back to camp," agreed Tolin, just wanting this day to be over.

"I'm starving," commented Daegel, leading the way. "I hope Kit has a meal ready and waiting for us."

"Me too," said Rook, racing his brother back to camp.

"So? How did it go?" Raven rode beside Tolin, asking him about Kit.

"I talked with her. And kissed her," he admitted.

"You did? So, did she like it?" asked Raven with a mischievous smile.

"I'm not sure," he said, his heart going out to Kit. "Raven, she's had a hard life. I am thinking about lifting her son's sentence and letting them go back to the bakery, to their home."

"Is that what you really want? To send her away? I thought you planned on getting to know her better." Raven said the words that made Tolin question every decision.

"I do want to know her better," he told his sister. "I am just not sure she wants to get to know me. At all. I think what she really wants is to return to her home and bakery. To make a good life for Parker and her sister. I can't blame her."

"Think about this long and hard before you make the decision, because you can't go back," she told Tolin. "Remember, you are expected to fill Father's shoes until his return. It won't bode well for him or for you or for any of the nobles if you let a thief go free."

"Parker didn't steal anything, I know that now and you know it too," said Tolin. "He's just a mischievous boy, that's all."

"I do agree with you; however you can't take a commoner child's word over that of a castle guard. It's just not right, Tolin."

"Well, what would you have me do? Put the boy in the dungeon?"

"Nay, of course not. Just let them serve out their time

until the end of Twelfth Night as planned. Then when it's over, make your decision if you want a relationship with Kit or not."

"I never said I wanted a relationship with her. I just said I was attracted to her and wanted to know her better."

"So, what does that mean?" asked Raven. "That you're going to bed her and then forget all about her? The way you do with the rest of your trollops?" Raven didn't give him a chance to answer. She rode away, leaving Tolin alone with his thoughts. He'd never felt as confused as he did right now.

The night was a long one. And cold. Tolin realized he never should have called for this hunt. They should have all stayed at the castle and continued to celebrate where it was warm and where the ale and wine were flowing freely. Rook hadn't wanted to come on the hunt, but Tolin played the Lord of Misrule card and made him do it. Rook was also angry with Tolin for giving his pallet to Kit and her family. Tolin's older brother had barely spoken two words to him the entire trip so far.

The sun had set and it was time for sleeping now. They had three tents. One was for Tolin, his brothers and Jarvis. The second was for the rest of the men of the hunting party, including Oliver. The last tent would be shared by Raven and Kit and the boy.

Everyone retired for the night and disappeared into their tents. That left Tolin at the fire. He stared into the flames wishing and hoping for answers. Life had been so fun and carefree up until recently. He hadn't liked sentencing the boy, and he didn't like worrying about Kit and her future. What the hell was the matter with him?

"My lord," came Kit's soft voice as she left her tent and came to join him. She grasped her cloak around her while her teeth chattered. "Will there be anything else before I retire?"

"Nay."

She started to walk back to the tent.

"Aye," he said, changing his mind. "I want you to come sit next to me by the fire."

"My lord?" she asked in question, her eyes darting back to the tent with her son.

"Just to talk. Nothing more," he assured her.

"Of course, my lord." She padded over the ground, her shoes crunching the snow that had fallen. It had thankfully stopped snowing for now. Kit settled herself next to him on the log that served as a bench. Her teeth continued to chatter.

"Come closer," he told her, holding out his arm.

She was reluctant to do so, but then did as ordered. He opened up his fur-lined cloak and pulled her next to his warm body.

"Thank you," she whispered.

"I don't want you to be cold. Your teeth are chattering," he told her.

"Aye, my lord. King is sleeping with Parker, but I will snuggle up next to them when I retire for the night so we can share each other's warmth. Will you require the dog to return to your tent?"

"Nay, it's fine, King can stay with Parker. Kit, I never should have commanded you and the boy to join the hunting party. I am sorry."

She slowly leaned in against him and her chattering

teeth finally stopped making noise, even though her body still shook.

"We have one more day and night of this?" she asked, sounding as if she felt doomed.

He chuckled lowly. "That was the original plan. However, in the morning I will announce that we will abandon the hunt and head back to the castle instead."

"Really?" She looked up at him in surprise. The flames from the fire reflected, the flames dancing in her big brown eyes. "Won't the others be disappointed? You've yet to bring down a deer."

"Nay, they'll be happy to get back to their families. After this, Rook will even be grateful to sleep on the floor in the great hall, now that I've given you his pallet."

"Oh, please. Give it back to him." She sat up straight and turned to look at him with concern on her face. "I don't want to take anything from a noble. It's not right."

"If not a noble, then who?" he asked. "You can't expect your pregnant sister to sleep on a bare floor."

"Well, she was very grateful for the pallet, my lord." Kit smiled, making Tolin's heart soar. He would do whatever it took to make Kit's life easier and to bring her happiness. He knew that now.

"I am very grateful for you," he told her, giving her shoulder a slight squeeze, his arm still around her.

"Grateful? For me?" She looked at him quizzically.

"For your baking. It tastes good."

"Oh." She turned back toward the fire. "I'm glad you approve, my lord."

They sat in silence staring at the flames for a few

minutes, even though it seemed to Tolin like hours. Finally, he found the nerve to speak.

"Kit, I've decided when we return to Blake Castle, I am going to lift Parker's sentence."

"Really?" She sat up straighter, looking directly into his eyes. "What exactly do you mean?"

"I mean that you and Parker will be free and able to go home. There will be no more accusations against your son."

"Oh. I see." She didn't sound half as happy about this decision as Tolin thought she'd be. He'd only wanted to make her smile, but she wasn't smiling anymore.

"That is what you wanted, right? To go home?" he asked her. "To go back to work in your bakery?"

"Yes, I suppose it is," she said, looking down and wringing her hands together. Tolin didn't understand this reaction at all. Then she yawned and slowly leaned her body against his again. Her head lowered against his chest as they continued to stare at the fire without talking. They sat in silence for a long time. Too long. Tolin thought he'd better take this opportunity to tell Kit how he really felt about her, after all. This might be the only chance he had if she planned on going back to town on the morrow.

"Kit, I like you. Actually, it is more than like. A lot more," he told her.

He thought he heard a slight moan from her but she didn't move and didn't answer. It unnerved him, but at least she didn't get up and walk away.

"I know you are just a commoner, and I am a noble and we don't belong together."

No response.

Tolin continued. "But when I kiss you, I forget all about

who you are. All I know is that you make me feel different than the way I've felt with any other woman I've been with. I want to do so much more with you than just kiss." He suddenly realized this was making him sound like a lustful cur. "Wait. Let me explain that better. I don't want to just love you and leave you, is what I mean. You deserve better than that. You have been through too much hardship in your life, and you don't need me creating more. Right?" Tolin stumbled over his words, wondering how he could be making such a mess of this.

Still, she didn't answer.

"Kit? Say something, please." He leaned forward to look in her eyes and that is when he realized she had fallen asleep lying up against him.

He smiled to himself, almost glad she hadn't heard him. He wasn't good at expressing himself and felt like a fumbling fool right now. If she had heard what he'd just said, she would probably really hate him and he couldn't blame her. God's eyes, why was it so hard to tell her how he really felt about her? Why couldn't he just say that he thinks about her constantly and wasn't sure what he'd do without her?

He reached over and kissed her atop the head. "Sweet dreams, my lovely lady," he whispered, knowing she wasn't really a lady, but to him she was so much more.

Tolin scooped her up into his arms and carried her back to her tent, his eyes focused on her angelic face as she slumbered. He ducked and entered the tent. King looked up, but didn't come over to greet him. The dog was under the blanket and Parker had his arms around the hound. It was innocent and precious and he'd never seen anything like it.

He didn't want to disturb this, but he also didn't want Kit to have to sleep without a covering. Tolin laid her down next to Parker, then removed his cloak and covered her with it before turning to leave the tent.

"Did you tell her?" came Raven's sleepy voice from the dark inside the tent.

"I told her," said Tolin, not pointing out that even though he'd tried to tell Kit how much she meant to him, she hadn't heard a word of it. "Go back to sleep, Raven. We head back to Blake Castle first thing in the morning."

CHAPTER 12

K it stirred the next morning, having been dreaming all night about snuggling up to Tolin under his fur-lined cloak and kissing his sexy lips. With her eyes still closed, she smiled. That is, until she felt something wet on her nose and cheek. She opened her eyes to see King's face right up against hers, and her arms were around the blasted dog. His tongue shot out to lick her again, but she bolted upright to a sitting position.

The sun had just started to rise. Through a slight opening at the flap of the tent, she could see Tolin outside stoking the fire.

King got up and shook, then trotted out of the tent. Kit stood up, clutching Tolin's warm cloak in her hands. How did she get this? And how had she gotten back to her tent last night without remembering?

The last thing she remembered was Tolin kissing her. And telling her that she and Parker were free to go home as soon as they returned to the castle. Had she dreamed it all? Looking down to his cloak in her hands she realized that she had not. She must have fallen asleep and Tolin carried her back to her tent and covered her with his cloak.

She brought the garment to her face, inhaling his manly essence, rubbing her cheek against it. All she had wanted all along was to go back home. But now that he'd told her she was free, all she wanted to do was stay. Kit found herself wanting to get to know Tolin better. Even though they had a rocky start, she had to admit that she enjoyed being around the man. Just when something good was happening, life took a wicked turn, as usual.

Kit exited the tent, and when she stepped out, Tolin looked up and their eyes met. Her heart jumped and her tongue seemed too big for her mouth. His smoldering perusal of her now led her to believe that had she remained awake last night, they might have done something more than just kissed.

"Good morning. How did you sleep?" he asked, still poking the fire. "Were you warm enough?"

"Good morning," she finally managed to squeak out. "I slept well, thank you. And yes, I was very warm and comfortable." She held up his cloak. "Thanks to you."

"You fell asleep on my shoulder," he told her, flashing a smile that showed his strong white teeth. "The boy was snuggled up with the damned dog under the blanket. I didn't want to disturb them so I used my cloak as your blanket."

"That was thoughtful of you. I appreciate it." She walked over and handed the cloak back to him. "But weren't you cold?"

"Nay. The fire kept me warm." He took the cloak from her and donned it.

"The fire?" she asked in surprise. "You slept out here all night?"

"Yes. I had a lot of thinking to do. Besides, I like nature."

"Mayhap so, but it's the middle of winter," she said, pulling her cloak tighter and looking at the thin layer of snow covering the ground. "So, what were you thinking about?"

"Huh?" He fastened his cloak.

"We did some talking last night," she said, trying to ease into the conversation.

"Yes, we did. How much do you remember?"

She was sure her face blushed. "I remember the kiss," she said quietly, glancing around, hoping no one else could hear their conversation.

"Anything else?"

"There was more?" At that thought, her anxiety rushed in and her body started to shake. Had she done more than just kiss with Lord Tolin and not remember? Kit hoped she hadn't acted like a strumpet. She'd been so attracted to him last night that part of her even wanted to bed him. God's eyes, she hoped she hadn't!

"Calm down," he said, noticing her reaction. "Do you always get this way around men?"

"Only ones I am extremely attracted to," she answered, looking up at him shyly.

"That's good to know. I mean, not good that you shake. I mean...I am attracted to you, too, Kit." He quickly reached out and stroked her cheek. "Now, tell me, what more do you remember me saying to you?"

"Saying?" she asked, letting out a deep breath of relief. Mayhap the intimacy between them never went anywhere past a simple kiss, after all. "Well, I remember you telling me that Parker and I will be free to return home once we get back to the castle."

"That's right, I did. Anything else?"

"Nay, not that I can remember. Why?" she asked cautiously. "Was there something else that happened that I've forgotten?"

Tolin bit at his bottom lip, looking for a moment as if he were going to say something. Then he slowly shook his head. "Nay. That's all. Now prepare to leave. I am about to wake everyone and we'll head back to the castle anon."

"All right," she said, turning and walking back to the tent. Parker bolted out of the tent, crashing into her. "Slow down, Parker. Where are you going?" she asked her son, catching him by his shoulders.

"I lost King! He's gone. I need to find him."

King barked, playing with Tolin.

"Nay, he's not gone. He's right there, with his master."

"King, King!" called the boy, running after the dog.

Laughing, Kit entered the tent to see Raven sitting there folding up the blankets.

"Oh, allow me to do that, my lady. It isn't something a noble should be doing." She knelt down to take over.

"Kit, I don't mind. Since I'm a mother I have a different opinion on what a noble should or shouldn't do. Speaking of that, did you have a nice talk with Tolin last night?" She sounded as if she knew something.

"Yes. We spoke." Kit continued to fold the blankets.

"So...what did he say to you?" She smiled and seemed eager to hear.

"Well, he told me that Parker and I are free to go home as soon as we return to Blake Castle."

"He did?" she said, sounding surprised and as if it wasn't what she expected to hear.

"Lady Raven, I swear my son is innocent. He never tried to steal the guard's sword. It was just a misunderstanding."

"I believe you, Kit. I didn't mean it that way. It's just that I thought perhaps Tolin said...other things to you too?"

"Such as what?" Kit wasn't volunteering the information about the kiss.

"Didn't he tell you that he was attracted to you?"

"Well, yes, as a matter of fact, he did. Just now, by the fire." Her eyes darted back to the flap of the tent.

"Just now?" Raven seemed confused. "Kit, how do you feel about my brother?"

"I like him," said Kit. "At first I didn't, but now I do." She said nothing more.

"Do you want to leave the castle and go home today?"

Hearing Raven say it made it seem so final. Kit thought she'd be happy returning home, but now that it was happening so soon, she found herself wishing she could stay. At least until Twelfth Night. "It is the Lord of Misrule's wishes."

"But is it really your wish to leave?"

She thought for a moment, not sure what to say. Then she realized that it would probably be best to go since she and Tolin did not belong together and never would. "It would be most beneficial to me and my family to get back home," she told Raven, not looking at the woman when she spoke.

"Oh, Kit! I had so much hope that you and Tolin might someday end up together. I suppose from now on I should stick to minding my own business." She got up abruptly and left the tent.

End up together? What did that mean, Kit wondered. Had Tolin released her because he didn't want her anymore? Or had he done it because he really did care about her?

Confusion filled Kit's mind. She wasn't sure what was going on, but mayhap once she returned home she'd be able to think about this with more of a clear head.

~

"We're ready to leave," called out Tolin a short time later. "Everyone mount up. Parker, you're with me." He looked over to see the boy sitting on Raven's horse with her.

"He's riding back with me," Raven told him.

"What? Why?" he asked. "Kit is supposed to ride with you."

"She'll just have to ride with you instead, I guess." Raven shrugged and took off atop her horse. King barked and ran along with her. Tolin spotted Kit putting out the fire and walked over to join her.

"Kit, it seems Raven took the boy so you'll have to ride back to the castle with Oliver or Jarvis instead."

"Nay, my lord," said Jarvis, riding past him. "Oliver has already left by Lord Rook's orders and my horse is too loaded down with the supplies to hold a person too."

"What about the spare horse? Where is it?" Tolin looked around.

"It was loaded with the spoils of the hunt," said Jarvis. "It's already gone as well."

"I won't have to walk back to the castle, will I?" asked Kit.

Tolin looked up at Jarvis and groaned. Jarvis had a dung-eating grin on his face. Tolin was sure Raven put them all up to this. Now he had no choice but to let Kit ride back to the castle with him.

"Nay, of course not. You will ride with me," he told Kit, leading her to his horse. Putting his hands around her waist, he lifted her into the saddle. Damn she felt good under his hands. And when he settled himself behind her and put his arms around her to direct the horse, their bodies were pressed up against each other. Being so close to her was driving him mad.

"Thank you," she said, dragging him from his thoughts.

"For what?" he asked.

"For letting Parker and me leave and go back home. Now my sister can give birth to her baby in her own bed."

"Are you happy to be leaving?" He wanted to ask her if she'd miss him, but couldn't bring himself to do it.

"Aye, of course I am. Why wouldn't I be?"

"No reason."

It was such temptation, holding Kit so closely. Every time they moved, their bodies smashed together. He could feel the womanly curves of her hips between his legs, making him hard since he liked her in that position. He rode faster, only wanting to be back. The girl didn't seem to have the same feelings for him that he did for her, so it was best she leave before he ended up making a fool of himself.

It wasn't long before they rode over the drawbridge and into the courtyard of Blake Castle. He saw Brother Ruford flagging him down. The monk had a young woman at his side. Tolin stopped the horse.

"Brother Ruford needs to speak to me," he told Kit, helping her dismount.

"Nay, I think he wants to talk to me," she told him, looking in the monk's direction. "That is my sister-by-marriage who is with him. Something must be wrong." Kit ran to them and Tolin followed.

"Vivian, what is it? Is everything all right? Why are you here?" Kit took the woman's hands in hers. It was evident the girl had been crying.

"Brother Ruford? What is the meaning of this?" asked Tolin.

"This woman is from town," explained Ruford. "There has been an unfortunate circumstance. I brought her here and am so glad to see you returned early."

"Unfortunate circumstance? What happened?" Kit asked the girl.

"Oh, Kit, I am so sorry. I know this is the last thing you need to hear after all you've been going through."

"What is? Vivian, please. Tell me. I need to know." Kit sounded frantic.

"It's gone! It's all gone," cried Vivian. "The townsfolk tried to help but it happened late last night when everyone was sleeping."

"What happened? God's eyes, tell me everything," spat Kit.

Ruford stepped in to explain. "The girl is trying to say that because of an unfortunate event, last night your bakery burned to the ground."

"What?" Kit gasped, her mouth falling open. Parker ran over and clung to her. Raven was right behind the boy.

"Mother, did he say the bakery burned down?" asked Parker.

"It was vandals," explained Vivian, tears streaming down her face. "Someone said they saw a man in the shop late last night just before the fire started."

"Who was it?" asked Kit. "Why would anyone do this?"

Vivian's eyes darted back and forth. She shrugged. "We're not sure. Oh, Kit, I am so sorry."

Kit sank to the ground, hiding her face in her hands. Parker cried, getting down next to his mother and holding her. King ran over and whimpered. The dog lay down with his nose between his paws.

"Kit! Kit!" Brenna hurried over. Oliver had dismounted and was with her in an instant. "Did you hear? We've lost our home and the business and everything we own. Ooooooh," moaned Brenna with her hand on her belly.

"I will send my men to town to find out all they can," Tolin offered. "Once the vandal is caught he will punished, I promise."

"My bakery. It's gone." Kit rocked back and forth on her knees crying, staring into space.

"This is horrible. But at least we have somewhere to live for the next ten days," said Oliver, meaning the castle.

"Nay. Nay, we don't." Kit looked up to Tolin with desperation in her eyes. "Lord Tolin granted Parker his freedom. We were to leave and go back home today."

"We were?" gasped Brenna, starting to cry as well. "So, I really will have to birth my baby in a barn after all. Oh, Kit, what will we do now?"

Oliver pulled Brenna to him to try to comfort her.

"You will all stay here until further notice," Tolin spoke up.

"What?" Kit sniffled and looked over at him. "But you said Parker's punishment is over. You told me we were free to go. Have you changed your mind about the sentence?"

Tolin realized they had nowhere to go. He'd seen how cold Kit and Parker were on the hunt. What were they going to do now since they were homeless and it was the middle of winter? They couldn't live in the streets. He wouldn't let them. They had no bakery, no home. Nothing. It sounded as if everything they'd owned was burned in the fire.

"Nay. There is no more sentence," Tolin clarified himself. "But you may still stay."

"Oh, Kit, Lord Tolin is letting us stay," cried Brenna. "Isn't that wonderful?"

"Nay, it isn't," said Kit, standing up and regaining her composure. She pulled her son to her and ran her hand through his tangled hair. "Thank you, Lord Tolin for your offer, but we cannot accept it."

"You can't? Why not?" asked Tolin, having hoped she'd be relieved by hearing his decision. She certainly didn't seem grateful.

"We will survive, we always have," Kit continued. "I will not have anyone feeling pity for me and my family. We don't want your charity. We will still leave today as planned."

Tolin didn't know what to say. He had offered them a way out of this mess and the fool girl wouldn't take it.

"Tolin, do something," whispered Raven.

"Wait!" he called out, as Kit and her family started to walk away. "It wasn't a request, but a command," he told her.

"A command?" Kit narrowed her eyes. "You said the punishment was over."

"Yes. And it is," he assured her.

"Then I'm confused. How is it a command and why?"

"We are in the midst of Christmastide and its celebrations, if I must remind you," he explained. "I am also the Lord of Misrule, so I order you, Kit Baker, to get back to the kitchen through Twelfth Night. I also command your son and sister to help you. And as Lord of Misrule, I want Oliver to get back to work in the stable, starting with my horse right here, right now."

"My lord?" asked Oliver in confusion. "You want me to continue working in the stable? Really?"

"Yes, I do," he said, handing Oliver his horse's reins.

"Lord Tolin, I know what you're doing," said Kit with a glare. "This might all be naught but a game to you, but it isn't to me. This is my life! My family's life. It is something that must be taken seriously and cannot be toyed with. As I told you, I will not have anyone feeling sorry for me and my family, and I mean it. You can't do this. You cannot make us stay."

"Ah, that is where you are wrong, sweetheart," said Tolin with a chuckle. "As the Lord of Misrule, anything I command anyone to do must happen. My orders must be followed. It is the rule of the game."

"That's right," agreed Brother Ruford. "I'm afraid you

and your family will have to stay until Twelfth Night now, Kit."

"Why doesn't the Lord of Misrule command that I get my bed back?" grumbled Rook, crossing his arms over his chest.

"I'd like plum pudding tonight, Kit. It is a must during Christmastime and we've yet to have it. You do know how to make it, don't you?" asked Tolin.

"Of course I do," she said through her teeth. "But I don't believe you do." She crossed her arms over her chest.

"Pardon me?" he asked.

"The fruit for plum pudding needs to be soaked in brandy overnight. The pudding itself needs to be steamed for at least eight hours. This isn't a dish, my lord, that can be produced at the snap of your fingers. Not even if the Lord of Misrule desires it."

"Oh, well then we'll have it whenever it is done, I suppose. In the meantime we'll have mincemeat pies, since I've yet to get one."

"Only because you keep changing your mind," Kit mumbled under her breath.

"Was there something that you'd like to make for Christmastide?" he asked her. "One of your favorite baked goods, perhaps?"

Kit's arms slowly fell to her side. She thought about it for a minute. "Well, Parker's favorite is my gingerbread. Would that be to your liking, my lord?"

"Very much so," he told her. "And from now on, through Twelfth Night, you will be the one to decide what you will bake and serve for dessert."

"All right, then," she said, releasing a deep breath and

nodding. "I will get to work at once." Everyone started to leave, but Tolin summoned Kit back to him.

"Kit," he called out.

She sent her son inside with Brenna and walked back to him. "Yes, my lord?"

"Later tonight, after the festivities are finished for the day, I'd like to see you in my solar."

"My lord? I don't understand. You want me to bring food to you tonight in your solar?"

"Nay, not food. However, wine would be good. I want to talk with you. Privately. Just the two of us."

She looked up at him in a suspicious manner. "Is this a command from the Lord of Misrule then?"

Sadness filled his being. "Nay, Kit, it is not." He reached out and gently laid his hand on her shoulder. "However, it is a request...from me. As Tolin. It is not, however, an order."

"I'm sorry, but I'm confused as to what this is all about."

"I want to spend time with you. And I hope you want to be with me, too."

Kit's body stiffened and then it started shaking the way it always did when she was around him. She had told him it only happened when she was around a man she liked a lot.

"Is something wrong?" he asked.

She shook her head. "White wine or red, my lord?" was all she said, once again asking a question rather than to answer directly. This woman named Kit Baker was more mysterious than anyone Tolin had ever met.

CHAPTER 13

"Sister, are you really going to Lord Tolin's solar? Now?" Brenna spoke in a hushed voice so others wouldn't hear their conversation.

The night's festivities were over, and the mincemeat pies were served. Kit had purposely eaten one, because it was said one could make a wish on a mincemeat pie at Christmastime and it would be granted. Her wish had been for things to be better between her and Tolin.

Kit's gingerbread had been one of the highlights. Both the nobles and the commoners complimented her on her baking, making her feel good inside. The musicians had finally stopped playing and all the Christmastide games were finished for the night. The trestle tables in the great hall had been removed and everyone was settling down for the night.

"He wants to see me," Kit told her sister. Her hands shook as she filled a decanter with red wine. "I saw him leave the great hall earlier so I am sure he has retired for the evening. He will be waiting for me to join him in the solar."

"Mother, I'm tired," said Parker, stumbling into the kitchen with his eyes half closed. The boy had been a big help tonight serving the gingerbread and assisting in cleaning up from today's main meal as well. "Lord Tolin took King back to his solar for the night, so I think I'll go to bed now."

"You do that, sweetheart." She reached over and kissed Parker on the head. "I'll be there soon."

Parker left and Brenna spoke to Kit again in not more than a whisper.

"Kit, if Lord Tolin is asking you to come to his solar alone, with wine, and at this time of night, you know there is only one thing he is expecting from you."

"I know what you think, but I am sure he only wants to talk. To get to know me better, like we did at the hunt." She picked up a goblet in one hand and the decanter in the other.

"Mmm hmm," said Brenna, with a knowing look in her eye. "And what if he wants to couple with you? Will you turn him away or give in?"

Kit froze. She was wondering this exact thing and wasn't sure what she'd do. "Do you think I should bring one goblet or two?" she asked her sister.

"I think you should stop ignoring my question with one of your own," scolded Brenna. "Tell me, sister, are you interested in Lord Tolin? I mean in a romantic way?"

If her damned body would stop shaking, mayhap she could think about this with a level head.

"I'm...not sure," she finally answered, releasing a deep

calming breath that seemed to do little to push away her anxiety. "All I know is that whenever I am around a handsome man that I am interested in, my body shakes. Just like it is doing now."

"Did that happen with Crispin too?" asked Brenna, speaking of the man who had sired Parker.

"It did," she admitted. "And it hasn't happened since then. That is, until I met Lord Tolin."

"I guess that is your body's way of telling you that you truly are attracted to the man."

Kit put the goblet and decanter down, holding on to the table with one hand, pushing back a stray lock of hair with the other. "Brenna, I admit that I am attracted to the man. I also need to tell you that I have dreamed of—of making love with Tolin."

Brenna smiled widely and rubbed her large belly. "Be careful, sister. You remember what happened last time you felt this way about a man." Her eyes shot down to her belly. "You ended up with Parker."

"Stop it, Brenna. I'm sure nothing is going to happen." She released a deep breath, feeling a little more in control. She picked up the decanter and goblet once again. "It was a request that I join him, not an order. That means, whatever happens tonight is up to me. I say, we are only talking. I will be sure to thank Lord Tolin for letting us stay here at the castle. For now."

"I thought you told him that you didn't want his pity or his charity."

"I don't," she spat. "But I realize now that he only did it because I think he cares for me. And for Parker too."

"He is a noble, Kit. We are commoners who have nothing at all right now but what he has given."

"You don't need to remind me of that, I am quite aware. It bothers me immensely."

"Even if something does happen between you two tonight, you won't end up together, you realize. You can't. You know that. Don't get your hopes up, because if so you will end up with a broken heart."

Emotions stirred within Kit making her feel as if none of this was real, nor was the situation fair. She never asked to be a commoner. And she certainly didn't intend to have feelings for a noble. For a man who could never be anything to her but her lord.

"That is why I told you, nothing is going to happen. Now stop worrying. Go to bed and keep an eye on Parker for me, please."

"Good luck, Kit," she heard her sister call out from behind her as she left the kitchen and headed to Lord Tolin's solar.

Once outside his door, she transferred both items to one hand, raising her fist to knock. That's when her thoughts turned to fear. What if Brenna was right? What if this man wanted to bed her? In a way that frightened her, but in another way it pleased her immensely. She hadn't made love with a man in years now. Even after marrying Gerold, the coupling had ended abruptly when she and Gerold realized they weren't attracted to each other at all. They'd stayed married for her sake and the sake of her son. But sometimes she wished they hadn't. True, Parker had a stepfather growing up, but honestly Gerold had little to do with the boy and it was only Kit raising him. Just like now.

Her nerves got the best of her and won out. Kit decided she had no business being here and that she should turn right around and go back to the kitchen where servants belonged. Slowly, she lowered her fist, not knocking on the door after all. Just as she started to leave, the door swung open and Lord Tolin stood there looking more handsome than ever.

"Kit. I thought I heard something." One hand on the door latch, he leaned his other arm on the jamb opposite the open door. "Well, aren't you going to come in? That was your intention wasn't it?"

"I—I," she couldn't find the words to speak as she drank in the sight of his toned, manly body.

He was dressed in a simple tunic that was open down to his waist. Her gaze swept down that sturdy chest with the dark curls of hair teasing her, making her want to reach out and touch them. At his waist, she saw he wore no weapon belt but only a pair of tight breeches. Her gaze slid down his long, lean legs until it got to his feet, which were bare. How, she asked herself, could she possibly even consider stepping into the room with this handsome, half-dressed man?

"Here. Let me help you." He reached out and took the decanter and goblet, putting them both in one large hand. Then he took her arm and gently guided her into the room. "Why didn't you bring two goblets?" he asked, closing the door behind her.

"I wasn't sure, my lord, who all would be drinking the wine."

"It's for you. And me. Both of us," he told her with a smile, holding up the wine. "I suppose we can share the goblet. It doesn't really matter." He walked over to a small bedside table and poured a goblet of wine.

"Share the goblet," she repeated, feeling anxiety getting the best of her again. Her body started shaking.

"Are you cold?" he asked, looking over his shoulder. "I can stoke the fire on the hearth."

"Nay. I'm quite warm," she told him, feeling the heat rise to her cheeks.

"You looked flushed. I hope you are not feverish." He walked over with the goblet, reaching up to touch the back of his free hand to her forehead. "I've never been good at telling if someone is feverish from a touch. I can summon the healer if you're not feeling well."

"Nay, please." She held up a halting hand. "I am fine. Just a bit...flustered, that's all."

"Flustered? Whatever for?" he asked with a deep laugh, taking a sip of wine. "Do I really make you that nervous?"

"I—I'm not sure. My lord," she added quickly.

"I see." He nodded slightly, drinking her in. "I do make you nervous. I didn't intend that at all. I'm sorry."

"It's not your fault. My body always shakes when I'm near a handsome man."

He was drinking again and stopped abruptly. His gaze lifted and he looked at her from over the rim of his goblet. "So you think I'm handsome?"

She bit her lip and squeezed her eyes closed. "Yes, I think you are very handsome," she admitted.

"Well, I must admit that I am feeling a little nervous in the presence of such a beautiful woman as you. If that helps make things any easier."

Her eyes popped open. Now that he'd called her beautiful, her knees shook uncontrollably too. This was more than she could handle. She felt as if she were going to fall.

"Please. Sit down," he told her.

She looked back at the only chair in the room, but his weaponbelt and clothes were thrown over it. "There is nowhere to sit." She became wobbly.

"Just sit on the bed." He grabbed her arm and led her to his bed, guiding her to sit. This only made her anxiety worse. "Here, take a sip of wine. It'll help you relax."

Needing to relax, she did as instructed. She half-expected him to sit down next to her, but he didn't. Instead, he removed the things from the chair and sat upon it, stretching out his long legs and plopping his bare feet on the bed next to her.

She took one more sip of wine before handing him back the goblet. "Thank you, Lord Tolin."

"Please, just call me Tolin when we're alone. Do have another drink of wine. I will refill the goblet." He got up to do so.

"I think I will," she mumbled, finding her attraction to the man growing. The firelight from the hearth flickered, causing his face to almost glow. He quickly retrieved the decanter, refilling the cup and handing it back to her.

"I should be refilling the cup, not you, Lord Tolin." Kit held the goblet of wine with two hands.

"I told you, it's just Tolin when we're alone." He put the decanter on the floor, sitting back down in the chair. "And you are off-duty for the night, so there is no need to serve me."

"I'm afraid there is, my lord. I am a commoner and you are a noble. Nothing will ever change that."

"You don't need to remind me." He retrieved the goblet from her and took a big swig of wine. "That is what I wanted to talk about, Kit."

"It is?" She didn't understand what he meant.

He finished off the wine and put the cup down next to the chair. "I like you. I really like you. You are a strong, beautiful woman, a good mother, and a fantastic baker."

"Thank you," she said, blinking several times in succession. The wine started to help her to relax. "You are a handsome, interesting lord."

"Interesting?" He raised a brow and chuckled. His blue orbs reflected the warm hue of the fire from across the room. "I'm not sure what that means, but I'll take it as a compliment, I guess."

"As it was meant to be," she quickly added.

"Kit, what will you do now that your bakery has burned down and you and your family have nowhere to live?"

"I—I'm not sure," she said, brushing back her hair. She felt tension inside her growing. "But we'll manage. We always have before."

"There you go being strong again. I like that." He put his hands on his knees and patted them. "Put your feet up here, Kit."

"What?" she asked, aghast that he would even suggest such a thing.

"I see my question has upset you and only made you more anxious. I know of a way to help you release all your worries."

"By putting my feet on your lap?"

"I like to walk around barefoot when I can. It relaxes me."

"It does?" She really didn't understand this. "How is the thought of possibly stepping on a stone or something sharp relaxing?"

"You'll see. Just give me your feet. Please," he said, looking her directly in the eyes.

"All right," she said, not wanting to disobey a noble. She hiked up her skirt slightly and rested her feet on his lap. Tolin took off her shoes and put them on the ground. "What are you doing?" Panic started to fill her.

"Shhhh," he said. "It feels freeing to have bare feet. But first you need to rid yourself of your hose."

"M-my hose? Oh, nay. I could never remove them. Not here, not now."

"Then allow me to do it for you."

Before she could object, he'd put his hands around one of her legs and slowly slid them upward higher and higher, until he got to her undergarment where her hose was attached. His lithe fingers untied the strings and then he rolled the hose from one leg downward, slowly slipping it off, leaving her foot completely bare. Then he repeated it on the other side. This time when he had his hands up her skirts she felt the tip of his finger flick against her womanly mound, not sure if it was an accident or on purpose. Neither did she care. It felt good and was awakening a part of her that had been dormant for many years now. She moaned slightly and closed her eyes while he removed the hose from her leg.

"You like that, don't you?" he asked, in a voice that sounded sultry.

"Yes. The air on my toes feels invigorating," she said, her

eyes popping open. He was staring at her with hooded eyes, making her feel lustful.

"If you think that feels good, wait until you feel this." He took one bare foot in his hands and started rubbing her foot between his large palms. It was absolute heaven! She moaned again in pleasure.

"I figure since you're on your feet all day in the kitchen, you must need them rubbed."

"I do admit it feels good, Lord—" He frowned at her. "I mean, Tolin," she corrected herself with a giggle. One foot was ticklish while the other wasn't. He smiled.

"That is better," he said.

She giggled some more. "Oh, please, you are tickling me."

"It is a good thing to laugh, is it not?"

"You shouldn't be rubbing my feet," she told him.

"Then mayhap there is another part of you that needs rubbing instead?" His eyes drank her in and he stilled his hands. There was a connection between them that neither one of them could ignore. It felt right to be here. She liked his touch and longed for more.

"I thought you wanted me to come here to talk," she said in a mere whisper.

"I never said that. However, we are talking." He put one hand on each leg and slid them up slowly beneath her skirts, getting closer and closer to her most private part.

"Yes," she whispered. "I suppose we are."

"Unless you'd rather not do so much...talking?" His hands slid up to untie her braies from around her waist. He scooted closer to her, bringing the chair with him.

"Perhaps," was all she said.

He untied her braies and slowly pulled them down until they were lying on the floor. She was naked beneath her skirts now and she couldn't deny the fact that she liked it.

"Perhaps I am being too bold?" He seemed to be asking her permission in a roundabout way. What she said next would determine how intimate they would become. With one word from her, she could be headed back to her room. Alone. Confused. Unsated. But with a different word, she could spend an intimate night with a handsome man who stirred something inside her, bringing her to life in a most delectable way. A flash of Brenna's warning went through her mind. The last time she'd made mad passionate love with a man and felt sated was when she became pregnant with Parker. Just remembering her time with Crispin sent a longing washing through her. Her body started to shake again, but this time it was more like a vibration.

Kit couldn't deny the feelings she had for Tolin. She also didn't want him to pull away right now. With the feel of freedom under her skirts, she wanted more than anything to accept what Tolin was offering. Still, she felt like she shouldn't be doing this. Not with a noble.

"You are not being too bold," she told him, feeling a searing heat from his hands on her bare legs again. "I am just not certain about...about this."

"Do you have feelings for me, Kit? The way I do for you?"

"Yes." She nodded. "I believe I do, Tolin."

"But you are being reserved since we come from two different worlds?"

"I suppose that is true."

"Then let's try a little more rubbing and see if it helps to ease your mind. After all, I am a man, just like any other."

He proved that to be a lie by what he did next. Kit had never had any man do this to her before. Tolin was not only a noble, but he was a man with experience, and she liked that.

He pushed her skirts up to her knees and then parted her legs. His eyes never left hers.

"What are you doing?" she asked, feeling her heart drumming against her ribs in excitement.

"I think you've been ignored too much in life. I want to pay special attention to your needs and wants." He knelt down between her legs, and then he lowered his head.

"My needs and wants," she repeated, mesmerized and shocked by what he was doing to her. "Oh! Ooooh," she moaned when she felt his fingers playing with her womanly folds, slipping his finger inside. Then he surprised her even more when she felt his hot breath as his mouth took his finger's place. Her eyes closed and her head fell back as Tolin worked magic with his mouth and tongue, awakening her, arousing her, making her feel so wicked and wanton! His lips were soft and gentle. His flicking tongue danced and dipped, causing sensations that she never wanted to end. She felt the slight scratchiness of the stubble of his face against her inner thighs and she liked it. Damn, he was good with his fingers, his mouth, and especially his tongue!

He pulled away only for a second to speak to her.

"Do you like this, Kit?" he asked.

Her eyes drifted open. Her body was already reacting. She felt excitement and insatiable pleasure like she'd never felt before. "I feel so naughty," she told him with a smile in a breathy voice. She drank in the sight before her. His handsome face was between her legs, her gown hiked up so high that she was exposed, feeling the cool air against her burning body.

"Naughty isn't a bad thing. It can be exciting and fun. However, I can stop if you'd like."

"No!" she cried, her heart racing. "Please don't stop. I want to feel naughty. I like it. Tolin, please don't pull away now. I need more. More!"

A cockeyed grin crossed his face and he lifted one craggy brow. "I thought so."

Without being able to wait, she took hold of his head and pushed it back down, squirming and clamping her knees around him as she felt as if she were about to explode with delight as he tasted her, causing her to feel as if she were about to scream her pleasure out loud.

Before she knew what happened, he'd stripped her clothes away and was laying her naked body back on his bed.

"You are beautiful," he said, drinking in her nakedness. "Kit, I can't play this game anymore. I want you badly. All of you. I am going to burst with need if I don't feel myself deep within you soon."

His words were only exciting her more. She squirmed in anticipation beneath him as he crawled atop her, looking like a panther, making her feel like his prey. She wanted this more than anything in her life right now.

"I think it will be hard for you to bed me while wearing all those clothes." It was her turn to raise a quirky brow. She played with him, and didn't want to stop this game. "I want to go to the finish."

"Oh, Kit. You have no idea what a happy man you have made me by saying that." He ripped off his clothes and threw them to the floor. She gasped when the firelight danced upon his manly form. He was hard and straight and so big that she couldn't stop herself from reaching out and wrapping her hands around him. He gasped and clamped his hand around hers. "Slow down, sweetheart, or this will be finished before we are both sated."

"Take me, my lord," she whispered, feeling as if nothing in the world besides this mattered at the moment.

"Oh, Kit," he said, reaching up and cupping her breasts in his hands. "My sweet, sweet, kitten." He rolled her nipples in his fingers, causing them to become taut. Then he mouthed her mounds one at a time while he ran his fingers through her downy hair, kissing her passionately on the mouth and thrusting his tongue inside, as his thumb played with her womanly nub and he slipped two fingers inside her below her waist. She arched up off the bed, spreading her legs on her own. This felt so damned good that she never wanted it to stop.

"No one has ever called me their kitten before," she said through ragged breaths. Her lips tingled from his kisses. Her breasts ached from his suckling. And the heat she felt below her waist made her feel as if she were on fire.

"Then it shall be my endearment and mine alone," he said, kissing her again. "You are my special girl. My little pussy cat." He removed his hand and entered her then, filling her completely with his want and need. With each thrust of his hips she rocked her hips back to meet him, and they did the dance of love. Her excitement grew, her body coming to life with Tolin like it never had for any other man.

"Oh, Tolin. Ooooh. This feels so good," she gasped, as they made love upon the noble's bed.

"Oh, Kit. Oh, Kit!" he cried as he neared his climax. "I hope you are nearly sated because I am not sure how much longer I can hold out."

"I was only waiting for you," she told him, throwing back her head, arching her back, and going for the ride of her life.

She not only climbed that mountain, but she found release from all the fears, all the anxieties, all the worries that had been plaguing her for her entire life. "Oh, Tolin," she cried.

"Oh, Kit," he said through ragged breathing, as the thrusts got deeper and faster.

Then she cried out his name as she found completion, and the colors of the rainbow exploded behind her closed lids. She heard him cry out her name as well. When she knew he'd released his desire within her, it excited her so much that she climaxed once again. Then he stilled, falling to the side, pulling her into his arms, both of them sated.

Kit breathed heavily, her eyes closing as she leaned into Tolin, resting her head on his chest. He was silent. So was she. And in the warmth and security of Tolin's embrace, she drifted off to sleep, where she could only dream that nobles and commoners could be together for a lifetime, and not only for one night.

CHAPTER 14

Tolin awoke the next morning hearing a pounding on his door. He rolled over, looking for Kit, but she was gone. He sat up abruptly, running a hand through his tangled hair.

"Damn," he muttered, yawning and then rubbing his eyes. The door to his room opened and in walked Jarvis with Rook and Daegel on his heels.

"Get up, brother. You've missed the morning meal again," said Rook.

"It was good, too," agreed Daegel, plopping down atop the chair. "That baker woman made herb-encrusted bread and even fruit tarts."

"What?" That got Tolin's attention. "Kit was there? In the kitchen? She made my favorite tarts?" He swung his feet over the side of the bed, reaching down to the floor to pull on his trews.

"Of course she was in the kitchen," said Jarvis, pulling

open the shutter to let in the sunlight. With it came a cold winter breeze. "Where else would the baker be?"

"Nowhere," mumbled Tolin standing up and stretching. When he did, his foot tangled on something. He reached down and picked up the item. Kit's hose dangled from his fingers.

"I have a feeling Tolin had a tart of his own in his bed last night," said Rook shaking his head.

"What?" asked Jarvis. He walked over to inspect what Tolin held. "Oh, that looks like a girl's hose. So, I see you had a little action last night, my lord. Congratulations."

"It certainly is a girl's hose," said Rook. "And my guess is the tart it came off of was none other than the baker girl."

"Brother, you didn't." Daegel's eyes opened wide. "You bedded the baker? How could you?"

"I think we know how it is done, just not why," said Rook.

"Shut your mouths. All of you." Tolin wadded up Kit's hose and stuck it into his pouch. Then he continued dressing. "Kit is not a tart and I won't tolerate you calling her that again."

"So you *did* bed the baker," said Jarvis with a nod. "I didn't see that coming."

Damn it, Tolin didn't mean to admit that. Too late now. "I care for Kit and she for me," he told the others.

"You're falling in love with a commoner." Daegel cracked a smile. "So it seems you're no different from the rest of our siblings, after all. I'm not sure Father is going to like that. He had high hopes that at least one of his children would marry for status and wealth. You know, a good alliance."

"My lord, you prided yourself saying you'd never fall for

anyone who had less money or status than you," Jarvis spit out.

"Thank you for pointing that out, squire." Tolin finished dressing and donned his weapon belt. "However, I never said I wouldn't bed a commoner. I mean, don't worry because it's not like we're going to get married or anything."

"Isn't it like that?" asked Rook, crossing his arms over his chest. "I recognize the signs, Tolin."

"Signs? What signs? What the hell are you talking about?" grumbled Tolin, wishing everyone would leave him alone and mind their own business.

"Don't forget, the same thing happened to me with Rose," Rook continued. "Yep. It is as clear as day. You are defending the girl, denying how much you are infatuated with her, and getting ready to smash your fist into the face of anyone who says anything bad about her. You're falling for the girl all right, and falling fast. I wouldn't be surprised if you two are engaged to be married by the time Father returns."

"Stop it. All of you," said Tolin, not liking where this conversation was leading.

"It looks like she won the game this time, Tolin," said Daegel. "She probably did it to save her ass, now that her bakery has burned to the ground."

"Nay, you're wrong," snapped Tolin. "Kit has too much respect for herself and also others to ever do anything like that. Say anything about her again and I'll—"

"Smash your fist into his face?" asked Rook. "Like I said, you're showing all the signs."

"For your information, I like the girl and felt sorry for her," Tolin told the others. "I only wanted her to have some sort of enjoyment in life after all that she's been through lately. Her life has been so trying. No one deserves what she's been through."

Tolin didn't mean to make it sound like he coupled with Kit out of pity. But he needed his brothers and squire to think so. If not, they'd never stop hassling him regarding his personal life. They would also get the wrong idea of Kit. True, he did feel sorry for Kit. But the reason he bedded her was far beyond pity. He truly had strong feelings for her, and it scared the hell out of him, though he'd never admit it to the others. He had always prided himself on the fact he was single and free. True, he did say if he ever married someday, he'd only do so with a woman who had more money or more power than he. What was happening to him? In the past he'd accused love as being the culprit that made Rook and Raven weak. Was the same thing happening to him now too? Tolin didn't enjoy being like everyone else. Or at least being like the rest of his siblings. He thrived to be different. And he strived to be in control and win every time, no matter what he was doing. Tolin didn't ever want to be called a loser.

"Wait until Raven hears about this," said Daegel with a chuckle.

Tolin grabbed his brother by the front of the tunic and slammed his body up against the wall. "If you or anyone says a word of what happened last night to anyone, I swear I will make sure you won't be able to talk for a fortnight." The last thing he wanted was Kit being on the tongue of the gossip flooding Blake Castle. Especially because of him.

"God's eyes, Tolin, stop it," ground out Rook. "You're going to hurt him."

"If Daegel is going to be a knight someday, then he needs to be able to stand up for himself," said Tolin.

"I can and I will." Daegel pushed out of Tolin's grip. "I'll meet you on the practice field and bring your sword. Because even if I'm not a knight yet, no one is going to treat me the way you just did, my lovesick brother."

∼

Kit had sneaked back to her little room off the kitchen early this morning, and thankfully before her son or any of the servants had awoken. She'd spent a wonderful night in Tolin's arms making love with him in his bed. But she couldn't let that happen again. She could see it all so clearly now. It was a mistake. She never should have gone to his room in the first place. Nothing could ever become of their little tryst, just like her sister had warned her. As hard as she tried, Kit couldn't think of anything but Tolin. She also couldn't push from her mind her infatuations of someday being his wife. What on earth was the matter with her?

Kit felt feelings for Tolin that she had never felt, not even with Crispin. Could she be falling in love with him? If so, did he feel the same way about her? Somehow she doubted that was the case here. To him, their lovemaking was probably nothing but another night with a wench to warm his bed, although it meant the world to her.

Unable to go back to sleep, she had made her way to the kitchen super early, using all her newfound energy to make herbed bread as well as Tolin's favorite tarts. Unfortunately, Tolin hadn't come to the great hall for the morning meal to break the fast. That made her realize that what they'd shared last night wasn't as important to him as it was to her. If so, he would have wanted to be here to see her.

"You never told me what happened last night," said Brenna, holding on to the table in the kitchen, slowly lowering her body atop a stool. Her pregnancy was really tiring her out lately. Kit was sure the baby would be arriving any day now.

"There's nothing to tell." Kit busied herself stacking up the dishes from her baking. Thankfully, Parker had found a few new friends to play with at the castle, and was spending time with them now instead of just with Tolin's dog.

"What did he want to talk about?" asked Brenna, brushing flour dust from the table into a pile using her hand.

"Nothing." Kit shrugged.

"I see," said her sister looking to the floor as Kit leaned over the table to get more dishes. "And did that nothing have anything to do with the fact you are not wearing hose this morning?"

"What?" Kit stood up straight, terrified that Brenna had discovered her secret. By her sister's smile, Kit realized she couldn't keep lying to her. Neither did she want to. After all, it would be nice to have another woman to talk to about her relationship with Tolin. "All right, so you know."

"How was it?" Brenna scanned the room and leaned over closer to Kit. "Was he any good in bed?" she whispered.

Kit scanned the room as well. When she was certain no one had heard, she leaned forward and gave her sister her answer. "It was beyond wonderful!" Just saying the words aloud made her heart flutter. "Brenna, he did things to me that no other man ever has. He made me feel things that I never felt before, not even with Parker's father." Kit was so excited about this that she felt giddy.

"Tell me more," said Brenna with wide eyes. "I want to know every detail about what Tolin did to you."

"Me too," came a woman's voice, causing both Kit and Brenna to turn in surprise. Raven stood in the kitchen, having walked up without them knowing it.

"Lady Raven," said Kit, with a small curtsey. "Is there something I can do for you?"

"You can watch your feelings when you're around my brother," said Raven.

"I'm sure I don't know what you mean," said Kit.

"I'm sure you do." Raven let out a sigh and crossed her arms over her chest. "Look, I like you a lot, I really do."

"We like you, too, my lady," said Kit.

"Then take some advice. Stop seeing Tolin."

"What?" Kit blinked, not sure she understood. "But I thought you were promoting me being with your brother."

"I was. At first," Raven told her. "But I just came from the practice field where I spoke with Tolin's squire."

"The practice field?" asked Kit. "Was Tolin there?"

"Aye, he was there. Fighting his brothers in anger."

"Why would he do that?" asked Brenna.

"Probably because they found out Kit and Tolin spent the night together and were giving him a hard time about it."

Kit frowned and let out a deep sigh. "So Jarvis knew and told you."

"Nay, he didn't," said Raven. "But you just did."

"But you said Jarvis told you—"

"What he told me wasn't about what you did with my brother. It was something else altogether."

"What?" asked Kit, feeling her heart sink. "Did Tolin say something about me? Please, I need to know."

"Yes, I suppose you do," said Raven. "Jarvis told me that Tolin said he felt sorry for you for all your loss lately. Also the reason he was with you was that he wanted you to feel some enjoyment in your life because you deserved it."

"So he used me?" Kit was ready to start crying. "I see he doesn't have feelings for me the way I do for him after all."

"I'm not sure Tolin can feel anything for a woman except lust. I'm sorry." Raven turned and left the room.

"Brenna, you were right. I never should have gone to Lord Tolin's solar. I must have just been feeling sorry for myself. I guess I deserve being used."

"Kit, don't be so hard on yourself. You didn't know his plan. Lord Tolin seemed genuine. It sure looked like he really cared about you. I thought so too. He just fooled us, that's all. I guess it is because he is so good at playing games."

"Yes, I guess so," said Kit, feeling sorely disappointed. "But I will not be fooled again. Brenna, pack your bags. We are leaving Blake Castle today."

"Leaving? Nay, Kit. We have nowhere to go. I have no home where I can birth my baby."

"You're right again," said Kit. "Never mind. I will find Parker and take him back to town, but you and Oliver stay here until the end of Twelfth Night, where you'll be safe and warm and fed."

"Nay, Kit," said Brenna jumping up off the stool. "I won't let you two leave without me. Oh!" she exclaimed, rubbing her belly.

"What is it, sister? What's the matter?" asked Kit.

"Kit, you really can't leave now."

"Why not?" she asked, picking up a stack of dirty dishes.

"Because I'm scared to be here without you."

"I want to see the damage that's been done to our home," Kit told her.

"Then I'll come with you."

"Nay, you can't. It's not safe for you to travel right now. Brenna, your baby is due any day."

"Then that is even more reason for you to stay here with me."

"I promise I will return as soon as I secure a place for us to live while we are trying to rebuild the bakery."

"Kit, we don't have money to rebuild." Tears filled Brenna's eyes.

"I know," said Kit. "That is why I am going to ask Raven for a favor before I leave."

"You're going to ask her for money?"

"Nay, of course not. I am going to ask her to help me send a missive to Ireland."

"Ireland? You're going to contact our parents?"

"Yes, I have to," said Kit. "They are the only ones who can help us now."

"They are also the ones who kicked us out and disowned us in the first place."

"True," said Kit with a nod. "But I thought about this hard and long. No mother can really be that cruel that she wouldn't ever want to see her children again."

"Ours was."

"Was she?" asked Kit. "I have a feeling that she was forced to make that decision by our stepfather."

"Even if it's true, Hasten will never let her help us."

"That is why I am addressing the missive to her only."

"Oh, Kit, do you really think Mother still cares for us?" Brenna rubbed her belly.

"I know the way I feel about Parker," said Kit. "I would do anything in the world to keep him safe and to make certain he has what he needs."

"Then why are you taking Parker with you?" asked her sister. "There is nothing for him back in town. He won't even have a place to lay his head."

"You're right," said Kit with a nod. "I will leave Parker here for now with you. Until I can find a suitable home. For all of us."

"You're leaving him behind?" Brenna's eyes opened wide in disbelief.

"It is what's best for him for right now," said Kit, swallowing the lump in her throat. "He'll be happier here with his new friends and with King. I am certain he will be safe being under Tolin's care."

"You'll be safe under Lord Tolin's care, too, so why are you leaving?"

Kit felt the emptiness in her heart. She didn't want to leave but wouldn't stay if she was naught but another trollop to Tolin. "It will hurt my heart too much to see Tolin when I now know he doesn't have feelings for me like I thought he did last night. I won't have him giving me pleasure just because he feels sorry for me. I want a man who loves me...the way I have fallen in love with him."

CHAPTER 15

Tolin spent the morning on the practice field, winning every time he sparred with one of his men. Then he played cards with some of the guards and won that too. Damn, it felt good to be back on his winning streak. What he didn't like was his siblings making him feel as if he'd lost where Kit was involved. He prided himself on his games and success. There was no way he'd let a commoner trump him. He could never admit to the others that he'd fallen fast for the girl. Nay. It would only make him seem weak. Tolin couldn't let the others think that Kit had bested him, winning over him. That is why he lied when he said she didn't mean anything to him, and that he felt pity for her and just wanted to give her pleasure.

Guilt ate away at him for acting this way. Still, it was the only way he knew. The way it had to be. Or did it? Since when did he care what others thought of him? If he had his eyes on a commoner, why should it even matter if someone didn't agree? He didn't know what to think anymore.

Tolin purposely avoided going to the kitchen all day long, not wanting to have to face Kit after last night. He felt like pond scum for not admitting his true feelings to his brothers. But Rook had acted much too smug, saying Tolin was falling in love with the girl. With a commoner. He might be Tolin's older brother, but he didn't know what the hell he was talking about. Did he?

Finally, Tolin headed back into the keep for the main meal. He couldn't even concentrate on the delicious feast because his mind was filled with thoughts of Kit.

"What activities do you have planned tonight?" Rook asked from next to him at the dais table.

"I...don't know yet," said Tolin. "I haven't given it much thought."

"Is that so?" Rook looked at him and made a silly face. He obviously didn't believe Tolin at all.

Tolin needed to give an answer. "What I mean is, there will be acrobats and games for the children to compete in that involve balancing eggs on spoons and racing with them, of course."

"I see. That sounds more like you," said Rook with a nod, continuing to eat. "What about for the adults?"

"We'll play Snapdragon," said Tolin, his mind elsewhere. Snapdragon was a game played at Christmas that involved raisins soaked in brandy. The raisins were set on fire. People would pick one up and pop it into their mouth to put out the flames. The trick was to do it without being burned.

"Snapdragon for the adults?" Rook made another face. "That is a game for children, brother."

"Aye, but once Raven found out I had it planned she

became angry and told me it was much too dangerous for children. So, the adults will play it instead."

"Shall we bring the dessert now?" asked a server, clearing the dirty dishes from the table. "Tonight we'll be having Ryschewys and flaming Papyns," she told them, speaking of the fried fig pastry and flaming custard.

"Oh, I can't wait," said Rook, pushing his empty plate to the serving girl. "I've never seen custard set on fire before. Just make sure to put out the flames before Lady Raven gets ahold of it or she'll complain and send them all back to the kitchen," said Rook with a chuckle.

"Lord Tolin?" asked the girl, waiting for him to acknowledge this order.

Tolin knew Kit would be delivering the dessert, and felt hesitant because this put him in a very awkward position.

"Tolin? The girl is speaking to you," Rook reminded him.

"Yes. Yes, bring the dessert," said Tolin, with a wave of his hand in the air.

"What the hell is the matter with you?" Rook asked once the server had left. "You seem as if you've got something on your mind tonight that is distracting you."

"Nay, I'm fine." Tolin reached down to pet King, who had his chin on Tolin's leg, sitting at his feet under the table. Odd that the dog wasn't with Parker like usual.

Before long, a procession of servers emerged from the kitchen. Each one of them held a tray containing the fried pastry as well as the custard that had been set on fire. A serving girl came to the dais, placing it on the table and dousing the flames.

"Where is the head baker?" Tolin asked the girl. "She is supposed to deliver the desserts to the dais."

"I'm sorry, my lord, but she is not here," said the girl, with downcast eyes.

"Where is she?"

"I do not know, my lord. I was instructed to bring the desserts to your table."

Tolin nodded and the servant left.

"Pass the sweets," said Daegel, stretching his neck to see them.

"Yes, take some and pass it over to us," said Rook, devouring the desserts with his eyes.

"I don't care for any." Tolin pushed the dessert over to his brothers. He had no appetite for food. Only for Kit.

"Huh? Why not?" asked Rook. "It is one of your favorite Christmas pleasures."

Just the use of Rook's word 'pleasure' made Tolin's guilt toward Kit grow. He couldn't stand this anymore. He needed to talk to her." He stood up abruptly to go to the kitchen.

"Where are you going?" asked Rook. "We are not done with the meal yet."

"Continue on without me," said Tolin. "I have something I need to do."

Tolin made his way from the dais and to the kitchen. His stomach was in a knot but he couldn't avoid Kit any longer. He had to talk to her about what happened between them last night. He walked briskly with King at his side.

He stepped into the kitchen and all the servers stopped whatever they were doing.

"Continue," he said with a wave of his hand, heading to the area where Kit always worked.

"King!" shouted Parker, running over and hugging the dog around the neck.

"Where is your mother, Parker?" Tolin scanned the room but didn't see her.

"She's not here. She went home."

"What?" His eyes snapped back to the boy. "What home?"

"Kit went back to town, my lord," said Oliver from a work table. Brenna was seated next to him and they were kneading dough. Brenna looked tired and uncomfortable.

"Oliver? Shouldn't you be in the stables?" Tolin didn't understand what was going on here.

"I'm sorry, my lord. I am taking a break to help with the baking, since things are behind in Kit's absence. The bread needs to be prepared for the morning."

"Why did she leave?" he asked, getting angry. "She didn't ask my permission."

"My lord, she told me that you lifted the sentence," said Brenna. "Please, don't punish my sister. She is only trying to help out our family."

"Doing what?" he demanded to know.

"She is staying with her sister-by-marriage in town while she tries to secure a place for us live," Brenna informed him.

"Is she going to return?" he asked, feeling his heart sink.

"I am not sure, my lord," said Brenna. "She will probably be back after Twelfth Night to collect us and to take us to our new home. If she finds one."

This was wrong. So wrong. Tolin couldn't just stand by and let it happen. He needed to talk to Kit and he needed to do it right now.

Tolin spun on his heel and headed out of the kitchen, planning on taking a ride to town to find Kit and explain how he truly felt about her. He decided he cared more about her than winning any stupid game. He didn't want her leaving. Especially since she had nowhere to go.

As he left, he bumped into Brother Ruford just outside the kitchen.

"Ah, Tolin, there you are. Just in time," said the monk. "The mummers are here and want to start the entertainment, but are waiting for the lord of the castle to sit down first."

"They can continue without me." Tolin still planned on finding Kit.

"Nay, my lord, they can't," said the monk, as Emeric the steward joined them. "It is tradition that the lord of the castle start the festivities with a toast."

"And don't forget that all the ladies of the castle are waiting for a dance with you tonight," Emeric reminded him. "They look forward to this once a year."

"Is that tonight?" The last thing he wanted was to take another woman in his arms when the only one he wanted was Kit.

"My lord, my lord," said Jarvis, pushing his way through the people in an urgent manner.

"What is it, squire?"

"Everyone is upset that the Lord of Misrule hasn't ordered anyone to do things in a while now. They want you to command something crazy."

"Yes, this is the one time the peasants can actually be treated like a noble, or have fun. You need to give them that," agreed Rook.

"Yes, I suppose so," Tolin said, releasing a sigh. With everything planned for the festivities, he could see that he would never get to town tonight. Mayhap it would just have to wait until tomorrow.

~

Kit stood in the middle of her burned down bakery, feel lost, alone, and hopeless. Everything was in ashes. She walked through the area that had once been her home. Now it was a smoldering pile of nothingness.

The ovens were just fine, being used to flames. However, the upstairs was gone and so was the roof. She looked up to see the darkening sky since nightfall was coming fast.

"Kit? Kit, are you in here?" Her sister-by-marriage came through the opening that used to be the front door.

"I'm back here, Vivian," she called out to the girl.

Vivian waded through the ashes and water damage, joining Kit in what used to be the kitchen.

"Oh, Kit, my heart goes out to you," said Vivian, with tears in her eyes. "It looks like you've lost everything you own."

"Yes," said Kit with a lump in her throat. She had worked so hard to build her business, and now in the blink of an eye it was gone. "But at least there were no deaths. My family is safe. For that, I am grateful."

"Why did you come back from the castle so soon?" Vivian had arrived with a broom in her hand and started sweeping the floor.

"Lord Tolin lifted Parker's sentence," said Kit.

"He did? That is great," said Vivian. "So, he isn't such a bad guy, after all."

"I'm not so sure about that." Kit bent down and started picking up shards of broken pottery.

"What do you mean?" asked Vivian. "He sounds like he cares."

"I wish he did."

"There is something you are not telling me." Vivian stopped sweeping. "Now spill it."

"All right." Kit stood and placed the broken shards atop what was left of the counter. "I found myself very attractive to Lord Tolin. He seemed nice. And caring, like you said."

"And?" Vivian raised a brow.

"We made love," Kit blurted out, looking out the remnants of a window rather than at her good friend.

"You did?" Excitement resounded in Vivian's voice. "That's a good thing. Isn't it?"

"I thought it was," said Kit with a sigh. "I thought he had feelings for me the way I did for him."

"So...he doesn't?"

"Nay. I found out he only coupled with me because he felt sorry for me."

"Oh, Kit!" Vivian dropped the broom and rushed over to hug Kit. "I'm so sorry."

"It's fine." Kit faked a smile and pushed away. "I need to get my life back together."

"You know that Willis and I will help you however we can."

"Thank you for saying I can stay with you for now. But I need to find a home, because after Twelfth Night my son and the others will return. We need a place to live."

"Won't Lord Tolin let you stay at the castle until you rebuild?" asked Vivian.

"I didn't ask him directly," said Kit. "Even if he would, it doesn't matter. I have no money so rebuilding my bakery is out of the question."

"What are you going to do?"

"I don't know. I wish I did. Actually, I wish we could find the thief who set my place on fire. Lord Tolin said he'd be punished. Mayhap even killed for what he did."

"Oh, Kit, no. No one deserves to be killed. Do they?"

"That's an odd thing for you to say. I thought you'd be more adamant about having the man who ruined my life punished for his actions."

Vivian wrapped her arms around her and looked to the ground.

"Vivian? What is it?" asked Kit.

"Kit, I'm not sure how to say this, but I think you need to hear it."

"Hear what?" Kit became impatient. "Tell me if you know something."

"It has to do with the man who caught your place on fire."

"Do you know who it is? Tell me. I need to find out. He needs to be punished."

"I'm afraid to tell you."

"Why? What does that mean? Please, Vivian." She laid her hand on the girl's shoulder. "I need to know. I deserve to know."

"Yes, I suppose you do." Vivian sniffled and then continued. "It was Willis, but it was an accident, I swear."

"Willis did this?" Kit pulled back her hand. She felt in shock to hear that Vivian's husband could do such a horrible thing to her. "I know he thinks Parker is a thief and doesn't want you by me, but this is going too far."

"It's not what you think, Kit. Honest, it's not."

"Then why don't you tell me exactly what it is." Kit was so furious that she felt like marching over to Willis and strangling him right now.

"He did it for me."

"That makes no sense."

"He wanted me to have some fresh bread for Christmas but you weren't here to bake it. I told him I didn't need it, but he insisted. He came here one night to try to bake it himself. But I guess he fell asleep. He's been so tired from working so hard lately. The candle fell over and then the bread burned, catching the place on fire. He was lucky to wake in time to escape without being burnt. He was the one to awaken the townsfolk, trying to put out the flames but he was too late. Can you ever forgive him?"

"I don't know what to say." Kit was so angry that she couldn't even look at the girl. "How can I forgive something like this? Accident or not, the man has ruined my life!" Kit picked up the broom and started sweeping the floor.

"It wasn't his intention to hurt you. Plus, he only did it for me. So I could have fresh bread."

Kit let out a puff of air. "When has Willis ever done anything just for you? Why was this time so important that he couldn't wait until I returned?"

"It was going to be a Christmas present for me since we are struggling and he couldn't afford anything else. He has been trying to save money. For our family to live on."

"What family? It is only the two of you. I have three others besides myself to support and feed. Now, because of him, all I have is this." She looked over her shoulder and nodded at the rubble and continued to sweep.

"I'm pregnant," came Vivian's soft voice from behind her.

"What?" Kit stopped her sweeping and slowly turned around. "But you've been married for a while now and have had no children."

"We didn't think we ever would," admitted Vivian. "After all, my brother Gerold never had children."

"But your brother Crispin did. Parker," she reminded the girl.

Tears filled Vivian's eyes. Her hands went to her belly. "I am not even sure I will be able to carry this baby. I have been feeling ill lately."

Kit's heart softened for the girl. She didn't want to forgive Willis, but she realized now his reason for breaking into her bakery. This baby that Vivian carried gave the two of them new hope. She couldn't take that from them, no matter how much she was hurting.

"I forgive Willis," said Kit, putting down the broom and giving Vivian a big hug. Over the girl's shoulder she saw Willis appear from the shadows.

"I am so sorry, Kit," said the man, looking like he truly meant it. "I haven't been very kind to you and now I am the cause of all your misery. Thank you for saying you forgive me. Even if I do not deserve it."

"Everyone needs forgiving at some time or another in their lives," said Kit, walking over and hugging the man as well.

"I will do whatever I can to help you and your family," Willis promised.

"Thank you," whispered Kit with tears in her eyes.

"If you forgave Willis, then will you forgive Lord Tolin as well?" she heard Vivian ask from behind her.

The question made Kit's insides twist into a knot. How could she forgive Tolin for using her and making her feel like a fool?

"I don't know," said Kit softly. "Mayhap everyone doesn't deserve forgiveness after all."

CHAPTER 16

It had been two days, and Tolin's responsibilities with all the Christmastide festivities had been so demanding that he still hadn't gone to town to find Kit. Finally, he'd had enough of this and decided he was going and no one would stop him.

He rode with his squire to town as the snow started falling.

"My lord, what will you do once you find her?" asked Jarvis.

"I am going to bring Kit back to the castle with me. Where she belongs."

"What if she won't come?" asked Jarvis.

Tolin hadn't thought of that. After all, the girl didn't have a home. Why wouldn't she return to the warm castle where food was abundant?

"We'll deal with that if it comes to it." Tolin slowed his horse as they rode into town when he saw the burned-out shell of what was once the bakery. It was on the end of a row of businesses, and luckily the only one that seemed to have been destroyed by the fire.

"God's eyes, that looks horrible," said Jarvis, hopping off his horse.

"Yes. It is most unfortunate." Tolin dismounted and handed the reins to Jarvis. Once inside the establishment, he looked around, almost gagging from the smell of smoke. Hot coals were still smoldering in parts. He heard a clanking from the back of the shop and headed over. His boots crunched the remains of the shop underfoot, remains of what was left of Kit's life.

"Kit?" He spotted the back of a woman standing by the ovens. She wore dusty clothes and her head was covered with a scarf.

The woman spun around. "Tolin," she gasped, dropping the bottles she'd been holding. They fell to the floor and shattered. She groaned. "Well, there goes what was left of my life. Not even old bottles will be able to be salvaged now."

"I'm so sorry," he said, looking around, heading over for her. "I promise I'll find the man responsible and see that he is brought to the gallows for what he did."

"Nay, you won't," she said, turning and busying herself by sweeping the floor. "I already know who it is and you will not raise a finger to harm him."

"Why not? What are you saying?" Tolin moved closer to her, not understanding at all what she meant. With the roof open and gone, snow fell, making a dusting on Kit's shoulders.

"The whole thing was an accident," she informed him. "Willis said he'll help me in any way possible, but he and

Vivian don't have much money. I can't expect him to give me money when he will need it to raise their baby."

"Are you talking about your sister-by-marriage and her husband?"

"Yes," she said, stilling the broom and looking over her shoulder at him. "They are to have a child, and I will do whatever I can to support them."

"Listen to yourself. That is nonsense," spat Tolin. "You have your own family to support. Kit, it is this man's fault that you've lost everything. How can you even consider helping him?"

"He is my family too," said Kit in a small voice. "I cannot abandon him or Vivian in their time of great need."

"I cannot believe how selfless you are. You need help for your family more than anything and yet you are putting others before it. You don't even have a place to live."

"Willis said that we can stay with them until we are on our feet again."

"All of you in one small shop?"

"I don't have another choice," she told him.

"Yes. Yes, you do, Kit. You can come back with me. To the castle."

"To do what?" She raised her chin and glared at him. "Warm your bed like the rest of those tarts you like so much?"

He took a few steps closer but when she backed away from him, he stopped. "The only tarts I want are yours," he said, meaning her baking. But when he saw the look on her face, he realized that it had not come out sounding the way he'd meant it to. "I mean your baking, Kit."

"Oh. So you want me as your servant is what you are saying."

"No. I want you at the castle as my...as my...guest." Tolin stopped himself from saying wife, even though it was what he wanted to say. But he couldn't. He didn't know Kit well at all. Their lives were so very different. And Tolin wanted to give his father what the man longed for regarding his children. That is, by marrying a noble. Or so he thought. Right now, Tolin still wasn't sure if he wanted to get married to anyone.

"Your guest?" she asked, sounding more than disappointed. "Tell me, how long would I be there as your guest, Tolin? Would I be expected to be in the kitchen, baking every day? And what about my family? Would we all be in servitude to you in exchange for this favor?"

"Kit, I am trying to help you and your family. Quit fighting me on this."

"Excuse me, Lord Tolin, but I have a shop to clean up." She continued to sweep.

"This isn't a shop," he said, looking around. "But it could be rebuilt."

"Without money, that will be hard," she said, without turning to look at him.

"Then let me help." Tolin risked everything by reaching out and putting his hand on her shoulder. "I have money. I will hire workers right away to rebuild your bakery so you don't have to do it."

Kit felt a surge of heat go right through her when Tolin touched her. She cried out in her mind for him—to feel him again inside her as they made love and held each other until they fell asleep. But that would never happen again. She couldn't let it. Tolin Blake was used to women falling at his feet and giving him everything he desired. She wasn't one of those women and he needed to know it. As hard as it was to reject his offer, she couldn't accept it. Accepting it, even though it would be an answer to her problems, would only say to the man that he could get away with playing with her feelings.

"What would you want from me in return for rebuilding my bakery?" she asked him curiously, wondering what he would say. She looked over her shoulder into his smoldering eyes, seeing his intent, knowing he longed to make love with her again, as much as part of her wanted it, too.

"Nothing," he told her, slowly shaking his head. His eyes never left her.

"Nothing?" She wasn't sure if he was telling the truth, although sincerity showed in his bright blue orbs. Still, she couldn't take such an elaborate gift without paying it back somehow. It just wasn't who she was. She didn't like taking without giving. Kit always repaid her debts.

"So, what do you say?" he asked, reaching up and gently stroking her cheek with the edge of his finger.

For a mere second, she wanted to close her eyes and bask in the warmth of Tolin's touch. His scent of leather and whisky drew her in. Her tongue darted out to wet her lips, almost able to taste his last kiss, still reveling in the softness of his lips. Damn, she wanted him more than she'd ever wanted anyone in her life. Mayhap she should go back to the castle with him after all, because in her heart she wanted to be anywhere close to him.

"My lord? Will the girl be coming back to the castle with us?" Jarvis walked in and Tolin quickly dropped his hand to his side. It was almost as if he was embarrassed to let Jarvis see him touching her. "Those breads and pastries aren't going to bake themselves for the rest of the Yuletide celebrations."

"Dammit, Jarvis, wait outside." Aggravation resounded in Tolin's tone.

"Yes, my lord." Jarvis looked confused, but turned and left as instructed.

"So, what will it be, Kit?" Tolin directed his attention back to her.

After hearing what Jarvis said, it made Kit feel as if Tolin only wanted her back to bake in his kitchen. Dropping his hand from touching her when Jarvis walked in told her everything she needed to know. He hadn't even mentioned making love with her, and neither did he ask her why she'd left the castle. Kit had almost been swept up in his charms once again, and she needed to be careful.

"I don't need or want your help, Lord of Misrule. Therefore, I will be staying right here for now until I am able to make a home again for me and my family."

CHAPTER 17

Life at the castle was nothing without Kit.

Tolin moped through his duties the next day, still hurt that Kit wouldn't return with him to Blake Castle. What did the girl think she was doing? She couldn't survive without his help. It would take years for her to rebuild the bakery even with the little help she'd get from the townsfolk. Hell, she didn't even want him to punish the man who burned her place to the ground. Tolin didn't understand Kit and he probably never would.

It was late in the day and Tolin was in the armory polishing his sword. His squire usually did this, but he was looking for excuses to stay out of the castle because it only reminded him of Kit and how much he missed her.

"Tolin? Tolin, I am talking to you. What's the matter with you?"

"Raven?" He looked up to see his sister standing there. Her baby was in her arms and she rocked little Sparrow back and forth. "What are you doing here?"

"Looking for you. Everyone is in the great hall asking about the Lord of Misrule. You are supposed to be entertaining everyone through Twelfth Night. You are not doing a good job at all."

"I suppose not, but I'm not really in a festive mood." He continued to polish his sword.

The baby fussed, and Raven talked in a silly manner to the little girl until she quieted down again.

"Did you really have to bring Sparrow up here? The armory is no place for a baby," he complained, just wanting to be alone. "Damn it, I can't seem to get this smudge off my sword."

"My daughter will someday use weapons like I do, so I see no problem introducing her to the armory now," replied his sister. "Brother, you were never any good at doing a thing for yourself. You are lost without your squire."

"What do you mean?" he asked, looking up at her.

"Here, let me show you how to polish a sword. Hold Sparrow for me." She shoved the baby into his arms before he had a chance to object. Then she grabbed the rag and the sword and sprinkled a little sand on the blade. Then she started rubbing, spitting on the sword and rubbing that too.

"I thought sand was just to get rust off of armor," he said, sitting there with a baby in his arms. "And did you really have to spit on it?"

"I am a mother. I know little tricks that men do not. Someday you'll be a father so start paying close attention."

"We're nobles, Raven. We have servants to polish our swords. I don't need to pay attention."

"Says the man whom I found polishing his own sword."

Raven looked at him and nodded. "I'm not talking about the sword, you fool." She held it up and he saw it shine. "I am speaking about babies and marriage."

"What?" he jumped to his feet, startling the baby. Sparrow started to cry and he couldn't stop her. "Take her, Raven. I cannot get her to settle down."

Raven smiled, put down the sword, and took back her baby. She had the child calmed in an instant. "It took me nearly eight months with Sparrow, but as you see, I am getting better. You'll learn in time too. If you ever get married."

"I haven't found the right girl I want to marry," he said, picking up his sword and inspecting it, not wanting to look at his sister.

"Mayhap you have but you are too much of a simpkin to realize it. You are too busy focusing on things that do not matter."

"I don't know what you mean." He looked at his reflection in the sword and smiled.

"Like that," she said with a sniff. "You would rather stare at your own reflection in a sword than spend time with a woman who really cares for you."

"Raven, if you have something to say then come out and say it and stop wasting my time."

"Kit Baker is a wonderful woman."

"Yes, she is."

"She is talented, smart, and a good mother."

"I agree."

"Do you even have any feelings at all for the woman? After all, everyone in the castle knows you bedded her."

Tolin cringed hearing this. He had hoped to keep his personal life private. But between his brothers and Jarvis, there was no chance of having a secret.

"Of course, I have feelings for Kit. More so than any woman I've ever met," he told Raven.

"Well, you have an odd way of showing it."

He frowned. "I don't understand."

"The gossip going around the castle is that you felt sorry for her and that is the only reason you bedded her. Because she deserved a little pleasure in her humdrum, horrible life. How could you do such a thing and then brag about it afterwards? No wonder the poor girl left. I would too, if I were her." Her baby started crying and she bounced it in her arms.

"That's why she left?" he said, not knowing this. "God's teeth. She must think I am some kind of ogre."

"Well, aren't you?"

"Nay. I only said those things to my brothers and Jarvis because they were making me feel like a loser. I swear, they're not true."

"Then mayhap you should try telling that to Kit."

"My lady, my lord, come quickly." Jarvis ran up to the door breathing heavily. "She's writhing in pain and screaming and I don't know what to do."

"Jarvis, slow down," growled Tolin. "Now what the hell are you talking about?"

"It's the baker's sister. She is having her baby," Jarvis blurted out.

"Brenna's in labor?" Raven's head popped up. "The midwife needs to be summoned immediately. Have you done that?" asked Raven.

"Well, nay," said Jarvis with a shrug. "I just came to find the two of you."

"I'll get the midwife. Jarvis, go to the stables and tell Oliver that his wife is in labor." Raven shoved her baby into Tolin's hands again.

"Wait. Why are you giving me Sparrow?" asked Tolin.

"Because you are not in your right mind so we'll handle this. You just watch your niece." She left the room. Jarvis looked over at Tolin and shrugged.

"I'm the one not in my right mind and yet she gives her baby to me?" mumbled Tolin. "Explain that one."

"Now Lady Raven's got you playing nursemaid." Jarvis grinned.

Tolin looked down to the baby in his arms. The little girl looked up at him and smiled. "You are kind of cute," he said, tapping the baby on the nose. The little girl grabbed his finger and started sucking on it. Unfortunately, this only made him think of Kit and the intimate night they'd spent together. It rattled him in every way possible. He needed to talk to Kit and this time explain to her how he really felt about her. "Take the baby," he said, pushing the child into Jarvis' hands.

"Me?" asked Jarvis. "Nay, I have to tell Oliver about his wife." He gave the baby back.

"I'm your lord, and you will do as I order. I'll find Oliver." Sparrow went back the other way again. "Now get the child to the nursemaid and then tell Raven that I have gone to town to bring back Brenna's sister."

"You're going to get Kit?" asked Jarvis, awkwardly holding the child. "I thought she refused to come back with you. How are you going to change her mind?"

"Don't be addled," he said. "The girl's sister is having a baby. She'll want to be here."

"Oh, aye. I suppose that will work." The baby wailed and Jarvis made a face, trying to jostle the baby to make her stop crying. "I'll never understand why anyone would want one of these," he mumbled, leaving the room.

"I do," said Tolin under his breath, knowing exactly what he was going to tell Kit and hoping she would forgive him for being such an ass.

∾

Kit was in the bakery cleaning up the mess when she heard the sound of hoofbeats stopping in front of her store. Willis and some of the men from town were trying to repair some of the walls. They had only a few boards and some hammers and nails. Vivian was still sweeping up the mess with Kit.

"Kit, isn't that Lord Tolin?" asked Vivian.

Kit looked over and stretched her neck to see. Sure enough, he was there again, probably devising some plan to get her to return to the castle.

"I don't care," she said, not bothering to look at him as he entered the door-less store.

"Kit, come quickly," he called out.

"I told you, I am not coming back to the castle, so stop asking." She continued to sweep.

"It's your sister. She's having her baby."

"What?" Kit threw down the broom and ran over to him. "Is she all right? When did it start? Has anyone called the midwife?" She untied her apron and threw it to the side.

"She's fine. I think. It started not long ago and Raven has

called the midwife. She and Oliver are there with Brenna. I came to get you because I thought you'd want to be at her side."

"Yes, of course, I do. Let's go." She hurried to the street.

"I also have something else to say," he added, clearing his throat. He needed to do this while he had the chance.

"What? What is it?" She turned back to him and everyone else listened and watched as well. "Tell me, quickly. We have no time to waste."

"I—it's not important," he said, realizing this wasn't the time or place to talk to her about his feelings. "Let's go. Your sister needs you."

~

Kit rode in front of Tolin atop his horse, not even caring that he had his arm around her waist. The cold breeze blew her hair up in the air and several times Tolin had to push it out of his face. She couldn't think about him right now. All that was important was that Brenna make it through this birth easily.

"I'm worried about my sister," she said aloud.

"I'm sure she'll be fine."

"How can you sound so unconcerned?" she asked over her shoulder. "Giving birth is a very dangerous thing."

"I understand," he agreed.

"How in heaven's name could you understand?" she bit off, still angry with him for being such a cur. "You think women are only there to play with and for your pleasure."

"I have a feeling we aren't talking about Brenna anymore, are we?"

They continued to ride.

"You should have come for me sooner," Kit scolded. "If anything happens to my sister or her baby, I'll never forgive myself for not being there."

"I did come sooner. I was here yesterday unless you've forgotten. I came for you but you refused to return."

"What?" Her head snapped around. "Was Brenna in labor yesterday and you didn't tell me?"

"Nay, of course not. Kit, I really need to talk to you."

"Isn't that what we're doing? Can't you make this horse go any faster?"

"Mayhap now isn't the right time to say what I want."

"If you have something to say, then do so," she demanded.

"All right, I will. I'm sorry."

"If you're apologizing for not coming sooner, I'm not sure I can forgive that."

"I am asking for forgiveness because I acted like an ass."

"I agree, but there is nothing we can do about that now. I just hope there are no complications with my sister birthing the baby."

"This isn't working." He slowed the horse and then stopped.

"What are you doing?" she cried. "We are not to the castle yet. Why did you stop?"

"Kit, there is never going to be a good time to talk to you, so I am just going to do it now."

"Now? My sister is having her baby!"

"Yes, she is. And she is in good hands. This will only take a minute—now please, look at me. I have something I need to say."

"What is it?" She turned to see him.

"I think you have the wrong idea about...about what we did together."

"I know you did it out of pity."

"Nay! That's not true."

"Raven told me that Jarvis told her that is what you said."

"Jarvis," he growled. "I am going to kill him."

"Can we go now?"

"Nay, we can't. I am trying to tell you that I have strong feelings for you, Kit."

"Yes, I know."

"You do?"

"Feelings of lust. Glad I could help you out with that."

"Stop it. I care for you, sweetheart. More than I've ever cared for anyone before."

"Well, you sure have a strange way of showing it."

"I might have said I bedded you out of pity, but it was only because my brothers were giving me a hard time. I didn't mean it."

"Tolin, it doesn't matter. It's over, so just forget it."

"Forget it? Is that what you want?"

"Yes. It is what I want because this is only slowing me down. Now please, I need to get to Brenna."

"I see. Yes, I suppose that is most important."

They rode back to the castle without saying another word. Once there, she slipped off the horse before he did, not wanting him to touch her waist to help her dismount.

"Kit, Kit," called out Oliver, seeing her and running over.

"Oliver, is Brenna all right?" she asked the man.

"I think so. The midwife and Lady Raven are with her but they won't let me into the room."

"Of course not. You're a man. I'll go to her at once." Kit ran off, not bothering to look back at Tolin because thinking of making love with him was the last thing she needed in her life right now.

CHAPTER 18

Tolin sat in front of the fire with a tankard of ale clutched in his hands. Parker played with the dog on the ground. No activities were happening right now because Tolin decided they would all wait for the new baby to arrive before celebrating another minute.

"I wonder what's taking so long," said Rook sitting next to him. "Rose went into that kitchen room hours ago to help out and hasn't come out yet."

"Sometimes it takes days for a baby to be born," said Jonathon, Raven's husband. "When Sparrow was born, it lasted two days, unless you've forgotten. It was the longest two days of my life. We just have to wait."

"My lord, everyone is becoming impatient," said Jarvis, coming to give Tolin a report. "Can't you start a game or at least let them dance to some music? They are bored. And if I must remind you, this is Christmastide, a time for continuous celebrating."

"Nay," said Tolin, watching Oliver pace back and forth in

front of the fire. The man was upset and anxious and rightly so. Tolin didn't want to put less importance upon the biggest day of this man's life. "However, you may ask the musicians to play some calming music, but there will be no celebrating or dancing or even eating until that baby arrives. We need to put our focus on what is really important in life." Raven's words, Rook's words, and even Kit's ran through his mind. Tolin wanted to prove that he could decipher what was important in life and this should prove it.

"My lord." Emeric emerged from behind Jarvis. "The cook says the food will be ruined if we don't have the main meal soon."

"That's right. We should at least eat," agreed Rook. "There is no need to waste good food."

"Is my wish falling on deaf ears?" asked Tolin in a raised voice. Everyone looked at each other but didn't say a word. Finally the monk spoke up.

"Lord Tolin." Brother Ruford got up from the table and walked over to him. "Your father has put you in charge in his absence. You need to carry out his wishes."

"I am," said Tolin. "But right now, we're going to wait."

"The girl is not even a noble," protested Ruford. "She is just a commoner. Surely you shouldn't require the nobles to go hungry for that."

"He's right," agreed Daegel from the other side of the table. "I am so hungry right now that I could eat a horse. Please, brother, stop this nonsense and let us eat."

Tolin was about to object again when Kit walked out to the great hall. She looked bedraggled and had blood on her apron. In her arms was a small bundle wrapped in a soft blanket.

"Oliver, come meet your new daughter," Kit called out, smiling down at the newborn she held.

Oliver rushed over to see his new baby. Tolin jumped up and followed him across the room.

"How is Brenna?" asked Tolin before Oliver had a chance to do so.

"She's fine. Thank you for asking." Kit looked up and their eyes interlocked. She had a glow about her holding the baby. Tolin could tell it meant the world to her. She seemed so natural. And happy. Love showed in her eyes.

"You look good holding the baby," he remarked, realizing that Kit truly was a good mother. She deserved so much more than the bad hand life had dealt her. Kit looked up at him but didn't say a word.

"Can I hold her?" asked Oliver.

"Of course," said Kit, giving Oliver the baby.

"Kit, thank you," said Tolin.

She looked at him and blinked. "For what?"

"For being here."

"Brenna is my sister. Of course, I'm going to be here to support her in any way I can."

"Of course," he said with a nod. "But I meant more than just that."

"Just that?" she asked, making him feel as if he'd belittled the event, but he hadn't meant to do so.

"You misunderstood. Yes, that is important, I agree. What I meant was...I want you to stay at Blake Castle." He meant forever, but she must have thought he meant only until Twelfth Night.

"I can't stay that long. However, I will stay until the

morning only. I need to prepare a home for the baby to come to."

"I told you, I'll pay to have the bakery rebuilt. You don't need to worry about it. Neither do you have to go back to town." His heart ached. Now that Kit was back here, he didn't want her to leave again.

"I have to and need to return. I told you before, I don't want your pity, Lord Tolin. We will survive without your help, thank you very much."

Tolin watched her walk away, feeling as if whatever they had between them was over. He longed for the right words to say to make her stay but his mind was blank. He wasn't good at expressing his feelings, and Kit wasn't making this easy for him.

"Can we eat, now that my cousin was born? Me and King are hungry." Parker stood in front of Tolin, looking up at him with wide eyes.

"Yes, of course," Tolin answered with a sigh, giving a nod to his steward to start the meal.

"Can King eat with me today?" asked the boy, dragging Tolin from his thoughts.

"Yes," he answered, trying to think of some way to make this up to Kit. "Do whatever you want."

"I can't do whatever I want," complained Parker. "I'm not the Lord of Misrule, you are."

"That's right," said Tolin, having an idea. He put his hand into his pouch bringing forth the bean that had made him Bean King to begin with. "Parker, I'm giving you the bean, so this means you will be the Lord of Misrule now until Twelfth Night." He dropped the bean into Parker's hand.

"I'm the Bean King? Really?" asked Parker, with wide eyes focused on his palm.

"Really," Tolin answered with a chuckle.

"So whatever I say, people have to do?"

"Yes, that's right." Tolin looked up and announced to everyone that Parker was the new Lord of Misrule. There were comments and complaints from behind their hands but Tolin didn't care. He could do whatever he wanted, even make an eight-year-old boy the new Bean King if he wanted. "Go ahead, Parker," said Tolin. "Give your first command as the Lord of Misrule."

"All right," said the boy, his eyes gleaming. "I want to sit at the dais to eat with King at my feet the way you do."

"You've got it," said Tolin raising a hand to call to his steward. "Bring another chair up to the dais for the boy."

"Nay, I want to sit in *your* seat," said Parker with a big smile on his face. "The chair with the arms on it."

"What?" That took Tolin by surprise. "Parker, that chair is for the lord of the castle," he explained, thinking that the boy didn't understand the game.

"You told me I could do whatever I wanted since I'm the Bean King, right?" Parker held up the bean to show him.

"That's right, brother," said Rook with a chuckle. "Since the boy will be in your chair, that means you will have to eat with the commoners below the salt."

"Wait a minute," said Tolin. "I don't think that is what Parker really wants, is it?" He looked over at the boy, shaking his head.

"Nope," said the boy with a mischievous grin.

"Good, good," said Tolin, once more motioning to his steward. "We'll need another chair at the dais, please."

"You can eat with my mother in the kitchen instead," said Parker. "Come on, King, I'm going to be the lord of the castle tonight." The boy headed to the dais at a run with the dog right on his heels. Tolin's jaw dropped and he found himself speechless.

"Well, you heard him, get going," said Rook, laughing. Daegel was with him, laughing as well.

"Off to the kitchen with you," said Daegel flicking his fingers. "The rest of the Christmas celebrations should prove to be very interesting now. I cannot wait to see what happens."

"More interesting than you think," said Rook, with a smile that Tolin wanted to slap right off his face. "I wonder what the Bean King will command next."

~

Kit washed up and changed her apron, feeling relieved that the birth had gone so well. There were no complications at all. Both Brenna and the baby were alive and well and that couldn't make her happier. She checked once more on her sleeping sister before heading to the kitchen to take Brenna's place with the preparations for the night. She stepped out, tying on a new apron, stopping in her tracks when she found Tolin sitting at her work table in the kitchen.

"Tolin? What are you doing here?" she asked. He looked sad or disappointed.

"I was ordered to come here and eat with you, Kit."

Hearing him say her name and 'eat' in the same sentence made her mind spin. All she could think about was his mouth on her in places a mouth didn't truly belong. It made her feel naughty just thinking about it. She tried to push away the memory. Right now she needed to stay focused on her family and to find them a home.

"What do you mean?" She giggled softly.

"It was a command from the Bean King," he explained.

"You're the Bean King, Tolin," she said, thinking he had gone mad. "If you wanted to join me for a meal, then just admit it."

"You are right, I did want to join you for a meal," he told her. "However, this was all initiated by your son."

"I don't understand. What does that mean and where is Parker? He needs to sit down and eat his meal."

"Oh, he is, I assure you. Come and see." He took her to the door that led to the great hall.

"Where is he?" Kit looked around the hall, but didn't see her son at the tables with the commoners.

"He's there. You are just looking in the wrong direction." Tolin took her chin in his hand and slowly turned it toward the dais.

Her mouth dropped open. "Parker is in your seat? I'm sorry, I'll remove him at once." She took a step forward, but he grabbed her arm and spun her around.

"Nay, you don't understand. I gave the bean to him. He is the Lord of Misrule now, and has ordered me to eat in the kitchen with you."

"Really." Her eyes went back to her son at the dais, looking so small sitting in the lord's big chair. Parker looked up and waved to her, Tolin's silver goblet in his hand. Then King's head appeared above the table and the boy handed the dog a big piece of meat. "You are telling the truth, aren't you?" she asked Tolin.

"I am. And I'm also looking forward to having a meal with you. I'm sorry I didn't command myself to do this sooner, when I was the Lord of Misrule."

"Please," she said, feeling her face blush. "You would never purposely eat in the kitchen with a servant."

"I would if she were you." He reached out and took her hand and she let him take it. "Let's go back to the kitchen and have some food. If I stand here any longer the boy might have me washing dishes next. I assure you that is a job I would not like in the least."

Kit smiled, feeling happy about this new turn of events. "Let me show you where the servants eat." She led him to the table and they both sat.

"I can't wait for some lamb. And I've been salivating all night smelling the aroma of that freshly baked herb bread."

"I hate to disappoint you, but the white bread is for the nobles only. Also, there wasn't an abundance of lamb so we'll probably end up with pottage and boiled cabbage instead. Most of the best food goes to the dais. We get the rest. Here, have a piece of rye bread." She picked up a loaf of the brown bread, ripping off a piece and handing it to him.

"Oh, thank you," he said, accepting the bread, staring at it looking like he'd lost his best friend. "What about the braised pork or the stewed rabbit?" His head turned as his eyes followed a serving wench with a tray full of the Christmas food. "Or the venison in a savory herb gravy? That is one of my favorite meals during the holidays."

"Don't get your hopes up. The kitchen servants eat last out of everyone, and that crowd is hungry from waiting so long. If we're lucky we might get some eel or sausage and bacon with beans. However, my guess is we'll most likely have to settle for umble pie," she told him, talking about the pie made from the entrails of animals that were leftover on the butcher's block. "Have you ever had it before? I can't say it is really tasty, but it fills an empty belly."

Tolin sighed. "Nay, I can't say that I have."

"Oh, I just remembered something." Kit snapped her fingers. "I believe today is the day when the peasants come to your gate to get their umble pies for their families."

"I suppose it is."

"Well, I am sure they've been waiting for hours since the meal has started so late."

"I didn't let anyone eat until Brenna had her baby." Tolin popped the whole piece of rye bread into his mouth at once and chewed.

"Why not?" she asked him.

"I did it for you, Kit. To show you that I care." He swallowed forcefully, grabbing a tankard of ale off a server's tray and taking a big swig to wash down the coarse bread.

"Then you'll want to show how much you care about the peasants as well, won't you?"

"What do you mean?" His eyes fastened to a tray of sweetmeats that went out the door next with a server heading for the dais. He looked so hungry that Kit almost felt bad about it. Almost, but not quite. Parker being the Lord of Misrule was going to work out in her favor and that is something that pleased her immensely.

"Come with me," she told him. "Be sure to bring your cloak."

"My cloak? Why?" he asked, following her. "We are going to eat now, aren't we?"

"Nay. Not until we hand out all the umble pies to the

peasants who have been waiting at your gate in the cold for hours now. Grab a tray, my lord. We have a lot of work to do. We will be lucky to get any food to eat at all tonight, since this will be a lengthy task. There are many beggars and peasants waiting, and we don't want to disappoint them or let them go home hungry."

By the time Tolin had finished handing out umble pies to the peasants and returned to the castle, the meal was over and all the trestle tables had been cleared of plates and food.

"Tolin, where were you?" Rook walked up with Daegel. Daegel had a piece of honeyed seed cake in his hand and was about to take a bite.

"I was handing out umble pies to the peasants and it took too long," said Tolin. "I am cold and starving. Mayhap I'll go to the kitchen to find something to eat."

"No time for that," said Rook. "Tonight is the big card tournament that you've planned as entertainment. You have even promised to teach everyone how to play your silly game, Tolinoffel. I've instructed the servants to bring out cards so everyone can play a card game of some kind. However, you need to give instructions for your game first so they'll know the rules."

"I don't feel like playing cards. I just want to eat and go to bed. I'm exhausted." Tolin's eyes were focused on the cake in Daegel's hand. The sweet yet spicy aroma drifted over to him in the air. "Is there any of that left?" Tolin licked his lips, already able to taste the sugar on his tongue. His mouth watered and his stomach made growling noises.

"Nay. This was the last piece," said Daegel, inspecting what was left. "I sweet-talked the kitchen maid to get it." He shoved the rest into his mouth, causing a pain to go through Tolin's heart. "However, I do think there is some white bread left in the kitchen that the servants are not allowed to eat. Mayhap you can get some of that."

"I'd eat trenchers right now and not care," mumbled Tolin, feeling his stomach twisting.

"My lord, everyone awaits you and the crowd is getting restless," said Brother Ruford, approaching with a worried look on his brow.

"Then go say a prayer or something while I get some bread." Tolin was hungry and irritated. He turned to make his way to the kitchen when he heard Parker call out to the crowd.

"Since I'm the Bean King, I want all the leftover white bread in the kitchen to be given to the dogs in the kennel."

"What?" Tolin spun around to see the boy standing on his chair. Tolin's dog was looking up at Parker, panting or smiling, he wasn't sure which. That was the same look his dog used to give him. Kit stood behind the boy grinning. Most likely giving the lad the lame idea.

"I also want King to have an entire loaf of bread to himself," said Parker, petting the dog on the head.

"Naaaaay," moaned Tolin, seeing his last hope going to the dogs.

"My lord," said Jarvis, hurrying over. "The games are late in starting and your presence is needed. You are in charge of the festivities and they can't begin without you."

"Aye," he said, turning slowly and shuffling over to the tables where the card games would take place. Perhaps giving the bean to the boy to show goodwill toward Kit and her family was not the best idea after all.

The night was extremely long, and finally Tolin was happy when it was over. Even if he'd had to stand in the cold handing out pies to peasants and was so hungry he could retch, at least now he'd have a good sleep in his warm bed.

"Good night, everyone." Tolin was so hungry and tired that he did not even care that Rook and Daegel had both beat him tonight at a card game that he'd invented. In his defense, he couldn't think straight, but it still made him a loser instead of a winner. It wasn't a good feeling at all.

Tolin yawned as he opened the door to his solar, hoping Jarvis had a fire burning on the hearth. He stopped in his tracks. Yes, there was a fire to warm the room, but there was something else inside his room that he hadn't expected to be there.

"Tolin! What are you doing here?" Kit sat up in his bed, clutching the blankets in front of her. Parker lay on the bed with her, sleeping. Even King was on the bed, sprawled out at the foot, looking up at him with half-closed eyes.

"This is my room. I'm going to bed. My bed, which you are in," he ground out.

"Shhhh," said Kit with a finger to her lips. "You'll wake Parker."

"I hope I do," he told her, storming into the room. "Then he can take himself and you back to your room off the kitchen where you belong." He was so furious that he was about to rip the covers off of her.

"The Lord of Misrule wants to sleep in your bed tonight, so you'll have to sleep in the great hall on the floor I guess," Kit told him, watching Tolin's mood turn from bad to worse.

"I'm sure you put that idea in his head, didn't you?" The corner of his mouth quivered when he spoke.

"Now, Tolin, please. My sister is using our room and has just birthed a baby. The infant cries a lot and Parker needed his rest. Plus, Oliver is using the extra pallet, staying with Brenna to assist her. There is no room for us in there, so this works out better."

"Works out better for you but not me!"

"Shhhh," she told him again.

"Don't shush me in my own chamber! And what the hell is Oliver doing sleeping in that room? I said he needed to stay in the stables or the great hall."

"Well, the Bean King said he could stay with his wife." She smiled at him smugly.

"Kit, you are behind all this, I know it. I don't like it in the least."

"Me?" She slapped her hand against her chest. "You were the one who decided to give Parker the bean, so don't blame me. Besides, I can hardly think that giving white bread to the dogs would upset you since that is exactly what you did when I first arrived."

"I told you I was sorry for what I said about you to my brothers. You are obviously still angry with me or you wouldn't be advising your son to do everything and anything to spite me."

"Now, what kind of a thing is that to say? My son has a mind of his own and you know it."

"I also know that you are enjoying a little too much the fact that he is Lord of Misrule now." He stomped over and yanked the pillow out from behind her.

"Oomph," she spat, her body falling back against the headboard. "What are you doing?"

"I am getting a pillow because the damned floor in the great hall is hard and cold." He tried to pull a blanket off the bed too, but the dog's big body was atop it and King refused to move. Tolin gave up and left the room, slamming the door behind him.

"Mother? What's that noise?" asked Parker, opening one sleepy eye.

"It's nothing, sweetheart, go back to sleep." Kit had been enjoying herself telling her son what to do, because she knew it would upset Tolin. But mayhap her games had gone too far. Tolin was a man who liked games, but it was obviously only when he was winning. He had told her he was sorry and had even given Parker the bean in good faith. Mayhap tomorrow she would have to tell Parker to give the man back his bed.

She lay back and pulled the covers up to her chin smelling the scent of Tolin upon them. Every time she closed her eyes, she kept picturing herself and Tolin atop this bed, making love and crying out each other's names in elation.

Kit missed his touch. She missed his kisses. And most of all, she was going to regret having to leave here soon and never see him again.

CHAPTER 19

Tolin awoke the next morning feeling cold, hungry, and achy, with King licking his face.

"Stop it, King," he mumbled, turning over the other way on the floor of the great hall, not even having had the good luck of getting a spot close to the fire. By the time he'd returned from getting kicked out of his room, most everyone had already settled in for the night. The only spot he could find to sleep was the floor under the dais table.

"Lord Tolin, it's time to get up," he heard Parker say.

Tolin opened one sleepy eye and then the other. The boy was kneeling down looking under the table at him.

"What is it you want, Parker?" he asked.

"I want you to take me for a ride in the wagon. King and some of his dog friends want to go down to the lake."

"You've got to be jesting. I don't give rides to dogs. Nay. Go away and let me sleep." He rolled over the other way.

"I thought you said as Lord of Misrule I could ask

anyone to do anything and they'd have to do it. Did you change the rules of the game again?" asked the boy.

"Nay, I didn't change anything," he answered with a sigh. He sat up, bumping his head on the underside of the table. "Ow!" he groaned.

"My lord?" Jarvis hunkered down and looked under the table next. "The wagon is ready for you. I've had the kennel groom put a dozen of the dogs in the back of the wagon for the outing. You'd better hurry, though. I'm not sure how long they are going to stay put."

"I'm not going," said Tolin, rubbing his head.

"Oh, yes, you are." Raven peeked under the table next. "If you don't follow the command of the Bean King no one is going to respect you. Now hurry up, brother. You need to be back in time to lead Hunt the Slipper. The children are looking forward to that game. And the men are really looking forward to the Mould-My-Cockle-Bread that takes place tonight after the children go to sleep.

"Hunt the Slipper is fine, but cancel Mould-My-Cockle-Bread," he told his squire running his hand through his long hair. The latter was a game where the women stood on tables and lifted their skirts and pretended to be kneading bread with their asses. He couldn't watch that and not think of wanting to make love with Kit. Normally he loved that type of entertainment, but now it was the last thing he wanted to see.

"Lord Tolin, King is ready," said the boy, holding the dog as it barked playfully, hurting Tolin's ears.

"All right, all right," he grumbled, crawling out from under the table getting a bath from King's tongue once again. "Egads, your breath stinks," he told the dog. "What have you been eating?"

"He had rabbit and eel and pork and deer yesterday," the boy proudly announced.

"King got all that and I didn't?" What was the world coming to? Tolin found himself jealous of a damned dog! "Let's go," he grumbled heading for the stables. "I can't wait for Twelfth Night to be over."

∿

Kit waited in the back of the wagon with the dogs, trying to keep them from eating the food she had packed up in a basket. It was her way of making up with Tolin. After keeping him from eating yesterday and then taking his bed at night, she was sure the man was in a foul mood this morning. Then again, he had the right to be. He was lord of the castle but was being treated worse than a servant. It was funny at first, but she started to feel bad about it. It wasn't right. No matter what the Lord of Misrule ordered him to do.

"We're here, so let's go on a dog ride." Parker hopped into the back of the wagon and King followed. Kit got stepped on by a dozen excited dogs.

"I'll put the board over the back of the wagon to keep the dogs from jumping out," said Jarvis, securing it in place.

That's when Tolin noticed Kit was in the wagon along with all the dogs.

"Kit? What are you doing here?" he asked. "Whispering more addled ideas into your son's ear?"

He obviously knew she had been telling Parker what to

command as the Lord of Misrule. "I'm going along on a ride to the lake today," she said with a smile.

"To try to drown me?" he asked under his breath, climbing up onto the bench seat. Jarvis hopped up and took the reins.

They hadn't gone far before Kit realized it was a mistake to sit in the back with the dogs. She crawled over to the front of the wagon with the basket of food over her arm. "Can I sit up there with you?" she asked.

"I don't know," said Tolin, staring off in the distance rather than to look at her. "Mayhap you'd better ask the Lord of Misrule, since my word means nothing anymore."

"I'm sure Parker won't mind." She started to climb over the sidewall onto the seat. The wagon wheels hit a bump in the road and she fell, landing right in Tolin's lap. Kit looked up only to find herself staring into Tolin's beautiful blue eyes once again. "Sorry about that," she said. "I'm a little clumsy it seems." It felt good to be in his arms again, even if it was by accident.

He cleared his throat and looked the other way once again, but held on to her so she wouldn't fall out. "It's fine."

"It's a beautiful day for an outing." She tried to make small talk, but he didn't seem to be in the mood.

"It's a beautiful day for sleeping as well," he grunted.

"I brought food," she said, finally getting him to look directly at her.

"Food? Where?" That took his interest. The man was probably very hungry.

"It's in the basket in the back. I'd better get it before the dogs eat it." She got off his lap and sat next to him. When she tried to reach for the basket, his long arm shot out and he got to it first.

"Get away, you mangy hounds," Tolin said, swishing the barking, jumping dogs away. "You ate my food yesterday and will not get it again today." He put the basket on his lap and opened the lid. "God's teeth, you are wonderful, Kit." His eyes lit up when he saw the roasted chicken and apple fritters.

Just that small endearment, calling her wonderful, made her heart soar. This was the first step in repairing the damage that had been done between them.

"Mmm, that smells good. What is it?" Jarvis looked over in curiosity.

"It's nothing." Tolin slammed down the lid. "Don't think you're getting any when you had the nerve to eat the last honeyed seed cake right in front of me last night. Jarvis, why don't you give me the reins. You can go in back with the boy to help keep the dogs from becoming too wild."

"I'd rather stay up here and have some of whatever it is in that basket." Jarvis looked over with hungry eyes. "All I managed to get this morning was a piece of dried salted beef that I brought with me but haven't had a chance to eat yet." He patted his pocket to show where it was.

"Jarvis, the dogs want to play with you," came Parker's voice from the back.

"There you go. The Lord of Misrule has spoken." Tolin nodded at his squire and raised a brow.

"Fine," grumbled Jarvis handing Tolin the reins. He flipped his body over the back of the wagon and immediately disappeared in a sea of dogs licking his face and sniffing his pocket. "Heeeelp," he squeaked out.

"Do you think he'll be all right?" Kit looked over her shoulder in concern.

Tolin chuckled. "Not with that beef in his pocket and all those dogs, but it's his problem, not ours." Tolin opened the basket, pulled out a leg of chicken, and held it in one hand while he gripped the reins with the other. "I love you," he said, sinking his teeth into the meat.

Kit's heart jumped. Was he speaking to her or the chicken leg? She was sure he'd only said the words meaning he was thankful that she brought food. Still, it was nice to hear it even if he meant naught else by it.

"Tolin, I'm sorry about having slept in your bed last night while you had to sleep on the floor."

"I don't mind you in my bed." He looked over from the corner of his eyes. "As long as I'm in it with you."

Kit looked down to her hands and felt the blush rise to her cheeks. So he was still attracted to her after all. That was good to know.

"You're not shaking," he noticed.

"Nay. I'm dressed properly for the cold weather."

"That's not what I mean. It seems you tend to tremble when you are close to me." He tossed the chicken bone over the side of the cart. Three dogs jumped out after it and Parker shouted for them to return. "Damn," he said. "I guess that wasn't a good idea."

"Do you think we should go back to get the dogs?" Kit looked back over her shoulder.

"Nay, they'll follow the wagon. After all, now that they know we have food they won't stray far."

"I didn't bring that much food." She opened the basket

and looked inside. "But mayhap we can share it with the hounds."

"Over my dead body. What else do you have in there?" Tolin reached down into the basket at the same time as she. Their hands ended up touching. Kit went to pull hers away, but before she could, his fingers closed around her hand, giving it a gentle squeeze. When he didn't release it, she looked up to see him staring back at her. That look of want had returned to his eyes. This time it wasn't just lust, it was something more, although she couldn't explain what. Admiration perhaps? Or mayhap a longing to break down the walls between them? She hoped for the latter.

"I'm concerned about you, Kit." His voice was deep and serious. "Where will you go? How will you live? You don't deserve the hand that life has dealt you."

"I'll be fine," she said, flashing a smile, not sure if she really believed it. She tried her hardest to be strong. "We will rebuild our bakery and our home. Eventually."

"It is going to happen sooner than you think," he said, leaving her feeling confused.

"What do you mean?"

"I left orders for some of my men to start rebuilding your bakery, starting today."

"You did what?" Her eyes snapped up to his. "Tolin, I told you I don't want charity."

"It isn't charity, sweetheart. I want my tarts and fresh bread and everything else you bake. The sooner you get your bakery back up and running, the faster I'll get my food. Right?"

"Oh. Yes. I suppose so." She smiled and looked down, still holding his hand. Even though she didn't want pity or charity, she did like having his concern for her well-being. But it sounded to her as if he only had his own interests in mind after all. Not hers.

"I told my workers to add on two extra rooms to the bakery."

"Whatever for?" she asked. "It was sufficient the way it was."

"Nay, that won't work anymore. Your family is growing. This way, you and Parker won't have to share the same room with Oliver and Brenna and their baby."

Kit's heart swelled. So he was thinking of her after all. Mayhap she was being too stubborn about this and should accept his help. "Lord Tolin, that was so thoughtful of you. It makes me very happy. Thank you."

"What would make me happy is if you stayed at the castle and never went back to the shop at all."

"Never went back home? I can't do that," she said, slowly slipping her hand out of his hold. "I am responsible for my family and cannot and *will* not leave them."

"Then why don't you all stay at the castle," he told her. "There is plenty of room. Think about it, Kit. Mayhap it is time your life changed."

"Live at the castle? You mean as servants," she said softly. "Nay, Lord Tolin, I cannot agree to that, I am sorry."

"Why not? It would be a better life for all of you."

"I am a free woman, if I must remind you. I am also a guild member and a business owner. I won't give that up to live as a noble's servant, even if it is in the castle. Not ever."

Tolin released a deep sigh and looked off into the distance again. After a few minutes he spoke once more.

"What if you all lived at Blake Castle but weren't servants?" he asked.

"What do you mean? How could we live there as anything but servants? We are commoners, not nobles if I must remind you."

"I am well aware of that, Kit."

"Then tell me. What did you mean?"

"You could...you could...marry me. And be my wife."

Her eyes opened wide and her mouth became so dry she couldn't swallow. Had he just proposed to her? Surely she must have heard him wrong. Their gazes interlocked once again. Her heart beat so rapidly she thought it would jump right out of her chest. "I...could, I suppose. However, I don't love you," she said in a mere whisper.

"It's all right," he said with a shrug. "Nobles seldom marry for love."

"But this won't be an alliance either," she pointed out. "And I am sure you don't love me either."

He looked deeply into her eyes, seeming as if he were searching his feelings. Finally, he spoke. "I am not sure what love even feels like," he admitted. "I have never been in love before. Have you?"

"Aye. Once," she told him. "With Parker's birth father."

"How did you know it was love? What did it feel like?" he asked, leaving her speechless again. She couldn't admit that it felt a lot like the way she was feeling at this very moment.

"I'd have to think about it," she told him, feeling confused and as if she needed to talk to another woman about this before she gave him an answer. "Tolin, do you really feel like this is the best thing for both of us? That a marriage between a noble and a commoner could really work?" Her body started trembling so much now that she couldn't control it. Was this really happening to her? Mayhap her luck was changing. Suddenly, she could think of nothing else but how it would feel to be the wife of Lord Tolin Blake.

"I think—oh hell, no!" He looked forward and his eyes opened wide. A deer ran across the road right in front of them. The horses reared up in surprise and he struggled to control them to keep them from running. The dogs saw the deer and they all jumped over the side of the wagon barking, chasing after the buck. "Damn it! It's going to be hell getting all those dogs back in the cart now." He stopped the wagon and jumped down. "Jarvis, Parker, help me hunt down the hounds. Do whatever you can to get them back here. They go wild when they see a deer as most of them are hunting dogs."

"Aye, my lord." Jarvis jumped out and helped Parker get to the ground as well.

"King will help us too," said Parker. "Go get the other dogs, King," the boy gave the command and surprisingly, the dog seemed to understand and ran off after the others.

"You're going to need something to lure them back." Kit picked up the basket and got to the ground. "I have a basket full of food that might help."

"Oh, nay," moaned Tolin. "Anything but my food."

"Come here, little dogs," called out Kit, holding a pork chop in the air and waving it around over her head as she walked. By the look of dread on Tolin's face, she could see this was the last thing in the world he wanted her to do right now. Secretly, Kit was happy about the whole situation because this would give her time to think and to calm her body from trembling. She'd been taken by surprise when Tolin asked her to marry him. Part of her wanted that more than anything. Yet another part of her wanted to stay in town at her bakery, taking care of her family on her own.

Life had just become so confusing that Kit wasn't sure which road to take. She needed a mother right now, but hers was inaccessible and didn't want her. The next best thing would be talking about this with her sister, Brenna. Now, Kit just needed to keep Tolin distracted until she could figure out how to give him an answer.

CHAPTER 20

"You did what?" asked Rook the next day, as he and Tolin oversaw the servants setting up for the outdoor snowball fight that would take place today as part of the Christmas festivities. It had snowed overnight enough to make not only snowballs and snowmen, but also forts. The best snowman would win a prize and the winning team would get extra wine as well as the right to smash the losers' fort.

"You heard me. I said I asked Kit to marry me." Life was changing so rapidly that it made Tolin's head spin.

"I knew it!" Rook clasped his palms together. "I told you it was only a matter of time and you'd be marrying a commoner too, just like me and Raven and most of your cousins. Join the club, brother." Rook chuckled, reaching out and shaking Tolin's hand. "Wait until Father hears about this. He'll burst a vein in his neck since he'll be so upset."

"Now, wait a minute. I didn't say she accepted."

"What?" Rook made a face. "What do you mean she didn't accept your proposal? A commoner getting the chance to marry a noble is a dream come true. Why in heaven's name would she turn you down?"

"She didn't turn me down, but neither did she accept. She wanted to think about it."

"So what is there to think about?"

"I don't know. Mayhap because we not really in love?" Tolin shrugged.

"Nobles seldom marry for love. That comes later."

"I told her that. But she is a headstrong woman and likes having a business and taking care of everyone, I guess. Everyone but me, that is."

"Tolin? Is this just about the sex?" Rook gave him a disappointed glare.

"Nay, that's not what I mean at all. It's just that I think I have feelings for her even though I'm not sure they are love. Yet. Kit, on the other hand, I don't think seems to feel the same way about me."

"You think? Or you know? This part is important."

Tolin threw his hands in the air. "When it comes to Kit, I know nothing." He plopped down in his dais chair and stretched out his legs, placing his feet on the table. "Nothing ever seems to go my way anymore. I am used to winning, but lately I feel like I am always losing."

"Are you talking about the fact that you had to use your food to lure the dogs back to the wagon?" Rook laughed aloud. "The knights and even the kennel grooms will be talking about that stunt for quite a while to come."

"It wasn't my idea to bring the dogs. I swear since I gave

the boy that bean, my life has crumbled and turned upside down."

"Hear ye, hear ye," called out Jarvis from the other side of the hall.

"What the hell is my squire doing?" Tolin narrowed his eyes and stretched his neck to see what was going on.

"I don't know," said Rook with a shrug. "Did you tell him to make some sort of announcement for the upcoming festivities?"

"Nay. Not at all."

"The Lord of Misrule would like to give another command," shouted Jarvis.

"Oh, hell no," complained Tolin, wishing he could hide. He was already expecting the worse. He pictured himself shoveling horse manure in the stables next. But when he heard what the boy said, it actually pleased him instead.

"I command Lord Tolin to kiss my mother under the mistletoe," Parker called out loud enough for everyone to hear him.

Tolin slowly stood, seeing Kit peeking out from the kitchen. Had she possibly told Parker to request this? It would please him immensely if he thought it was true, but how could it be? She never even gave him an answer when he took a huge risk and asked her to marry him.

"Well, go on," said Rook with a jerk of his head. "Go kiss the girl. I know you want to."

"I'm a little hesitant," said Tolin.

"What the hell for?"

"Because if I kiss her, I'm not going to want to let her go. Ever. But if she doesn't want to stay with me, then there is nothing I can do to keep her from leaving."

"Would you just get over there and kiss the wench? And stop worrying about winning or losing. Just live for the day, brother."

"Live for the day," he mumbled, walking blindly to the center of the room where the biggest kissing bough was fastened above their heads.

Raven took ahold of Kit's arm and brought her out to the center of the room. If it wasn't Kit's idea, then it surely was his sister's. Either way, he wouldn't fight it. Tolin had been longing to kiss Kit again ever since the night they'd made love.

Being urged on by Rook, Tolin walked up and stopped under the kissing bough. Raven all but pushed Kit until she met him there, toe to toe.

"You heard the Lord of Misrule," said Jarvis. "Kiss."

When neither of them took the first move to do so, Jarvis got the whole crowd to start chanting. "Kiss, kiss, kiss!" came the shouts.

"You hear them," Tolin told Kit.

"Yes. I don't suppose we should disappoint them," said Kit, not able to look him in the eye.

"After all, it is the command of the Lord of Misrule," he said, taking a step closer to her, gently placing his hands on her shoulders.

Then, staring deeply into the eyes of the woman who could someday possibly be his wife, Tolin decided to live for the moment like his brother told him. He pulled Kit into his arms, kissing her passionately, not caring that everyone was watching. She returned the kiss, her hands going to his shoulders. It felt right. It was good. Damn, why didn't she just accept his proposal, because this kiss sealed it for Tolin. This time, he was sure he had fallen in love with Kit.

~

Kit slowly opened her eyes, feeling like she was in heaven. Being in Tolin's arms again, pressing her lips up against his was exactly what she'd needed. She had talked to her sister last night. Brenna told her not to worry about her and Oliver and baby Glenda. Brenna was healing quickly and decided that she and Oliver could run the bakery with the help of Vivian until they learned all they needed to know and were able to join the guild.

Willis had felt so bad about burning down their bakery that he was the one who had offered his wife's help. Vivian was already a bakers' guild member, so this should suffice the guild masters and all their rules. That meant the shop wouldn't be taken away from Kit after all. It was tempting. Nay, it was more than that. It was the answer to all her prayers.

"Kit, you never gave me an answer," said Tolin in a hushed voice, still holding her in his arms. "Will you marry me or not?"

"Is this what you really want?" she asked him, so only he could hear.

"It is," he said, staring at her. She saw the sincerity in his eyes and heard it in his words. "Kit, I told you that I don't know what it feels like to be in love, but I think I am starting to learn. I believe I am falling in love with you. I don't want you to go back to town. I want you at my side, as my wife. Always."

"And Parker? What about him?"

"Parker is your son. He'll stay with us, of course. If you allow it, I would like him to be my son, too."

Her heart swelled. Tolin really did care about them. She cared about him too. How could she live without him?

"I'd like that."

"My offer still holds. Brenna and Oliver and their baby can stay too, if they want. We'll find something for them to do at the castle that isn't considered the job of a servant."

"Nay."

"Nay?" He sounded so disappointed.

"My sister wants to run the bakery with Oliver. They want to stay in town."

"So, what does that mean, Kit?"

"It means, you built an extra room onto the bakery for nothing." She smiled. "Yes, Tolin Blake, I accept your proposal. I think I am falling in love with you, too. I would like nothing more than to be your wife."

Everyone in the room started clapping. That is when Kit realized they were all listening to their conversation after all.

"Oh, Kit, this makes me so happy." Tolin kissed her again, and then picked her up and spun her around. He put her back down on her feet and they both laughed.

"Mayhap that extra room at the bakery won't be wasted after all." Brenna came forward with the baby in her arms. Oliver was next to her, and so was someone that Kit hadn't seen in a very long time.

"Mother!" gasped Kit. "What are you doing here?"

"I got your missive," said her mother, looking like she felt guilty. "Kit, I've already explained it to Brenna. I never wanted to shun either one of you. It was Hasten who didn't want you girls with us. I should have stood up to him years ago, but I was afraid. You see...he often hit me."

"Oh, Mother! I had no idea." Kit ran to her mother and hugged her. "I don't want you going back to that horrible man."

"I won't. He died, Kit. He can't hurt me anymore."

"He died?"

"Hasten took to a fever and never recovered."

"So, are you back in England to stay?" asked Kit.

"Only if you and Brenna can forgive me and will have me."

"I forgive you, Mother," said Brenna. "Oliver and I want you to live with us. At the bakery, as soon as it is done being rebuilt."

"Kit?" Her mother looked over with worried eyes. "I won't accept it unless I know you feel the same way."

"I learned to bake from you, Mother," Kit told her. "You will be just what the bakery needs."

They hugged again. Kit felt a tugging at her skirt. She looked down to see Parker looking up with wide eyes.

"Who is that, Mother?" asked her son.

"Oh, I'm so sorry. I almost forgot. Mother, you never met Parker. Parker, this is your grandmother."

"What a sweet boy. He looks so much like your father, Kit." Her mother hugged Parker.

"I'm the Bean King, Grandma." Parker lifted his chin in pride. "Is there anything you want? I can get it for you from Lord Tolin."

"Parker!" scolded Kit.

Tolin cleared his throat from behind them.

"Mother, I'd like you to meet Lord Tolin Blake. We are going to be married."

"I heard. Congratulations," said her mother, curtsying to Tolin.

"If there is anything I can do to help you, please let me know," said Tolin, being the kind and considerate man that he was.

"The first thing you can do is take the bean back from Parker," said Kit, holding out her hand. "Parker, hand it over."

"All right," said Parker pouting, but doing what she asked. Kit handed the bean back to Tolin.

Tolin looked at the bean in his hand and then at Parker who continued to pout. "Parker, now that you're going to be my son too, I'll need you to take good care of King for me. Can you do that?"

"I can!" exclaimed Parker.

"Actually, King is going to be your dog now."

"Really? Yay!" yelled the boy. "I can't wait to tell him. King? Where are you?" Parker ran off to look for the dog.

"Tolin, there are a few days left before Twelfth Night," Rook reminded him. "Everyone is expecting more games and festivities. You wouldn't want to disappoint them."

"Nay, and neither shall we," said Tolin, pulling Kit into his arms. "Everyone is invited to join us for our wedding which will be on Twelfth Night as soon as my parents return to Blake Castle," he announced.

"That soon? Oh, Tolin, I'm worried." With their arms around each other, Kit looked up at him. "What if your father doesn't agree to this marriage? What if your parents don't like me?"

"I wouldn't worry about a thing," he told her. "If they give me any trouble about marrying a commoner, I will tell them something that they'll have to obey."

"I don't understand. What do you mean?" asked Kit.

Tolin chuckled. "I'll just tell them that our marriage is a wish of the Lord of Misrule."

CHAPTER 21
TWELFTH NIGHT

The time for the wedding had come quickly. Kit was so nervous and excited that her body started to tremble once again. So much had happened over the past few days that it seemed to her like a dream.

"Kit, it's time," said Brenna, handing Kit winter greens mixed with holly and mistletoe as her bridal bouquet. Raven had given Kit one of her royal gowns to wear, and today Kit really did feel like a noble.

Her cotehardie was made of soft velvet in the color of gold. This was not a type of cloth that Kit had ever worn before. It was trimmed with ornate edging. Gold buttons lined the fitted sleeves. Kit wasn't used to such wealth but truly did love it. Over her gown she wore a cloak that was trimmed in fur. The cloak was so long that it dragged behind her sweeping across the floor like the garment of a queen.

"Daughter?" Katherine, her mother, held out her arm, ready to walk Kit to the altar. Brenna led the way as Kit's maid of honor.

The wedding was taking place in St. Basil's Cathedral. It was a beautiful church with tall stained-glass windows that curved at the top. The church was filled with people, all well-wishers who were there to witness and celebrate the union between Kit and Tolin.

Kit walked down the aisle, clinging to her mother's arm. Kit's body trembled. As she walked, she saw Tolin's entire family whom she had met over the past few days.

Tolin's cousin Lady Eleanor and her husband Sir Connor watched with smiles on their faces. Eleanor was a red-haired raving beauty. She was pregnant and nearly ready to give birth. Kit swore the girl's face glowed with happiness. Connor was first a noble, then an executioner, and now a noble again as well as a knight. Eleanor's brothers, Gar and Evan, were there too, as well as Gar's very pregnant wife, Josefina. The siblings' parents, Lord Garrett Blackmore, who was Lord Warden of the Cinque Ports, and his wife, Lady Echo, who used to be a pirate, also joined them. This family had a colorful past.

The musicians played soothing music while Brother Ruford and the monks chanted a melodic tune. Their voices echoed off the walls and filled the huge church with rich tones that bounced off the massively high ceilings. It sounded so angelic that Kit felt as if she'd entered Heaven itself.

Next, Kit passed by Tolin's cousin, Lord Robin and his wife, Lady Sage. Sage had been a common healer when she and Robin first met. Their little boy Martin wandered out into the aisle, and Robin ran after the one-year-old, scooping up the boy into his arms and bringing him back to the bench, where Robin's two sisters, Regina and Dorothy, took the child from him. Robin's sister Lady Martine held the hand of her husband, Lord David, who used to be an innkeeper. They'd just found out a few months ago that they were expecting. The Blake family was really growing. Their parents, Lady Abbey and Lord Madoc, who used to be a thief, watched with smiles on their faces.

On the next bench Kit saw Tolin's Scottish relatives, who happened to show up with Lord Corbett when the man decided to return to Blake Castle earlier than expected. Probably to check on Tolin to make sure he hadn't done anything horrible to his castle in his absence. Lady Lark, Tolin's Scottish cousin, was a beautiful woman with bright blonde hair. Her young daughter Jorie was next to her. Lark's husband, Lord Dustin, who used to be a scribe, held their baby daughter, Elspeth. With them was Lark's brother, Hawke, and her sister, Heather. Their parents were there too. Lady Wren, even though a noble, was once blind and the leader of a group of female renegades. Wren's husband, Storm MacKeefe was well-known and the laird of his clan in the Highlands. Their son, Renard couldn't make it to the wedding since he acted as laird when Storm was gone.

As Kit reached the front, Tolin's immediate family was seated there. Lord Corbett had a stoic look upon his face. He hadn't been happy about Tolin marrying a commoner, but his wife, Lady Devon, gave him the talk about true love and got him to accept it. Lady Devon was the kindest woman anyone would ever want to meet. She understood commoners from below the salt. Mayhap it was because before she knew she was noble, she'd been raised in a monastery and was even a servant of her husband.

Lady Raven was next to her mother, beaming with pride

when she saw her gown on Kit. Her husband, Lord Jonathon, who was once a blacksmith, held on to their daughter, Sparrow. Lord Rook was there too, with his wife Lady Rose. Rose used to be a gardener before they were married. She was also the one who had put together Kit's wedding bouquet. Their son Beowulf was fussing, while Raven's daughter Sparrow was good. That might be another reason why Raven looked so happy.

As Kit approached the altar, she saw Daegel, who was acting as Tolin's best man. Tolin never looked as handsome as he did today. Dressed in his finest clothes, Tolin's long black hair fell down over his shoulders. She could see his bright blue eyes staring at her before she even got near. His gaze heated her and made her feel special.

Kit's mother went to sit with Oliver and baby Glenda, as well as Kit's son Parker, who had brought King to the church. The dog was lying under the bench wagging his tail. Brenna straightened out Kit's cloak behind her and then came to her side and took the flowers from her.

"Stop shaking," whispered Brenna. "He's going to be your husband now, so there is no need to be nervous."

All the more reason to be nervous, Kit decided, feeling the rapid pounding of her heart.

"You look beautiful, sweetheart," said Tolin, taking her hand in his.

"You look so handsome. I can't believe this is real," she replied.

"Believe it," he said, flashing her one of his gorgeous smiles.

"Are you ready?" asked the priest, standing with a book in his hands. The music and chanting stopped, and then it was time to take the vows that would join Tolin and Kit in marriage, a union that would last forever.

They both nodded, and repeated their vows as the ceremony progressed. Daegel handed a ring to Tolin and Tolin slipped it onto Kit's finger. Before she knew it, they were married and the priest was telling Tolin that he could kiss his bride.

They did kiss. It was a long and very passionate kiss right there at the altar before the eyes of all the witnesses, their family, their friends, the peasants and servants, and most of all before God.

Daegel cleared his throat causing Tolin and Kit's lips to finally part. Kit felt the blush rising to her cheeks when she looked out at the sea of onlookers all watching them intently.

"So, we're really married then," she said rather than asked.

"Aye," said Tolin, holding her hands, still smiling at her. "Kit, you're no longer shaking."

"I'm not," she said in surprise, seeing that her new husband was correct. Mayhap now that she was married to the handsome man, her nerves wouldn't be so jittery around him anymore. She let out a breath of relief. "I like it. Nay, I love it. I love being your wife, Tolin." She smiled back at him, noticing that sexy look in his eyes.

"You do realize we're not officially wed until we consummate the marriage. Which I think we should do right away."

"Right away?" She scanned the room of onlookers again. "What about the dancing and celebrating first? And the feast that is planned? I know how much you enjoy those things."

"I can think of something I enjoy even more." With a smoldering look on his face, he raised her hands and kissed them. "Let them all wait," he said, speaking of the crowd.

"Tolin, I'm not sure that is such a good idea. Your father won't like us making everyone wait."

"It is still Twelfth Night, Kit," he reminded her.

"Yes, but why does that matter?" she asked.

"Because I still have this." Tolin pulled the bean out of his pouch and held it up and smiled even more. "Anything I say, goes. Until the end of the day at least."

"Oh, I understand." Kit smiled back, realizing exactly what he meant. "I want you to know that I will eagerly be awaiting anything you want to do in the bedchamber, my husband, my love, my **_Lord of Misrule._**"

FROM THE AUTHOR

I hope you have enjoyed *Lord of Misrule* and will take the time to leave a review for me.

I must admit that when I wrote *Sweet Mead for Lady Martine*, I thought I was finished with the *Below the Salt Series*. Not so. Lord Tolin Blake wanted his story told, so I knew I had to add at least one more book to the series.

This has been a fun journey. I love pushing the envelope and that is why I decided to write about nobles who fall in love and marry commoners. Of course, back in medieval times this wasn't a usual occurrence. Nobles married for alliances, not love. And they married someone of their own or higher status. Not to mention the wealth.

You might have been surprised to see football mentioned, but they did play this game back then. It was just different from what you know it to be today. And Blind Man's Buff, known later as Bluff, was a game named after a small push. The blindfolded player was often struck or buffeted as they would say back then, by the other players.

I included a family tree at the beginning of this book. Of course, there are still more siblings who need their stories told so anything can happen. Even if their stories don't come out through the *Below the Salt Series*, you might find them popping up in a new series, since I have ideas on the back burner.

If you'd like to read more about Tolin's brother, Rook, you can do so in *A Rose Among Thorns*. Tolin's sister Raven's story is *Picking up the Gauntlet*. And if you'd like to find out more, farther back in the family roots where things first got started, read the **Legacy of the Blade Series.** There is a free prequel where you will see Lord Corbett Blake as a boy. This sets up the rest of the stories about him and his siblings.

Here are the books in the Below the Salt Series

Below the Salt Series:

Picking up the Gauntlet – Book 1 (Lady Raven is the daughter of Corbett and Devon from Lord of the Blade.)

A Rose Among Thorns – Book 2 (Lord Rook is Raven's twin brother.)

Love Letters for Lady Lark – Book 3 (Lark is the daughter of Storm MacKeefe and Wren from Lady Renegade.)

Dancing on Air – Book 4 (Lady Eleanor is the daughter of Garrett Blackmore and Echo from Lady of the Mist.)

Winter Sage – Book 5 (Lord Robin is the son of Madoc (Echo's twin brother) and Abbey from Lord of Illusion.)

Riding out the Storm – Book 6 (Gar is the son of Echo and stepson/nephew of Garrett from Lady of the Mist.)

Sweet Mead for Lady Martine – Book 7 (Lady Martine is the daughter of Madoc and Abbey from Lord of Illusion.)

Lord of Misrule – Book 8 (Lord Tolin Blake is son of Lord Corbett Blake and Devon from Lord of the Blade.)

If you'd like to know more about my books, please visit my website at http://elizabethrosenovels.com. You can also follow me on **Amazon, Bookbub, Goodreads, Facebook,** and other social media. Be sure to sign up for my newsletter so you won't miss sales, free books, and new releases. You can do so by going to https://bit.ly/3aK66i2.

Thank you all for your support,
Elizabeth Rose

ALSO BY ELIZABETH ROSE

Medieval Series:

Legendary Bastards of the Crown Series

Seasons of Fortitude Series

Secrets of the Heart Series

Legacy of the Blade Series

Daughters of the Dagger Series

MadMan MacKeefe Series

Barons of the Cinque Ports Series

Holiday Knights Series

Highland Chronicles Series

Pirate Lords Series

Highland Outcasts

Medieval/Paranormal Series:

Elemental Magick Series

Greek Myth Fantasy Series

Tangled Tales Series

Portals of Destiny

Contemporary Series:

Tarnished Saints Series

Working Man Series

Western Series:

Cowboys of the Old West Series

And More!

Please visit http://elizabethrosenovels.com

ABOUT ELIZABETH

Elizabeth Rose is an award-winning, bestselling author of over 100 books and counting. She writes medieval, historical, contemporary, paranormal, and western romance. Her books are available as EBooks, paperbacks, and some audiobooks as well.

Her favorite characters in her works include dark, dangerous and tortured heroes, and feisty, independent heroines who know how to wield a sword. She loves writing 14th century medieval novels, and is well-known for her many series.

Elizabeth loves the outdoors. In the summertime, you can find her in her secret garden with her laptop, swinging in her hammock working on her next book. Elizabeth is a born storyteller and passionate about sharing her works with her readers.

Please be sure to visit her website at **Elizabethrosenovels.com** to read excerpts from any of her novels and get sneak peeks at covers of upcoming books. You can follow her on **Twitter, Facebook**, **Goodreads** or **BookBub.** Join Elizabeth's **newsletter** so you don't miss out on new releases or upcoming events.

Milton Keynes UK
Ingram Content Group UK Ltd.
UKHW031201251124
451529UK00004B/325